PECKERWOOD TWIST

By Nathan Lichtwar

"Peckerwood Twist"

This is a work of fiction. Names, characters, places, and incidents are the product of the author's imagination or are used fictitiously. Any resemblance to actual persons, living or dead, events, or locales is entirely coincidental.

Cover Design by: Kristin C. Klaiber
kristyklaiberdesign@yahoo.com

Book Design and Layout by: www.integrativeink.com
Editing Provided by Joyce Shafer, jls1422@yahoo.com

ISBN: 978-0-6152-0231-0

DEDICATION

Linda Mays, my wife who made every one of our
adventures possible.

The tribes of the Amazon and people of Peru.

ACKNOWLEDGMENTS

Joyce Shafer — my editor and advisor.

Keep the River on the Right by Tobias Schneebaum, Grove Press ~ "The saying kept us alive."

If I have offended anyone with this book, it may be that the truth can be painful. Evil is always around; but for the most part, we can tell on it and show it for what it is.

CHAPTER 1

Heat is something I never seem able to escape. It's not just about climate. Heat comes in many forms and follows me wherever I go, or maybe the truth is that I'm drawn to it like the proverbial moth to a flame. Like in this small town on the east coast of Florida. Nighttime in Port Selerno is as hot as if it were midday. If you frequent some of the places I do, it can get even hotter.

Almost as soon as I leave the air-conditioned mall I can't exit quickly enough, sweat starts to bead across my forehead and trickles past the neckline of my T-shirt. My boot hits the tarred parking lot and I notice the surface is mushy. The word *mush* registers in my brain, and my lips press into a thin line as I recall when and how that word took on new meaning in my life. I start to walk and hear the sound of my boot soles sticking and releasing with every step. I've been in stickier circumstances.

I need to get away from the hoards of shoppers, most of them parents exhausted by screaming, irritable children unhappy at not leaving with a trunk-load of junk they'll forget about as soon as they get home. I know that one other thought on their minds is in order to get home they have to get into cars that are more like saunas. The ride won't be pleasant. That won't be a problem I have to deal with, I'm on foot. Dusk is setting in and I have somewhere to go. I place my fairly new brown felt cowboy hat on and start walking. The heat of my body under my black denim pants and jacket bothers me some, but I'll cool off as soon as I sit down.

My destination is close—a section of gaudy stucco buildings that house the many bars that dot Highway A1A. I pause for a moment to watch the multicolored neon lights buzz and sizzle

1

back to life. The electric hues don't help the area's appearance, though. A time-warp happened here, and everything got stuck in the 1930s, including, it seems, upkeep.

The bar where I usually warm a seat is the Peckerwood. The owner named the bar after his brand of homemade hot sauce. The sauce comes in two temperatures: *Damn It, This is Hot* and *This is Really Fuckin' Hot*. The milder sauce is green, created for people who wouldn't try the red sauce on a dare. The red is for the initiated or those who have an EMT on call, or maybe enjoy the near-death experience they feel when the chemicals reach the brain. The owner, Jake, was clever and made the labels sort of a brand, as well. People want to collect the labeled bottles with their cartoon-like characters sometimes more than they want the sauce. My favorite is the one modeled after the Roadrunner. This is because I'm the one who suggested it to him, and for reasons I've never shared with anyone.

The barroom is large enough to hold two tournament-size pool tables and two arcade games that bark out gunshot sounds followed by moaning, as though some poor sucker gets shot over and over. The actual bar is large, circular, made of oak, and seats thirty with nearly double that many drinkers who usually stand around it. Just like steins had glass bottoms so men could watch their enemies and drink at the same time, the bar is circular so everyone can watch everyone else at all times. It's called survival. Usually, the only thing that gets the attention of the regulars is a new face. If a newcomer is perceived a no-threat, everybody goes back to what they were doing.

When Port Selerno was in its heyday, thirsty fishermen and seafarers came here after their long sea voyages with pockets heavy with wages and pants heavy with a particular need—which attracted women eager to help lighten both burdens. The men never minded. Wealth and stability might have caused them to believe they had to settle down to marriage and family. To be land-bound was a form of imprisonment for any true sailor. It's still that way.

The sea could also make a certain kind of man religious real quick. Many became men of the cloth and that's why there are so many churches here. Those who founded churches could take themselves out of a seaman's life, but couldn't entirely take the seaman out of themselves, so most of the churches have nautical names. Port Salerno became a place of twos: Two famous hot sauces and two popular places of worship—the churches and the bars.

I walk in and nod at Jake who's tending bar tonight. I don't even have to order. He puts my usual in front of me before my butt touches the circle of wood I'll eventually have trouble staying on as the hours waste by. The regular odd assortment is here tonight…hard-working fishermen with the women who follow them and those who look like they crawled out of the Everglades to make it here.

There's a man sitting at the bar—skinny, unshaven, wearing a boa constrictor around his neck. He's holding a baby in his arms. His male companion is just as skinny and looks as though he's said the wrong thing to the wrong man one too many times. To their right is an old gent, already drunk, who has a cast on one of his arms that goes from his wrist to his shoulder. He also has a woman hanging on each arm. Each of them has seen better days, or I hope they have, and now try to camouflage the ravages of time and hard living with too much makeup, too many cheap baubles, and too much cleavage. Also at the bar is a gorilla posing as a human. He has a friendly kind of face, but his nose is pushed in, his ears are large and cauliflower-like, and his head rests directly on his shoulders as though the assembly line ran out of necks that day. His hands are the size of ham hocks.

It's still early yet, so some of the stools to his right are empty; six of them, in fact. The seventh stool, the one with the man who's quickly downed half his beer already…that's me, Sam Paris, son of German Jewish parents, both long gone. When my parents left the insanity happening in Germany and came to the States, they took on a new last name. What it used to be no longer matters to me; there's nothing I can do to change what happened. Besides, watching my back in the present keeps me busy enough.

I'm in my sixties, six-feet tall, trim, with hair that went solid gray while I wasn't looking, and brown eyes. I'm a used-to-be. Used to be handsome, used to be younger, used to do drugs, never smoked. But, I drink. Booze is my companion and will probably kill me one day, if someone doesn't beat it to the task.

Habit born out of self-preservation and lessons learned the hard way cause me to always keep an eye on my surroundings, even familiar ones like the Peckerwood. This is why I notice a Lincoln Continental pull into the parking lot and why I keep watching after the young couple gets out and makes their way into the bar. The sticker on the windshield is one of Alamo's, which means they're paying thirty-nine bucks a day to either drive in comfort, look as though they have money, or both.

It's easy enough to drive into the parking lot here, but to walk into the Peckerwood, or around this area of town, is another matter. About a month ago, the three-table diner adjacent to the Peckerwood lost their short order cook when someone shot and killed him because his gator stew tasted a little rancid. The blue-collar patrons put up with a lot in their lives, but bad stew or a chef trying to get away with something isn't one of them. You either have to be uninformed or have the guts to come to this neighborhood, and this bar, in particular. Only time would tell which category these two fit into.

I admit my focus is more on her since she's an eyeful. Attractive face, shoulder-length platinum blond hair, built to the point of distraction, and she knows it. She's tall, even without the heels—a height most men would like to climb—and dressed in a low-cut, tight-fitted bit of red silk. When she walks, she moves her body in sections like a model on a runway; first one part, followed by another. Every eye in the place tracks her movements.

Her companion is an inch taller than she is, broad-shouldered; and I'm willing to bet there are washboard abs to match the other bulges under his expensive gray pullover and precisely-creased darker gray slacks.

The couple takes the two empty stools to my right. I shouldn't care where they sit, but I do because I'm here to numb thoughts that play like a film in my head. I watch Jake walk over to them.

"What can I get you folks?" he asks them.

"We're here to buy a case of your hottest Peckerwood sauce," the man replies.

I take more of a look now and see the man is probably in his thirties, also blond, fair complexion, and speaks with an accent, though only a slight one. I guessed maybe Spanish, as in Spain, but I could be wrong. They'd both glanced in my direction as they sat, and I'd noticed they both had gray eyes. You seldom see one person with that eye color much less two at the same time.

One thing's for sure, both of them are going to burn like hell in the Florida sun.

"It'll be a while before I can get the case together for you. I'm tending bar solo tonight," Jake says.

The man turns to the woman. "Should we wait?"

"We came all this way."

"I'll start putting your case together," Jake says. "You want one particular label or a mix?"

"A mix is fine," the man answers.

"Mix it is. You got here just in time, too. It's Friday night, so I join my customers in celebrating the weekend. Kinda makes life, the bugs, and the heat bearable. But, hey! It sure the hell beats living in Minnesota."

"We might as well have something to drink, then," the man says. He glances at the woman, "Two beers?" She nods her agreement. "Two of whatever your best beer on tap is."

"Coming right up," Jake says as he walks off.

"You'd better drink your beer out of bottles," I comment, keeping my eyes on Jake. "The water here smells of sulfur and makes everything taste like it. Plus, Jake doesn't own a glass that isn't chipped more than some of the regulars' teeth."

"Jake," the man calls out, "make that your best bottled beer instead."

Jake glances at me and I hold up my own bottle in salutation. He puts the glasses back on the shelf, grabs two amber bottles from the cooler, opens them, and slaps them down on the bar in front of the couple then starts getting their case of hot sauce together between orders for drinks.

"You're right about how these people look," the man says to me, "like characters out of a Dickens' novel."

"Either talk more softly or keep your thoughts to yourself. That guy over there wouldn't hesitate to break your arm like he did his buddy's last night."

The woman leans over and looks into my eyes. "What was his reason for doing that?"

"Who knows," I answer. "They'd kill the other and cry into their beer over their loss. It's depraved, but it's a good show; better than television and why I come here night after night to watch."

Her eyes light up. "Do you think something like that might happen again tonight?"

I take a moment to look at her. "It's possible. Gorilla man over there isn't happy with the man sitting near him."

"He objects to the snake?" she asks.

"He objects to the baby."

"What do you think he'll do?" She almost purrs her question.

"Break his jaw, probably. And, maybe soon by the look in his eyes. When it happens, it'll happen fast."

"Good." As she says this, she moves off her stool and starts her slow slink towards Gorilla.

Her friend turns to me. "Why do you do it?"

"Do what?"

"Come to this bar. There are others, surely, that are nicer."

The woman is still within earshot. She turns and says, "But other bars may not have real men there."

I smile, partially at her, partially at a memory. "She's something else," I say to him. The man doesn't comment, just grins at me.

"I guess," I continue, "I feel safe here."

"Safe? Here?"

"I'm accepted. I've put my time in and no one asks too many questions."

"You don't look like you fit here."

"What makes anyone fit anywhere? By the way, you're something of a nosey bastard."

He smiles. "Yes, you could say that, I suppose; but, I'm willing to pay good money for a good story. You look like a man who has one to tell. I know because it's how I make my living, writing short stories."

"For what, Reader's Digest?" I ask before drinking the last of my beer. I hope he picks up on my sarcastic tone.

"Those types of articles, yes."

"Well, buddy, money and keeping the booze coming will get you some entertainment."

"Good." He catches Jake's eye and calls out, "Give this gentleman another beer, please, and another for me, as well," then turns back to me. "Why don't we take a table and you can tell me your story."

"What about your friend over there?" I nod my head towards the woman.

"She can amuse herself."

She is, too. She's chatting up the guys and even bought a round of drinks.

Jake puts two more bottles in front of us. My new friend picks them up, and gives a quick glance at the woman. "Life's a bitch, then you marry one."

"That's an old line. Still, she has a way about her… But, she's asking for trouble."

"Never mind her, she can handle herself."

Right. This evening could turn real interesting real fast with someone getting hurt; but, it won't be me. She's his problem. I follow him to a nearby table and take a seat facing the bar.

"I should introduce myself," he says. "Harry Parker."

"Sam Paris." Neither of us extends our hand to shake. "You know, Harry, I don't like that scene over there. Not at all."

"Forget about her for now, Sam. Start your story."

"Sure. Why not? I landed in this God-forsaken town in the summer of '83, hot, broke, and most of the time drunk. But it's far enough north of the Miami Trades."

"What are the Miami Trades?"

"It's an expression used in south Florida that means Cuban affluence. I didn't want any part of them or their stinking money. I was just passing through, but got caught up in Jimmy Buffet music and margaritas. I'm still just passing through, God willing."

"You're religious, Sam?"

"I don't believe in the guy who sits on a throne; but I believe in… Let's just say I've seen things."

"I'm sure that's very interesting, but I want to hear *your* story, Sam."

"My story is…either 90-percent true or the complete opposite. I'll leave it up to you to figure out which. Let's start with the fact I had a bad time in Vietnam. Landed in a Veterans' hospital on Staten Island."

"You were injured?"

"Nothing that couldn't be mended back like it never happened, but my mind was fucked up. I was a drugged-out, boozed-up nut case. Society didn't want me. And the family I had left didn't want me, either. You know, Harry, I went into the

Marines with a John-Fuckin'-Wayne attitude. My hippie cousins turned, both *on* me and north to Canada to avoid the draft. I should've joined them, now that I know better. Shit, John Wayne never did service. All those movies he made about the war led men to believe it was glamorous. Bullshit. So there I was, fucked in the head with no job, no prospects, and no future. I couldn't go back to my pre-war life, so ended up on the streets of New York City. Grand Central Station, actually.

"During the day, I begged for handouts. I spent my nights in a cardboard box off the beaten track of a subway rail siding. Shared space with the rats. Did you know rats make good pets? I had four one time. I brought them food and they protected me while I slept."

"The rats protected you? How, and from what or who?"

"From the sick rats, the ones that bite for no reason. Rats have a hierarchy just like people."

"Sam, I don't really give a fuck about rats."

"You should, Harry. They're smart. I learned a lot by observing them. If you lay out poisoned food, the healthy ones hold off until one that's demented from sickness tries it. If it dies, the healthy ones won't go near the food. That means something, Harry."

"Like what?"

"Like there are some healthy fucking rats in this world, and some smart bastards, as well."

"Can we move past the rat lecture?"

"Okay. But I'll tell you, Harry, rats come in all forms. Order another round of beers."

"Sure."

I watch as Harry makes his way to the bar and gives a quick look over at the woman. She's enjoying herself and has several of the regulars hanging onto her every word. Gorilla can't take his eyes off her; neither can I. It's the way she moves, I suppose. So like *her*. A strange feeling starts up in the pit of my stomach and I hope Harry hurries back with the beers. I also hope his pockets go deep.

CHAPTER 2

"So, Harry, the city had what they called 'clean-up week' two or three times a month. This meant we were sure to get hauled in to get cleaned up, and get a check-up and a meal. AIDS had just turned up at the party, and there was a thought that maybe those of us who lived on the street were the carriers.

"After the blood tests showed us clean of at least that disease, we were given a nice bus ride out of town to the suburbs. They wanted us to become someone else's problem. That lasted until those communities made a racket about it.

"I ended up back at Grand Central, crossroads for millions. One day, one of those millions happened to take an interest in me. I was clean-shaven and almost looked human that day. Still, I was pretty surprised when this attractive blond tall-drink-of-water, who looked to be in her late forties, give or take a few years, approached me and said her name was Ursula Jung."

"Was she Chinese?"

"No, German, in fact. Weird fucking woman, as it turned out. Anyway, she offered to feed me at the nearby hamburger joint if I'd listen to what she had to say. If she was horny, she wouldn't be looking for a homeless guy, even if I still looked pretty good then; so I figured I'd let her talk and get a meal out of it. Besides, it had been a long time since a classy, good-looking woman had given me any attention.

"Turned out, she had some fucked-up notion I could help her out. Said she'd pay me a lot of money if I agreed. I figured what the fuck? My dance card had lots of room on it."

"What did she want you to do?" Harry asks before he takes a pull on his beer.

I pause long enough to do the same. "She wanted me to go with her to Peru. Said she was concerned about her uncle, a doctor, who was working in the jungle. She'd lost touch with him and was worried. She was between jobs, so it was now or never. But she didn't want to travel without a companion and though I was a bit scruffy, I looked as though I could handle myself. I had nothing to keep me where I was, so I agreed to go."

"You didn't see a problem with her asking you to do this?"

"Listen, Harry, I don't trust anyone. But at that point, who cared? I was offered money, food, clothes, and travel with a beautiful woman. What could be worse, death? Fuck death. At that time, I welcomed it. Life sure wasn't holding its doors wide open for me before she showed up. The people who gave me coins when I was begging treated me like shit, worse than shit. They'd pick up their dog's crap, but made sure not to touch me when they dropped their change into my hand."

"So you and this woman, Ursula, flew to Peru?"

"Not right away. She gave me some money and a place to stay, but committed me to a drug rehab for twenty-eight days. I came out a new man, sort of. It wasn't my first time, as I told you."

"You're obviously drinking again."

"I can stop anytime."

"Sure you can."

"Fuck you, Harry."

"Easy. I'm not judging, Sam. Please continue."

"Yeah, okay. She gave me books to read, most of them about Peru, some on the Amazon, some on Third Reich bullshit. I asked her why the fuck I was reading about Nazis and she tells me she's paying me to read, not question her reading choices. She was right, and I wanted the money; so I kept turning pages.

"She called me one day and said she had to get to Machu Picchu. Now. Next thing I know, we're on a flight south to Lima, Peru. I've been in some real fuckin' hellholes, and this was one more. I'd rather beg in the States than there any day. Anyway, we flew from Lima to Cuzco, a town in the Andes. You know it?"

"I've heard of it."

"It's not bad, kind of nice. It's an old Spanish-style village with well-preserved Inca ruins everywhere. Ursula had rooms, if you can call them that, at the American Embassy. We left the heavy stuff there and took just our backpacks with us so we wouldn't pass out from trying to haul a load into the higher altitude. Cuzco's about 9,500 feet above sea level."

"You can leave out stuff like altitudes, Sam. I'm not writing for National Geographic."

"And you can go fuck yourself. You're paying for the booze, but it's my story. My story comes with scenery."

"Fine. Just keep it to a minimum, if you can."

"You just keep the beer coming and I'll keep talking. Ursula got us a side trip to some of the ruins being excavated. We added a tent, bedrolls, and supplies. I remember wondering how we'd make it with the heavier load, especially in thinner air, but all of it was actually pretty light. I'd imagined more of a first-class kind of deal, but what the hell. If she wanted to do some sightseeing while looking for her uncle, that was up to her and it was her dime. What I thought was going to be a fairly simple trip, turned into something else entirely."

We were looking down into what's called the Valley of the Gods while standing on top of an Inca ruin called Ollantaytambo. It's next to a section of the Urabamba River that twists through the most important valleys in Peru. On top of this ruin is a famous sacrificial stone, which is also part of a wall that faces the Valley of the Gods. Ursula said the Incas would bind a prisoner by his arms and feet and leave him like that all night so he could ponder his fate, which he'd meet at first light. The intention was for the doomed person's last image to be the sun rising over the valley.

We decided to set up our tent and spend the night atop the ruin so we could see for ourselves how this must have looked and felt to the person being put to death. Actually, that was her idea; I just went along with it.

The high elevation not only makes the temperature drop sharply when the sun sets over the Andes, but puts you closer to the sun. This is a combination that can quickly freeze-dry skin in a very short time. If you keep moving in and out of sunlight, that speeds up the process.

The view was incredible. The inked blackness of the night sky was dotted with bright beacons I knew were thousands of light years away; yet seemed so close. I couldn't see the horizon because of the mountains, and the thin air at that altitude created a surreal vista.

In New York, we never exchanged as much as a friendly hug. I'm not a man who details his time shared with a woman, but I'll tell you that in that tent with our bedrolls next to each other, Ursula and I shared conversation and what amounted to a heavy make-out session two teenagers might have. Ursula said it was delicious. That's all I'm going to say about that.

When morning light started to push its way across the valley, we left our warm comfort and crawled out into the cold to position ourselves at the sacrificial stone. The Urabamba River seemed like a giant serpent in hot pursuit of the sun, never quite able to catch it. The sunlight touched the top of the farthest mountain and caused a golden shimmer on the river so it looked like flowing gold. The shaft of light moved through the length of the valley and climbed the ruin walls until it looked as though it were a spear.

I caught my breath when the light hit Ursula who'd placed herself at the exact position of the condemned person. I asked her why she wanted to do that and she told me everyone wonders about their death, but she wanted to sense what someone might experience in this scenario. Would it be terror or peace as they anticipated the knife? I'd already decided she was unusual, which didn't bother me, but this seemed a little intense; and, as far as I was concerned, unnecessary and naïve. I'd lived terror every moment I was in 'Nam. I didn't need to imagine it.

As the sunlight continued to fill the sky, it was as though molten gold was poured over the mountains and valley. There seemed to be gold everywhere, including over Ursula who seemed to turn even more golden than she already was. Pure gold. Even her eyes shimmered with that color. I felt my heart pounding and I stepped towards her. Soon as I did that, the color began to shift to red, red like the blood that was spilled when the knife slit the condemned person's throat. Ursula told me afterwards that she felt she'd died on that stone. I tried a couple of times to get her to talk more about her experience, but she wouldn't. But I will say that the look in her eyes and the expression on her face fascinated and frightened me.

"I have to interrupt you, Sam, and ask if you're talking about an affect of sunlight or real gold. If there were deposits mixed in with the soil that might explain it."

"Who knows, Harry; all I know is you're not keeping up with the beer."

"I'll be right back."

I watch Harry walk to the bar. He nods at the woman, who looks over briefly at me, then returns her attention to her throng of admirers. Jake notices his approach and gets the beers ready before he reaches the bar, so Harry's back at the table in moments.

He sits down and puts a bottle in front of me. "Ready when you are."

I feel my throat and mouth grow dry, as though they fill with the dust of old memories, and put the bottle to my lips and drink half, hoping it'll make a difference.

Then I start.

Spanish armies had chased after the Incas and forced them further into the jungle. Machu Picchu was one of the last strongholds; but I learned the Incas had gone even deeper into the jungle than that. The Spanish conquerors, smitten with the gold bug, also found Inca ruins as they pursued their quarry, which gives you a sense of how ancient the Inca culture really was.

Neither the Spaniards nor the Incas prevailed. The jungle and disease did that. Thousands on both sides were felled until desire for gold was replaced with a desire to survive. After not too long, the conquerors retreated back to civilization, such as it was then. Over time, rumors started of Inca ruins buried under centuries of growth in the deepest parts of the jungle. Tales of buried cities said to have large vaults of gold waiting to be picked like fallen apples, attracted attention everywhere.

Enter modern times with better tools and pharmaceuticals that let explorers and treasure hunters go into the jungle and stay there for longer periods of time. Ruins *were* discovered and uncovered. Gold was found, and some of it was taken out of the jungle and placed in museums in Lima. Even more was smuggled out of Peru. It wasn't long before the jungle was flooded with adventure seekers who came from all points of the compass.

They came when there was a depression in the world and they came when the world was torn by war. These men had dreams, dreams of finding Inca gold and of what they imagined it would bring them. For most, it was the last stop on a wild journey.

The gold hunters who had the good fortune to avoid the arrows of the many Amazonian tribes of the region had the misfortune of falling prey to disease, since not all of these interlopers knew what to prepare for. Many had gold fever so bad threat of disease was the last thing on their minds. There certainly were explorers who made it to some of the more abandoned ruins and then returned to the large cities to tell what they'd seen; but for some reason, had no hard-core evidence to prove their stories were true. Sometimes a story is told so many times it becomes warped out of context; and in the end, it's believed to be nothing more than a fantasy. But, who wouldn't like to find gold?

An outsider can see how this fever can lead to disaster. Once you're standing in the middle of the myth, though, you can easily get sucked into that vortex. I did.

Anyway, we came down from the ruin and made our way to a main road where we hitched a ride on a truck carrying potatoes that was headed back towards Cuzco. We decided to rest up for two days, then head out for Machu Picchu by train. At some predetermined mile marker, we'd depart the train and do the rest of the trip to the site on the Inca trail. Those were our plans; they never materialized.

We were in Cuzco at the local watering hole, filling up on a potent drink called Pisco which is a kind of brandy made from white Muscat grapes. We'd heard this beverage is beneficial for dealing with the altitude and the cold, so we thought we'd get a head-start.

Four French hikers, two men and two women, who also planned to do the trail the next morning, were there getting their fill of Pisco, as well. Everyone at the bar was pretty excited, so conversation flowed like the liquor. The more Pisco that was drunk, the more the stories got bolder and, of course, grander. But one story about some gold seekers made us pay special attention.

One of the four, a young storyteller named Jean-Paul, went on to say that back during the end of the Second World War, some American bush pilots scouting the valleys for Inca ruins, reported seeing *que los flujos de oro*–the gold that flows. They pushed themselves to find the flowing gold and reportedly crashed in the jungle. Only one of the three men on board survived—the pilot flying the plane. The survivor was so obsessed with what he'd seen he walked the valleys for years searching for it. The Frenchman said this man became quite mad, and that eventually some natives took him in. The story was the man was still alive, living on the Island of Tequile on Lake Titicaca. The other man, Francois, joined in to corroborate the story, though his version was slightly different stating the pilot had died, and with him, his findings.

I could tell by the look on Ursula's face that she was more than a little interested in the story. This was confirmed when she leaned towards me and asked, "I wonder if we should go to Lake Titicaca?"

We talked separate from the others about making the trip; and I realized she had quickly become obsessed with finding out more about the pilot, which I took to mean what she really wanted was to find gold.

For someone looking for a possibly-missing uncle, she seemed easily distracted. This was brought home even more when she said first she wanted to go to Puño, and ignored me when I asked why.

This town could be reached by bus or train from Cuzco. Either way, it would be a hardship. The winding roads and train tracks positioned along the edges and ledges of the Andes are treacherous; and though the view is stunning, the landscape is also dotted with skeletons of vehicles and trains that have fallen over the side. After a lot more discussion, we chose the train or, rather, we chose it at Ursula's insistence. I figured if we went over in a smaller vehicle, there was a better chance of surviving than if a string of linked cars tumbled over the side. She convinced me when she promised we'd travel first class, which I discovered in the Andes means no cattle in the car, just chickens.

At the train station in Cuzco, Ursula and I watched a young Peruvian, probably no more than sixteen or so, bring several large burlap bundles into our car. Four young women, also around his age, helped him and boarded with him.

When we departed Cuzco, this Peruvian youngster spent a great deal of time pacing up and down the length of the car.

Every time he'd pass by me, he'd make eye contact. It was almost as if he expected me to say something to him. All this activity occurred as he clutched a black leather bag. He seemed to become frustrated with my not engaging him, and tried to stuff the bag by my feet. I balked at his doing this because it would infringe upon what little space I had, plus, he was up to something and I didn't want to get involved. I asked Ursula if the young man was speaking Spanish.

"It sounds like Spanish, but I don't recognize the words," she said.

I glanced back for a second as he made his way towards the rear of the car. "Good," I said. "Let him bother somebody else." Ursula turned to watch him, as well.

The train tracks followed the Urabamba. Sometimes the tracks were level with the river; but at other times the train climbed to breathtaking heights. At one point, we stopped at a small train station where we changed locomotives. I figured the climb higher up the mountain probably required a different engine. Local natives were there selling food and alpaca sweaters, and we made some purchases of both while we waited for the switch.

Once the new locomotive was attached, we found ourselves traveling through completely wild country. There were no towns and the area seemed to lack homes or roads. The scenery stayed the same for hours. After a while, the sound of the wheels on the tracks had Ursula nodding off, and I wasn't far behind her.

I woke to the loud screech of metal-on-metal and thought we must be on a descent down a mountain because the conductor was applying the train's brakes awfully hard. I tried to see ahead, but the train was rounding a curve to the left and since that's the side of the train we were on, all I could see were the cars in front of us.

The train seemed to level out and went more or less on a straight path. Suddenly, the brakes were applied so hard, all of us lurched forward as we came to an abrupt halt. Everyone got quiet. I noticed the look of anxiety on the faces of the other passengers. That is, with the exception of Ursula who'd slept straight through the noise and braking. I nudged her and told her we'd stopped.

Ursula stretched her body like a cat, looked around and asked, "Are we in Puño?"

"No. I think something's up."

Opaque steam poured past our window and obscured our view. Ursula and I pressed our faces to the filmy glass and tried to see through the smoky clouds. Whatever had made us come to a stop had to be on the other side of the train.

After five minutes or so, we were boarded by the military, or at least a group of young boys, mid-teens probably, dressed in military clothing. Whoever they were, their weapons were real. There was no doubt in my mind they should be taken seriously.

They walked up and down the aisle and started to search passengers' luggage. I say luggage, but their possessions were stored mainly in large burlap bags like the young man brought on board. It seemed that almost every bag in our car had cacao leaves hidden in them. These so-called soldiers tried to pin down the owners of the bags they found cacao in; but of course, no one claimed them. Ursula and I stayed quiet, but there was a lot of yelling by both the passengers and soldiers. Our car quickly took on the odor of fear-saturated sweat.

Another soldier who looked a little more mature than the rest came on board. He walked straight over to the young man who'd tried to stuff the leather bag under my seat, put a pistol to his head and led him off the train. Some of the other soldiers gathered the young man's burlap bags and piled them up outside. I noted they knew which bags were his and that I couldn't readily see the black bag. Outside, they forced him onto his knees and bound his hands behind his back. About ten minutes or so later, they dragged him to his feet, put him into their jeep with a few of their men, and drove off. Three of them stayed behind. They'd left Ursula and me, and our bags, alone. In fact, they passed by us as though we didn't exist.

"Of course they left you alone," Harry breaks in. "Neither of you are Peruvian. No threat."

"Maybe. Maybe searching for cacao was a ruse, or not. It was obvious they were looking for the young Peruvian. By the way, Harry, how's your woman doing?"

"Still controlling the bar. Go on."

"They detained the train for two hours before they let us go. At that time, I could only imagine the fate of the smuggler. I thought it was interesting they hadn't bothered with the young women who'd boarded with him. Those four kept a very low profile for the rest of the trip."

"The soldiers probably killed him."

"That was my thought."

Anyway, I found out that cacao use is allowed in the higher elevations to fight the dreaded *soroche*, or altitude sickness. Lower than fifteen hundred feet, the leaves become a police matter.

As soon as the train started to move again, Ursula said nature was calling and got up to find the restroom. When she got back, she said, "Take a look at what's behind the door in the restroom. It will certainly interest you."

So I went, and behind the door was the black bag our young smuggler had tried to put under my feet. The bag was fairly light and I figured it was stuffed with more cacao leaves. I thought about leaving it there; but since the train had already been searched and we were moving, decided to take it along. Ursula and I might need to use some of the leaves where we were going or we might be able to use the cacao to bargain with later on.

I also thought about the fact this bag could get Ursula and me into some deep shit. South American jails are not for the faint of heart. Ursula surprised me when I told her I wanted to keep the bag. I thought she'd argue, but she agreed. Some people can fall asleep like a light-switch being turned off. Ursula seemed to be one of them because she was sound asleep as soon as the word *okay* slipped from her lips.

The train started climbing again to a higher altitude. After the unexpected delay and an hour of going back and forth on a siding on the outskirts of town, we finally reached Puño.

CHAPTER 3

If there was a good side to the town of Puño, I never saw it. The sun was almost gone and we needed to find the hotel a man we spoke with in Cuzco had suggested. He said it was the only one in the town so we should book ahead. Ursula handled it since, as she pointed out, I didn't speak the language.

We hoisted our gear onto our backs and walked until we finally found a building with HOTEL posted on the front of it. On the way there, we passed several clusters of men who stared and whispered among themselves while never taking their eyes off me. A few even nodded at me. It would have made sense if they'd been watching Ursula. It almost looked friendly except for the puzzled and sometimes intense expressions they wore. It was as though they were studying me, but not sizing me up the way men often do with each other.

When we got to the hotel door, Ursula reached to open it and I said, "Hold up a second. I'm not sure why, but I feel uneasy here. Did you notice how we, rather, I was watched on the way here?"

"I didn't notice anything unusual. We're strangers. Naturally, they'd be curious."

"I think it was more than that. This town has the look and feel of one where we may want some protection; maybe hire someone, if that's possible. If not that, maybe a gun or two would be a good idea, instead."

Ursula glanced back towards some of the men still watching us. "You may be right."

"Most women don't want to go anywhere near guns, but I think we both should have one."

"I'm not most women," Ursula said as she opened the door.

19

"I noticed."

We entered the lobby, if you could call it that. The front desk was four feet back from the entrance and amenities were sparse. I'm being sarcastic, amenities were non-existent. We were in luck, or at least I was, that the man behind the counter asked us in English if we had a reservation.

"Yes," I responded. "We called ahead. I'm Paris, this is Jung."

He'd only glanced up briefly when we'd entered then made a big deal of pulling out a book and a pen. Still not looking at us he said, "Welcome. My name is Carlos. Your passports, please."

If Carlos stood five-foot-four, that was it, and that might be stretching it. He was unshaven, stocky and fat, especially around the middle where his belly protruded out of his shirt from too many lost buttons, and he had a full head of black, curly hair. His clothes were shabby and from the smell of them, didn't see soap and water too often.

He used our passports to write down whatever was needed from them then handed them back. This time he noticed Ursula and decided to take a longer look. She accommodated him with one of her killer smiles. I half expected her to bat her eyelashes at him just to amuse herself.

His eyes finally pulled away from her and focused on my face. After a moment of looking surprised, he smiled broadly and said, "This is a good hotel, Señor. The rooms are safe, and each one has a bed, of course, and a toilet. Your room is on the next floor, number four."

I noticed he said *toilet* as though he was really proud they existed at his hotel.

We climbed probably the narrowest staircase ever constructed and found ourselves on the second floor in front of a door with our room number crudely painted on it. I realized this was a four-room hotel; and as far as I could tell, not only would it be our *home* for the night, but we had only Carlos to share it with. The man who'd advised us to book ahead either had a sense of humor or didn't know this wasn't the height of tourist season in Puño.

The skeleton key Carlos had handed to us opened the cheap rusted lock. The door, which was no more than a plywood board, would need only a gentle push to be opened, locked or not. We entered the room and I noticed a small light bulb mounted on a pipe. The lamp was true make-shift, like a bag of hardened concrete with a pole stuck into it. A wire ran along the outside of the pipe, then along the floor and up a wall to where it plugged into the ceiling fixture. Once I saw this rigging, no way would I attempt to turn it on. I said so to Ursula. She shrugged and followed me inside.

Using the light from the bulb hanging low outside our door, I looked around. At the far side of the room was an old army cot, almost double-wide. In a heap on top, were two worn and obviously scratchy, faded green blankets; no pillows. It wasn't that I minded being that close to Ursula if we did share the cot, but we'd have to coordinate any turns we made so we wouldn't push each other onto the floor or one of us wake up with a black eye.

I stared at the toilet and it stared back. What Carlos sounded proud of was a plywood box with a hole crudely cut in the middle of it, with no partition or curtain for even minimal privacy. I peered into the toilet to see how deep it was and couldn't see the bottom. It was a mixed blessing that it was so cold in the room because that kept any odor out. In fact, heat in the hotel seemed nonexistent.

A basin stood on a tree stump that still wore its bark. Next to the basin was a square can that looked like it might hold about two-gallons of whatever. Electrical wire was fashioned as handles on two sides. Next to the can was a water valve that came out of the wall about two feet off the floor. I turned the handle, but nothing came out.

It was just for the night, only three dollars American, and safe. Or, so Carlos claimed.

Ursula said that morning would not be a good time to wait to get water and I agreed. My thought was that by morning, in this cold, we'd have to break through the ice that was sure to form on top.

I picked up the can, got to the door, then turned and said to Ursula, "Lock the door behind me. See this bolt? Use it. And, don't open it for anyone other than me."

"Sure, Sam. Since a hard sneeze could blow the door open, I'll lock it so if anyone tries to break in, at least I'll hear them coming."

"Smartass."

"Be careful."

21

"Don't worry. I have this for protection," I said, holding the can up.

I started down the stairs and found Carlos standing at the bottom step, looking as though he was just about to head up.

"May I be of some help, Señor?"

"Glad your English is so good, Carlos. Perhaps you can be of some help."

He saw the can and grinned, like maybe there was a tip in it for him. "How can I assist you?"

"Carlos, we feel in need of a little protection." His expression changed, but he stayed silent. "We need a gun." Again, no response. "A revolver," I added. I recalled a word from the many old movies I'd watched over the years. "A pistola. Preferably, two of them."

"I see," he replied and walked back behind the counter.

"In fact, better make that two pistolas and a really good knife."

Carlos draped one arm around his belly and rested his other elbow on it, posing like Thinking Man Standing. I couldn't tell if he was really giving the matter thought or trying to impress me—maybe both, because he did some pantomime with his facial expression that made it look like he was wracking his brain on my behalf. He kept this up until I got irritated that he was wasting my time.

"Carlos?"

He stopped this charade and calmly said, "The bag."

"Bag?"

"Yes, Señor. The bag from the train. You know, the black leather one left behind by a friend who seems to have lost it."

I didn't know if I should tell Carlos that his young friend had, indeed, lost it…possibly in more ways than one.

As I stood there thinking about what I should and shouldn't say, Carlos said, "You know I must get the bag, Señor. You have nothing to worry about in Puño. We are a very gentle people." He was wearing an expression I felt like knocking off his face.

"Stop the crap, Carlos. If you want the bag, get me what I want first. Two revolvers and one knife by early morning, and we'll…"

Carlos stopped me before I finished, "Señor, no! Lo siento mucho. I will get what you want."

"That's better. How much time do you need to…"

Carlos held up his hands, like he was showing me they were empty. Then he slowly reached under the desk, keeping his eyes on mine. When his hands came out, each one held a small caliber pistol. He placed both pistols on the counter and pushed them towards me. The guns were identical, both Beretta semi-automatics, both blued. I wondered how the hell he'd gotten them in this neck of the woods.

Granted a .32 caliber is better for closer encounters, but even a small gun is better than no gun. The almost five-inch length meant they'd be easy to conceal. I checked the safety on both guns then checked the clips. Loaded.

"Any more bullets, Carlos?"

"Señor, you did not ask for more bullets." He reached into his right pocket and pulled out a six-inch switchblade which he flicked open and pointed towards me. His hotel and clothes might be filthy, but the blade was clean and appeared sharp.

We stood there and looked at each other for a moment. Carols smirked, then closed the knife and placed it on the counter.

"Now you bring me the bag, Señor. When you return with it, I give you the pistols and the knife."

We both smiled. He was smiling as though he'd just proven something. My smile was because I wanted him to believe he had.

"Carlos, fill this with water while I get the bag." I held the can out to him, but he didn't take it.

"Señor, there is no water until the morning. You can leave the can with me to fill then."

"Actually, Carlos, I think I'll just take it back upstairs."

I returned to Penthouse Four, knocked on the door, and called out Ursula's name. No answer. "Ursula!" I called louder. I knocked again and pushed on the door. It didn't open. Shit, why wasn't she answering? I decided to break the door in.

I'd just readied my body to bust through the door when I heard a muffled, "Coming." She undid the latch and opened the door.

"What the hell took you so long?" I noticed she had braved turning the light on in the room.

"What's *your* problem?" she snapped.

"Never mind." I closed and locked the door. "No water until morning. Listen, I made a deal to swap the leather bag for two pistols and a knife."

Ursula stared at me for a moment then said, "I should have done the negotiations. I would have thrown water *and* heat into the bargain. Sam, I'm not giving Carlos the bag."

"I have no idea what's going on, but Carlos knows something about the bag. He knew who carried it onto the train, that's for sure. The exchange was his idea. I think we should give it to him. Probably better if we're not caught hauling around a bag of cacao."

She wore an expression I couldn't read. "It's under the cot," she said a moment later.

I went to the cot and retrieved the bag. "Lock up. I'll be right back."

Ursula closed and locked the door behind me. For a moment, I thought she might change her mind and fight me about the bag. One of the things about Ursula was just when I thought I had her pegged, she'd surprise me. Women generally confuse men, but unpredictable women not only confuse us, they entice us because they're like a riddle we feel obligated to solve.

I went back down to Carlos who looked as if he hadn't moved since I left him. "Here you go, Carlos. A deal is a deal."

He took the leather bag and gave me a cloth bag. I gave a quick peek inside to make sure it contained what it was supposed to.

"At first light, you and Miss Jung must leave the hotel. It is advisable you board a collectivo back to Cuzco. We will both keep quiet about the bag and the guns, yes?"

"What's up, Carlos? The bag can't hold that many cacao leaves to be worth anything to the drug cartel."

He gave me a blank stare for a second then moved straight into looking confused. "Cacao leaves?" Gut instinct told me to stay quiet. "Yes," he said. "I think I understand. I will make sure that the bag reaches the *right* man, Señor. I told you Puño is safe, but it is no longer safe for you. As soon as it is morning, you must leave."

"You said it's no longer safe here for me. You mean us, right?" The rest of what he'd said made no sense to me, so I fixated on the part about my safety.

"No. Only you, Señor Paris. I have that right, yes? You have been seen by too many and so have an unusual problem."

"What's my unusual problem, Carlos?"

"I think I have said all I should say." He looked so serious, I decided to believe him.

"Don't you worry, Carlos. At first light, it's adios."

Christ. What was going on? What unusual problem; and why was so much attention paid to my being here? "A boat to La Paz leaves very early from the town dock. Miss Jung and I will be on it."

"La Paz. It would be good for you to go there."

"Trust me, Carlos, come tomorrow morning, I plan to get as far away from here as I can. If we ever meet again be sure not to say hello." I turned, cloth bag in hand, and headed up the stairs.

My head was spinning, literally. I had to tell Ursula about Carlos' warning, but the altitude was beginning to get to me. I knocked on the door and waited a few seconds before a drowsy-looking Ursula stood in front of me.

"I have to lie down," I said. "I don't know why Carlos acted so strange about a bag of cacao leaves; and I didn't understand most of what he said to me, even though he spoke English."

Ursula closed the door and locked it while I headed over to the cot and sat down She stood there looking at me.

"Yes?" I asked. Nothing. Then she started to laugh, softly at first, then really loud.

"I think the altitude's getting to you, as well."

"It was money, Sam."

"What the hell are you talking about?"

"The bag was packed full of money—hundred dollar bills. American."

"What the fuck... I never thought to look. I thought it held cacao leaves. I assumed the weight felt about right. If you knew this on the train, why the hell didn't you tell me?"

"I never looked inside until you left to get water."

"Ursula, you should have told me when I came for the bag."

"Don't worry, Sam. I filled the bag with two alpaca sweaters and dirty underwear. I tried to match the weight as close as possible."

I was off the cot and pacing. "Shit, Ursula! I traded the bag for weapons, for Christ's sake. Carlos saw we had that bag and wanted it from the first minute we got here. He was waiting for it. He didn't check it when I gave it to him, but if he hasn't looked inside already, he's going to. Then, we're not just in trouble, we're fucked. Give me the money. I'll take it down to Carlos and explain... What I'll explain, I don't know, but I'll think of something."

"No."

"What d'you mean, no? Don't play around with this, Ursula. Did you take a good look at this town? We've gone back in time, here. Our friend downstairs told me things that make no sense to me, but it sounds like we should pay attention. And, let's not forget the original guy who had the bag, that guy they took off the train at gunpoint if you recall. He's probably dead. Executed, most likely. Carlos was very clear that we're no longer safe here. We're in Puño, what, maybe an hour?...and, we're no longer safe."

"Then, let's get out of here now."

"No good. There's only one way out of this place—the hotel *and* the town, as far as we're concerned. We can't start walking and there's no transportation available at this time of night. I don't want to risk asking anyone for a ride, either. Damn it, I blabbed and told him we're getting the boat to La Paz in the morning. Fuck. I don't believe this. And you, how could you do this and not tell me?"

"Look, Sam, it's possible Carlos doesn't know what should be in the bag."

"He sure knew it wasn't supposed to be cacao leaves."

"Maybe he hasn't looked or maybe he's not supposed to even think about looking inside it. Be logical. You've been back five minutes already. If there was a problem, the door should have been kicked in by now. Besides, we have guns."

"Fuck, Ursula. He knows we have guns, he gave them to me. But, they *are* small guns. He might have a bigger gun, and I'm not in the mood for a shoot out."

"Sam, let me just show you something."

Ursula walked over to where one of the green blankets we'd found on the cot was now rolled up. She flipped it open and it unrolled like a red carpet for royalty. Bundles of money flew in all directions. She walked to the middle of the blanket and sat down. I walked over and stood there looking down at her.

She looked up at me and said, "Each bundle contains $10,000 dollars. There are twenty-eight bundles, or $280,000, to be exact."

The only time I'd ever seen more green was when I went past a golf course. Spread out in front of me was enough cash to buy anything I wanted and with no interest and no time payments. My shoulders dropped in resignation.

"Hell, Ursula, this is drug money. We have to get ourselves back on the right track, whatever that is."

"Carlos."

"What about him?"

"I'll make a deal with him. Sam, give me a gun." She paused then added, "Twenty-eight."

"What?" The woman could make my head spin worse than the altitude.

"Twenty-eight," she repeated. "Sam, what if two bundles are missing? Or what if there were fifty at the start? We easily could have gotten the bag after someone else had dipped into it. Who can prove otherwise?"

She stood up, opened the cloth bag, took out one of the guns, and popped the clip out.

"Both clips are full," I said. "I already checked. Where did you learn how to handle a weapon?"

"My father was a gun collector. Since he had them in the house, he thought I should know how to handle them safely." She slipped the gun into her jacket pocket. "Just in case."

"Jesus. I thought we might need protection, but not this soon."

"Don't be such a flincher, Sam. I'm sure it's going to be fine."

She unlocked the door and took off down the steps. I wouldn't be able to stop her and I didn't want to leave the room with the money bundles spread out on the floor even if we did seem to be the only ones there. I went to the door and tried to watch or hear what she was doing, but couldn't.

I was about to roll the money back into the blanket when a dizzy-spell hit again, only worse this time. My head was really spinning and it began to ache like a bastard. I fell down and started to crawl towards the cot, dragging myself over the money. This was worse than any drunk-time or hangover.

I managed to climb onto the cot. *Damn it*, I hadn't closed the door. Then a familiar feeling came over me; I was going to throw up. I forced myself to crawl to the toilet. I heard a sound like a car backfiring. A massive wave of nausea hit and I forgot about everything until I realized someone was standing in the room with me.

"Who's there?" I barely heard myself ask this.

"What's wrong?"

I was relieved to hear Ursula's voice. "Altitude has caught up with me, bad. Time to throw up."

"Let me help you get to the window. Considering the toilet, I don't think it's a good option for this."

"Anything," I said. "Just hurry."

Ursula helped me up and we both moved as fast as we could to the window. As soon as she opened it, I fell onto the sill, knees on the floor, and took the position of praying to an alley in Puño. Heaving made my head ache even worse. When there was nothing left inside of me, I placed my chin on the outside of the brick facade and stared down into the alley. The spinning was coming under control, but I didn't dare move yet. "What went on with you and Carlos?" I finally asked. Silence.

I stood up and positioned myself against the wall so I wouldn't fall down. I was still woozy, but I could feel my head clearing. "Talk to me, Ursula."

"I thought maybe I could reason with him." she started. "You know, see what he'd say; but when I went downstairs, he wasn't there so I came back up."

"No one saw you?"

"No one was there *to* see me. Carlos is probably long gone. All we have to do is keep the money safe until we can figure a way to smuggle it out of the country. At dawn when light starts to appear, we'll leave just like nothing happened and get the boat. We'll see where we go from there. How does that sound?"

"Speaking of sound, what was that sound?"

"What sound?"

"Like a car backfiring."

"I didn't hear anything, Sam. The altitude must be really getting to you."

I admit the thought that maybe Ursula had dispatched Carlos as opposed to his leaving on his own, occurred to me. I didn't want to believe it. If she had, wouldn't we be getting the hell away now? What started out to be a possible search-and-rescue for an uncle had quickly gone strange. I didn't like the feelings I was having about her either—not exactly frightened, but definitely wary.

Ursula took the cot while I sat with my back against the wall next to the window in the event I needed to purge again. Also, it seemed like a good idea not to get too comfortable so if anything happened, I'd be ready to move. I put one of the guns next to me on the floor. I dozed, but I know I was awake more than not. Ursula, damn her, slept through everything, including the racket some dogs made when they got into a fight over something they found in the alley.

Just before dawn, I gently woke Ursula. We'd slept in our clothes, so were ready to move. The money was in her backpack and as she picked it up, I said, "Maybe I should carry that."

"Sam, if we get stopped for any reason, it's more than likely I won't get searched. Peruvians have respect for fair-haired women, and especially one who speaks their language."

"Maybe you're right, but maybe you're not," I said. Her face and body language clearly told me she wasn't going to part with the backpack. I pitied anyone who tried to take it from her. And, I realized she didn't know me any better than I knew her. She might wonder if I'd take it and run. Ursula was on her adventure; and me? Who the fuck knew? I just wanted to get back to the States in one piece and alive.

We went downstairs as quietly as possible. Carlos had been nowhere in sight, inside the hotel or outside. Nobody else was hanging around either, at least, not that I could see. We made our way to the dock without a hitch.

I'd been to Vietnam and had definitely seen action from both sides of a rifle; but the thought of Ursula killing Carlos and being so cool about it was more than a little unsettling. Everything considered it was as if I was in a movie, or having a weird dream, or had drunk too much bad booze, or all three happening at once.

As we walked in the direction of the dock, Ursula put her hand on my arm to slow me, "Sam, I was thinking of how I, we, might approach the pilot."

"I forgot about the pilot. Besides, I think we should focus on one thing at a time, like getting away from here. We may not find him. Remember the second guy said the pilot died."

"Don't worry, Sam. We'll get out of here with no problem."

"You sound a lot more confident about that than I feel."

"We're fine. I think the pilot's alive. If we talk to the right people, follow the trail, we'll find him. Anyway, my thought is that as fellow Americans, and having both actually seen the flowing gold, we might become new best friends, sort of. I'm certain I could get him to tell me—us—what he knows about the Inca gold."

I listened to her and found myself thinking one good reason to still have the money was if we did find the pilot, flashing cash at him might motivate him to open up to us. Even if he'd found gold, nobody turns down free money.

Ursula's gold fever was contagious because images of finding it were running through my mind. So were images of telling her half the $280,000 was mine. Conscience isn't supposed to be flexible, but I found mine bending. Shit. This broad had me thinking everything was okay. A deeper part of me knew we could get into real trouble, but another part of me said, *What the hell.* Here we were, walking down some of the most dangerous streets imaginable, carrying a load of cash and weapons, and the sun was just starting to rise.

I'd had worse starts to a day in Vietnam. But in that country, I knew people wanted to kill me and why. The danger was a known. Here, the full extent of possible danger was mostly invisible, an unknown, but palpable. However, this did beat my life in Grand Central Station.

It was also the first time in a long time any real thought about the future entered my mind. Life had become a matter of existing—finding a dry spot to sleep and the next meal. It almost scared me to think of the word: Hope.

The temperature was frigid, and I almost wished I was wearing one of the alpaca sweaters Ursula had stuffed in the black bag. We had extras packed, but I didn't want to take the time to put one on.

Ahead of us, through the narrow streets, was a lake with a turquoise hue unlike anything I'd ever seen. Lots of boats lined the water's edge. There were so many tied up, I wondered if there was one boat for every resident. The boats were kayak-shaped, but larger, and made of reeds. Sitting in each boat was either a man or a woman, though mostly women, all of them dressed in traditional colorful Peruvian clothing.

The shoreline was rocky beach littered with wooden docks. One dock had a larger version of these water taxis tied up so that the craft was positioned sideways along the pier. We approached a man standing near that boat and Ursula confirmed, in Spanish, it was the one that would take us to the Island of Tequile.

"What about La Paz?" I asked.

"No longer a good idea. Besides, we were going to Tequile anyway."

Ursula seemed to always be at least one step ahead of the game, and me.

Our transport was more like a large rowboat with what looked like a small car engine exposed at the center of it. That explained the film on the water and why the air reeked with the odor of gasoline. The smaller reed boats that were rowed started to look better to me, less chance of an explosion.

The lake seemed like it was at least a hundred miles across. The mountain ranges appeared to be farther back than that. The mountains, themselves, were massive and grand with their peaks hidden in clouds that hung low over our heads. Unless someone sees the colors, lines, and shapes in person, they can't imagine it.

There was obviously a distance between the mountain ranges and the shoreline, but none seemed to exist, like in the two-dimensional effect of a painting or photograph, more of a curved-space effect than linear. I felt visually saturated to the point of overload. And, illogically, connected to my surroundings in a way I didn't understand.

I allowed the beauty to sweep me into it. For a moment, I forgot about the hotel and Carlos—who might or might not still be breathing, drug money, armed soldiers, a young man taken from a train whose mother might be weeping over his death, and the danger I probably was getting into with Ursula as we tracked down a man who might know where X marked the spot, a man who might never be found because he was dead.

CHAPTER 4

I lean forward in my chair and fix Harry with my eyes. "I'll be right back."

"Where're you going?

"Gotta make my bladder gladder. I'd appreciate another round waiting when I get back."

You're like a dry well, Sam."

The Men's room is over by where Harry's woman is still entertaining the regulars, Jake included, I notice. I give her a brief glance as I walk by, and she gives me the same. On my return trip, she fixes her eyes on me, wearing an expression I can't read beyond definite interest, but not the sexual kind. That much, I'm sure of. Back at the table, Harry has two new beers waiting.

"You know, Harry, a lot of shit's hit the fan in that country; but I have to tell you, the area from the valley of the Urabamba to Lake Titicaca and the history and myths are as exciting as they are foreboding.

"The Incas molded themselves to their harsh environment quite well. They developed a way to freeze-dry meat and designed terraces on the mountainsides for farming that allowed them to use vast amounts of space not available to them in the valleys. They created a culture with a governing society and a religion that historians believe may have had its inception on the Island of Tequile. It's a religion that parallels that of the so-called civilized invaders who considered the Inca savages. They may have been considered savages by others, but the Incas, even in their savagery, were far more merciful to captive Spaniards than was the contrary."

"You're rambling National Geographic shit again, Sam. I get it, you were impressed. Now, can you get on with your story? You left off at the docks in Puño."

"It's not like you're paying me by the word, Harry." I take a long pull of beer.

He's right. I am rambling; but not much about my time there seems linear in how it happened. Some visions engrave themselves in a person's memory forever. My own memories are a blend of painful events and almost heart-stopping beauty.

We boarded the boat and were getting settled in when I heard a man's voice yell, "Espera! Espera!" I couldn't decide whether to feel relieved or grab my gun. Carlos was a distance away and jogging as fast as his pudgy body and short legs could move.

"I don't know if I'm happy or not to see Carlos," I told Ursula. "What's he yelling?"

"He wants the boat to wait for him."

""Fuck. We don't need this."

Not far behind him were the two French storytellers we'd met in Cuzco and the two women who'd been with them. I decided to call them the Cuzco Four. They were moving their feet and mouths a hundred miles an hour and left Carlos in their dust. There was something about them I didn't like; I just couldn't pinpoint what. I took a good look at each of them and called it for what it was: A bad feeling.

The man Ursula had spoken with yelled out, "Todos bordo."

Carlos was still a long way back, hardly moving, and bent over holding his side as he slowly staggered in our direction. I could see his mouth moving, but he must have run out of air because no sound seemed to come out.

The Cuzco Four got into the boat so smoothly it led me to think they'd done it before. In fact, rather than acting casually as they had at the bar, there was something of a military precision in their movements and manner. It was difficult to believe it was coincidence or just bad karma that we'd be sharing the boat to the Island of Tequile, instead of La Paz, as I'd told Carlos the night before. Everyone got settled into their seats on both sides of the boat. Ursula and I ended up next to the engine and facing it. No one made an attempt to strike up a conversation.

The engine sputtered to life and I whispered to Ursula, sitting to my left, "There are no life preservers."

She glanced around, "I guess not."

The lines were cast off and we began to move. "Glad our helmsman left before Carlos could make it," I said.

"I heard him say it would be too much weight in the boat."

Engine popping loudly, the boat's bow sliced through the water, creating a gentle wake that caused the reed boats still tied to the docks to undulate on the surface.

Ursula suddenly flashed one of her killer smiles at me and hugged me tightly, so I returned both gestures. At first I thought it was fear or anxiety that caused her to do this, but when I looked at her, I realized she was acting affectionate. There was something else, though, excitement. Another man might have hoped this random affection meant something promising was coming later. With all we could have done and hadn't, I wasn't going to hold my breath.

Granted, with Carlos alive and well, she wasn't a killer; but my gut told me to stay on guard when it came to Ursula. What was also in my mind was, in spite of feeling new hope, what the hell had I been thinking to take this trip with her? Money had been the primary reason, but was it enough? Sure, she certainly wasn't boring and I felt the effects of the landscape, but the rest of it was nothing short of fucked up. We had a lot of cash now. We were ahead. Logic said we should just return to the States, split the money, and say our goodbyes. Maybe even spend a day or two engaged in some of that physical interaction that wasn't happening here. Another part of me asked *What if a gold find is just around the corner?*

The engine coughed and the sound brought me back to the present. When I looked at the engine, I noticed the carburetor gas line had a rag wrapped around it to try and restrain a leak. Twenty minutes later, the rag burst into flames. Ursula and I, the ones closest to the engine, found ourselves climbing onto the tops of the seats to get away from the fire and heat. The engineman quickly snuffed out the flames with a large damp rag. The craft never lost headway and the engine kept up its endless *pop-pop-pop* beat. Though extraordinary for us, this was apparently a common occurrence for him because he not only put out the fire like it was no big deal, when he sat down again he placed the tiller between his knees and started to knit.

I had Ursula ask him about the knitting and learned the men knit constantly, as well as look after the children while the women tend to what would usually be considered a man's job in other countries. His wife was taking care of business in the village today, so had him take over the boat.

Needless to say, Ursula and I spent some time waiting for an encore of flames, though I seemed more concerned about it happening again than she did. However, the gentle rocking of the boat soon brought on a welcomed sleep. Naturally, Ursula was the first to nod off.

We woke at the same time. I looked around to get my bearings and noticed the Cuzco Four staring at us like vultures waiting for the last breath to leave a body. Ahead was the Island of Tequile. What I could see of this part of the island was very rocky and devoid of vegetation. The boat glided towards a large dock in front of us.

On shore was a long, steep rock stairway that went up at least five hundred feet and was built into the high cliff —a strenuous enough climb at sea level. I wasn't looking forward to making my way up it. Several people, dressed as colorfully as our engineman, stood at the top of the stone steps watching our approach. We disembarked onto the rocky shore. The Four, who had not said a word to us, yet had been so chatty in the Cuzco bar, literally stood at attention.

We learned upon docking, the only way visitors can stay on the island is if a family takes them in. Visitors not claimed by a family have to leave.

One of the Four, Jean-Paul, finally spoke and said to me, "We are in luck. There are enough families here for the people on the boat."

The Cuzco Four led the way up the stairs. Ursula was behind them, with me, gasping almost as soon as I started to climb, behind her. We reached the top several minutes behind the Four. The choice of who went with which family was made quietly by the women. The Peruvian men knitted away and never missed a stitch while selections were being made. Jean-Paul and Francois went with one family and the two women went with another.

There with us, faces blank of expression, was the remaining couple. He was knitting at rapid speed, needles clicking away. The woman at his side gave us a wide smile, exposing her blackened teeth and mouth. A slight nod from the woman indicated we were to follow them. Ursula exchanged a few words with the woman, who turned and began leading us along a rocky path well-worn with time. No one offered to carry our gear, which was fine with me considering what we'd packed in ours.

The terrain was glacial-like, just without the ice. Stone houses were scattered here and there, each one with what seemed to be a barn made of the same stones. The woman led us past their house and into one of these extra structures. We realized it was our lodgings, and that we had a pretty good view of the lake. The husband stood there knitting and the wife, smiling, as we looked around. Then, just as silently, they left without a word.

Ursula dropped her gear down in a corner of the room. "So, what do you think, Sam? Not exactly the Hilton, is it? And we can even afford room service now."

"Very funny."

Ursula suddenly started to sing and dance around. I thought a lack of oxygen probably made her feel as though intoxicated. I wasn't dizzy, but was lightheaded. What the hell. I joined her antics until both of us fell to the floor, holding on tight to each other to keep from falling off the planet. Our mouths came together. Both of us started to breathe heavier. This wasn't as sexy as it sounds, though, because all elements combined, I passed out.

CHAPTER 5

"Sam," Harry interrupts, "I think you're deliberately leaving out what happened next. Come on… You're alone with a beautiful, exciting woman and you want me to believe you passed out? I promise it won't be included in the story. I'm a married man. Let me have a little vicarious fun here."

"That's what happened."

"Bullshit."

"It's not bullshit. I woke up in nearly total blackness. I tried to focus, tried to make out a figure that was standing in the doorway."

"Sam," Ursula called out. She held a lantern up to her face then moved it two feet away from mine.

"Get that light out of my eyes, will you. What happened to the sun?"

"You've been asleep for three hours," she said as she put the lantern down on the dirt floor. "The sun's been gone for two of them. Guess what? I found out the pilot's here on the island, though hasn't been seen for years."

I stood up, but not very easily. My knees refused to work right, same for my body and brain. This altitude and thinner air was knocking my socks off. "Years, huh? Either he's real good at hiding or someone's yanking your chain and he's dead. Maybe we came here for nothing."

"I didn't word that right. It's been years since he's stayed on the island, but does show up from time to time."

"How are we supposed to find him?"

"They say it's not so easy."

"Who told you this?"

"I discovered a little tearoom in town. Sam, the pilot is here and it seems he spends his nights on the lake in a *junco barco*—a reed boat, but comes ashore on occasion."

"The locals at the tearoom gave you this information?"

"Not exactly. The Cuzco Four, as you call them, were there."

"And you believe them, of course." She didn't answer me, just stood there. "All right, what now?"

"Nothing, now. We have to wait for morning. You probably noticed there's no electricity, no toilet, and no running water. There is a well we have to fetch water from in the tin can over there," she said pointing. "The toilet, I leave to your imagination. Don't look at me like that, Sam. Come out here and see the sky."

I wobbled to the doorway and joined Ursula who was turning in slow circles with her arms out-stretched. I'd been impressed with the night sky at the sacrificial stone, but this was like having our own planetarium. We were under a dome of stars that seemed to be within reach. I thrust my hand skyward to touch the magnitude of melding lights. My fingertips seemed enveloped by the heavens. Ursula and I stood together. Our breath misted and mingled in the air like small clouds that we watched float above our heads and linger longer than I thought possible.

"Ursula, I know it's not realistic, but at this moment, it's like you and I are experiencing something no one else on Earth is."

She didn't speak, but wound her arm through the crook of mine and leaned into me. We stayed like that until the cold made us numb. Trance-like, we walked back to the barn. We put our bedrolls next to each other on the ground and lay there surrounded by stillness until we nodded off.

Morning sunlight penetrated my deep sleep and desire to stay in the moment. Ursula and I were lying with our bodies wrapped so close together you couldn't run floss between us. At the lower altitude, our bedrolls had been warm enough. Higher up, without the benefit of extra blankets beyond the thin ones we'd *borrowed* from Carlos' hotel, we'd huddled together and slept in our clothes as we'd done every night since we'd arrived in Peru. I learned, after the fact, that the way to stay warm at night in the Andes is to remove all clothing. If Ursula knew about this, she never mentioned it. Another kind of man would have discovered this on his own the first night he'd spent next to a woman like her. Ursula and I had kissed and touched, but she'd never indicated she wanted to do more. Whatever else I've been and done, I follow a code regarding women. Unless I get a green light, it's a no-go. I wasn't sure about Ursula, but the feel of our bodies so close did remind me I was still a man and that a man has needs. However, other bodily needs were more pressing.

There wasn't anything that resembled an outhouse around, so I found a private spot in nature and nearly froze my parts off while taking care of business. I walked around a bit, trying to loosen stiff muscles and saw a well about fifteen yards from the house. I grabbed the tin can from the barn and went to fill it up. Our hosts were used to the water, but I wished a good filter was on hand to run the water through before using it even just to brush my teeth.

When I returned to the barn, I told Ursula I wanted her to take me to the tearoom. She put her backpack on without a word and walked out. I followed, of course. Many paths led from our doorway, and Ursula went straight to one and started down it. I wondered how she'd known which path to take last night, but she could easily have asked our hosts while I was unconscious. We walked the path to town in silence.

We came to the building that housed the tearoom. I stopped and looked around. It appeared that all rocky paths led to the front door. We entered and crossed the room to a table near a window where we had a view of the large expanse of lake. The table was made from scrap wood and was built almost like a picnic table. The chairs, the first we had seen on the island, were crudely constructed and made of bark-covered branch segments with woven reeds fashioned for seats.

A young girl wearing colorful traditional clothing came to the table with a pitcher of steaming tea and a plate of pancakes. The pancakes looked as though they'd been cooked on a flat stone over a bed of ashes. Obviously, asking for a menu was out of the question.

I didn't hear anything, but movement in the doorway caught my attention. Silently, the Cuzco Four filed in one at a time and took up position on the other side the room. I watched them, but not one made eye contact with me or Ursula.

"I wonder if this is the only place to eat here, or if the Cuzco Four followed us?" I said in a low voice.

"Don't act so paranoid, Sam. They're not bothering us."

"Maybe they don't bother you, Ursula. From what I can tell, not a lot bothers you. I'm not comfortable with the fact that since we met them in Cuzco, every time we turn around, there they are."

"Whatever, Sam."

We finished our meal without further conversation between us. As we left the tearoom, I waved to the Cuzco Four who not only didn't wave back, but seemed to have no reaction at all.

Daylight gave us a chance to explore our surroundings on the island. Somewhere on this rock or out on the lake, was our pilot, our latest objective, if he was indeed alive. If alive, it seemed he stayed on his boat and only came ashore whenever he needed to.

We circumnavigated the whole island by way of one path, which unlike the others, did not lead to a house or barn. Instead, this path went only to the upper portion of the island on the side where the staircase was that we'd used at the dock. On the far side of the island, our path descended gradually; and after a good distance, went almost to the water's edge. Here, large boulders at least twelve feet in diameter, jutted out about one hundred feet until they fell deeply at a sharp angle to the seemingly bottomless green water, which made it look almost impossible for a boat to land.

The scene here was like one of the biblical plagues. Frogs covered the stones for as far as I could see; but as we neared them, they hurriedly scrambled into the water.

We sat on one of the boulders near the water. Ursula took off her backpack, reached inside, and pulled out a large bottle of Pisco.

"Ursula, there are times when you are my kind of woman, and this is one of them."

We took turns sipping from the bottle. Pisco is always potent; but at this altitude, a few slugs can make a person zonked. It acted like a drug on me. My eyes closed and my chin drooped towards my chest. I snoozed until I was disturbed.

CHAPTER 6

"You're on my rock," I heard a voice say. It wasn't Ursula. My head popped up like toast.

"What did you say?" I asked. My mind felt like it was in a fog and it took a few seconds for my eyes to focus. Ursula wasn't near me where she should have been. I looked around and could just barely make her out in the distance throwing rocks at the water.

"I said you're on my rock."

I turned my attention back to the man standing over me. Though he was wearing a pancho, he looked and sounded American. He stood about five-eight, and my guess was he weighed around 160 pounds. He wasn't rugged looking. In fact, he had a friendly, unlined face and a head full of wavy brown hair and blue eyes that commanded attention.

"Everyone who lives on this island," he said, "is given a rock of his own by the socialist committee. The one you're on is mine."

"I'll move."

"You might as well be my guest since you're here, but there is a price."

"And that would be what?"

"A decent pull or two on that bottle of Pisco. My name's Frank," he continued, "Frank Buero. And what do I call you, my trespasser friend?"

"Sam, and that's Ursula over there," I said as I handed the bottle to him.

Frank sat on the rock, took the bottle, and drank a good amount of Pisco. "Whew! This must be from Cuzco. It's the good stuff! Better than the slop they serve in P-town."

"Are you from Boston, Frank?"

"Nope. What's left of my accent is from North Carolina. What made you think Boston?"

"P-town, to me, means Provincetown, on the tip of Cape Cod."

"I meant P, as in Puño, though Puño stinks like pee."

"I hope you don't run a travel agency."

He looked out over the water, took another healthy slug, handed the bottle back to me and smiled. "No, but I could, I suppose. Thanks for the Pisco. I have to get going. The sun's starting to set."

"What happens? You turn into a pumpkin or something?"

Frank didn't respond as he stood up, just smiled again. Didn't say goodbye, either; just started to leap from rock to rock until I lost sight of him when the shoreline merged into a large bend at the coast.

I sat there for a while, taking smaller sips of Pisco. Something on the water headed towards me. It was Frank in a reed boat larger than any I'd seen so far. He pulled up as close as he could to his rock.

"You came here to ask me some questions, didn't you, Sam?" he shouted. "Be here tomorrow, same time, same place. Wear warm clothes and bring a compass. Have you got one?"

"I've got a real good one."

"Consider tomorrow a boys' night out, so don't expect to be back until sunrise the following morning."

"What are we up to?"

"You'll see. And, Sam, bring Pisco. Mañana."

Frank started paddling slowly but steadily away from the island. He stopped rowing after a few minutes and discarded the pancho to reveal he was dressed like a World War II pilot, then resumed rowing at a steady pace.

There are a lot of oddballs in this world, but one thing I felt sure of, especially with him in that get-up, was that he had to be the pilot, and he knew we were looking for him. Jean-Paul had said the pilot had gone mad searching for gold in the jungle. Frank didn't seem crazy to me, but maybe he'd turn out to be a few cards short of a full deck.

I watched him until he was only a speck on the horizon. We'd come here to look for him, and he found us...well, me, at least. The thing was the guy we were looking for should have been older, a lot older. I put Frank around my age, maybe younger. But, I've never been good at guessing a person's age. And what was with the costume? I was mulling over these questions when Ursula sat next to me on the rock. I was kind of startled when she did that because I hadn't heard her approach.

"Well, Ursula, your pilot or his imposter just paid me a visit."

She looked at me like I'd lost my mind. "Too much Pisco, Sam. Looks like you damn near finished the bottle by yourself."

"How'd he know about me or where to find me?"

"Who?"

"Frank. Didn't you see him? If you hadn't walked off, you would have met him."

"Maybe you need to take it easy on the Pisco or the tea from now on. I forgot to mention the tea they make at this elevation has cacao in it."

"I'm not drunk and I'm not hallucinating. While you were off tossing rocks at the water, some guy who called himself Frank showed up. Yeah, we drank Pisco, but... I wish you wouldn't look at me like that. I'm telling you, Ursula, he was here. I can't believe you didn't see him sitting with me or when he paddled off towards the horizon. He's real, all right; and I'm supposed to meet him here tomorrow at this time. I know you were the one who wanted to talk to him, but he didn't invite you. Maybe he's our pilot and maybe he isn't, but something in my gut tells me I need to be here when he shows up."

Ursula stood and so did I. I was wobbling, so grabbed onto her. "Para falta por oxigeno," she said. "The potent Pisco has had its way with you. It's decreased the oxygen in your brain and caused you to imagine things. You probably fell asleep and dreamed it."

"Just because you didn't see him doesn't mean he wasn't here. He was here."

"You have a point. From what you said, he didn't stay long, and I wasn't paying attention to what you were doing."

As we made our way to the top of the island, I thought of Frank out on the lake. Nightfall was almost upon us. What was he doing out there? Mañana seemed a long way off.

"This path will lead us back to the teahouse and some food," Ursula said.

The way back was dotted with stone houses. Every time we passed one of these dwellings, we became the objects of curiosity to the people inside. The sound of our footsteps on the rocky path brought children from the darkness of their homes to the doorways to peer out at us. I saw many shy round faces, most with runny noses. As we moved past, the parents joined in on what was most likely the only entertainment of the approaching evening.

The women appeared to be much older than they probably were. The men were constantly knitting, even as the day came to an end and light started to fade. Both men and women alike were missing rows of teeth, and their gums were black from cacao use. Ursula had explained the blackening happens when they chew on the leaves then put a cooled ember into their mouths. They let this odd combination sit in the saliva until it turns cocaine-like. We were at an elevation that allowed cacao and was why, as Ursula had said, tea served everywhere was loaded with it. For residents, it was a staple.

Near the teahouse was a church in what appeared to be the center of town. It was a church unlike any we'd seen elsewhere in Peru. Most churches had lavish Spanish facades. This one was drab in comparison, practically nondescript except for the small, plain cross on its roof. The path that led to the front steps of the church was not nearly as well-worn as the one that went to the teahouse.

We by-passed the church and went inside the teahouse. I wasn't happy and was definitely uneasy to see the Cuzco Four there again. This time, we drew their attention, and it wasn't because I was still wobbling a bit, well, more like stumbling. I did note Ursula didn't seem to be similarly affected by either the altitude or Pisco, at least not to the extent I seemed to be.

The Four were watching us as if in anticipation of something, so I called out, "Hello, everybody." The Cuzco Four looked away and Ursula and I crossed over to a table at the opposite side of the room.

"Ursula, I have the feeling the Cuzco Four were expecting someone else and we disappointed them."

"I get the same feeling, Sam. I know I disagreed with you about them earlier, but they are kind of strange. I'll avoid them tomorrow night while you're meeting with Frank."

"Glad you decided to accept my meeting him happened. Maybe you should stay in tomorrow night, or" I added quickly when she started to object, "you can make sure wherever you go is not where they are. If you show up anywhere without me, it may draw attention. Do you think they were waiting for Frank?"

"Who knows? Fuck 'em. Let's eat."

The meal was the usual gastronomical non-event found in this area. It was just as well, since I noticed something was doing a number on my stomach. I did take out the bottle of Pisco, which seemed to help a little after a couple of sips.

"Ursula," I said, looking across at the Cuzco Four, "I can't help but wonder what brought them here. At the bar, they didn't indicate they were looking for Frank, but maybe that was their intention. Your interest in the pilot and the gold was obvious to them. If they were headed elsewhere, they changed course. We may be competing with them for Frank's information about where to find the gold. I wonder if they've already approached him."

"Forget them. You probably made first contact. Anyway, that's what I believe. And even if they did meet Frank, you're the one he asked to meet tomorrow night. We should head back to our *suite* now."

Almost on cue, the Cuzco Four got up and walked out. When we tried to exit the teahouse, all four blocked our way.

"Excuse us," I said somewhat firmly.

One of the women sneered, "You should leave this island. These people are innocents; your kind destroys. We saw you both drinking in front of the natives, carrying on. You," she said pointing a finger in my face, "could barely walk when you came into the teahouse. This island is a sanctuary from all sins."

"Who died and made you God?" I fired back.

"We are the Church of the Christ workers," the other woman said.

"Maybe you should consider re-visiting what acting like a Christian means," I added.

"Goodnight," Ursula mumbled as she pushed me past the four.

"Those two are suddenly chatty," I said. "Back in Cuzco, they never opened their mouths at the bar."

"Considering what just came out, they should keep them shut."

"And, let's add hypocritical since all four of them were freely downing Pisco when we met."

We started up the stone path. Moonlight was all we had to steer ourselves in the dark. I reached over and grabbed Ursula's hand so we stayed together and steadied each other.

"My gut feeling is that they're full of shit," I finally said.

"I didn't like the way they behaved back there, but why do you think they're full of shit?"

"They said they're church members. Did you get a look at the church? Nobody takes care of it, there's not even a real road in front of it. This island doesn't seem to me to be influenced much by the church. Maybe tomorrow I can find out from Frank what's really going on."

When Ursula and I arrived back at the barn, a single lantern was lit and sitting in front of our door. Maybe it was the Peruvian equivalent to turning down the sheets at a swankier hotel, but without the chocolate mint on your pillow.

Suddenly not up to dialogue, I told Ursula we'd leave any discussion about anything until the morning. I had no trouble falling asleep like the dead as soon as I got into the bedroll. The events of the day, the blend of rarefied cold air and Pisco in the belly, and the walk back, surpassed any sleeping aid I'd ever used. Just before I fell asleep, Ursula told me she was going to sew the money into her bedroll.

"You're the one who has to sleep on it," was all I could muster before I was out for the count.

CHAPTER 7

I woke at dawn. When I felt I could brave the chill, I grabbed the tin can to get fresh water, but first, selected a new private spot in the great outdoors so I could take care of priorities. My muscles felt stiff from all the walking I'd done the day before, but the cold motivated me to move in double-time. I returned to the barn, put the full can of water down just inside the doorway, and turned to stare out at the lake.

"Where do you think Frank goes?" I said this more to myself than to Ursula who had joined me.

"No idea. All I know is it's time for our morning shot of cacao tea."

Ursula swung her backpack into position. She seemed to handle the cumbersome pack with greater ease than when we'd started our trip. Unless she'd stitched in the dark, the money was still in there. As for me, I had no problem leaving my backpack in the barn. Our hosts didn't appear the kind to bother anything. I could tell they'd left the lantern for us and hadn't disturbed anything inside. The knife and pistols were in Ursula's backpack, as well; so if anyone did mess with our stuff, all they'd find was clothing and some other items we could easily replace.

The walk to the teahouse seemed a lot easier. Maybe I was getting better acclimated to the altitude or maybe it's because it was mostly downhill. The quiet that surrounded us seemed to quell my usual desire to move with haste from place to place as I did in New York City. Even while living on the street, I still rushed as though I had appointments to keep.

Ursula didn't seem possessed by that typical big-city syndrome. At our first meeting over hamburgers, she told me she'd been born and raised in the Finger Lakes region where things happened at a much slower pace. I'd noticed, however, that when our pace quickened from time to time in Peru, she used it to her advantage. In fact, I'd noticed she sort of manipulated time by virtue of flowing with it, and among the things that intrigued me about her, that was one of them. I always seemed to rub time the wrong way, like sand added to oil.

Once again, we entered the doorway to the teahouse. I was relieved to finally be freed from the company of the Cuzco Four who were nowhere in sight. I expected the young girl to show up as before, with tea and pancakes sprinkled with ash, but a woman appeared and showed us the nearest thing to a menu they had. It was in Spanish, so I turned the task of ordering over to Ursula.

"You know, Sam, I gave some thought to our meeting up with the Cuzco Four. In fact, I'm actually anxious about them. You're probably right about their being up to something. A couple of times, they seemed almost military-like."

"I noticed that about them, too. One thing that got my attention was the attitude switch. They were chummy in Cuzco then totally different when they got on the boat. And, ever since."

"Oh, good! Food's here. Doesn't look too bad; does it?"

"Looks like some kind of brownish and greenish stuff to me. You sure this is what you ordered?"

"It'll be fine. I'm starving. Pass the tea, please."

Breakfast turned out to include more than what first came to the table, and since we weren't in a hurry to get anywhere and there was nothing else to do, we dragged the meal out until almost noon. We talked about what was going on from time to time; but for the most part, both of us seemed to be occupied with out own thoughts. Mine were about Frank and what he might tell me about the gold. What if we actually found a mother lode? I played out all kinds of scenarios about how to get a share of it into my life in the States, until I finally told myself *You have to find some first.*

The Cuzco Four never showed, though I couldn't help but glance at the door on occasion in anticipation of their arrival. They'd been our shadows so much of the time it almost irked me more not to know where they were. No one else came to the teahouse while we were there, so the hostess watched Ursula and me eat since we were the only action around.

I got tired of being the main attraction. "Let's go," I said.

Ursula put money on the table and we moved outside to the street. We saw a crowd of natives walking ahead of us. The Cuzco Four were there, as well. I told Ursula we should follow them, so we caught up to them but stayed at the back. One of the Four happened to notice us, said something, and three more heads turned to look.

The group moved towards the highest part of the island. It seemed we'd joined some kind of pilgrimage. We reached the top and everyone started to scrutinize the horizon. For a moment I wondered if they were looking for Frank, then wondered if there was a problem we should know about. I quietly voiced my concern to Ursula.

"Easy, Sam. Let me ask one of the locals what's going on."

Ursula spoke with a few of them. The women gestured like crazy while they talked and the men stitched even faster. Ursula's arms indicated the horizon. Heads shook first in an affirmative way and then in a negative way.

I didn't understand anything said, but it appeared two cultures separated by thousands of miles and time, were able to meld together with a smile. I felt this way as I watched Ursula smile and behave like a most gracious inquisitor. The Peruvians grinned at her in return. To me as an observer, both sides seemed to show no prejudice, just what appeared to be unquestioned respect or regard for all people. The Peruvians probably felt that way. Ursula was the queen of bullshit, so it was anyone's guess as to how she really felt.

While all this was taking place, I'd noticed the Cuzco Four had taken up a position well away from the general gathering. Instead of watching Ursula and the locals as I had, all four were fixed on me. Three of them moved their mouths in what seemed like unison. Were they praying? Since they couldn't seem to take their eyes off me, were they praying for me? The fourth member was writing something on a notepad. *Screwy bastards*, I thought. I tipped my hat to them. That caused them to turn away.

"Sam," Ursula called out as she returned to me with a smile from ear-to-ear, "it wasn't about Frank, but I went ahead and asked about him. I'd guess he's okay. No one seemed to have anything new to report about him, good or bad. But listen to this." She took my arm and moved us away from prying ears.

"Legend has it that gold flows over the Andes and fills this lake, like what we saw on the Urabamba River."

"Since it's not flowing now, when is that supposed to happen?"

"The legend says it happens when the water in the lake lowers so that the flat rocks appear. Those rocks are right in front of the big round ones where we were yesterday. After the water lowers, they say the lake fills with gold until only the round ones are seen again. They said it's almost time."

"Did the locals you spoke with tell you they usually see it?"

"They haven't seen it, but we've seen it before, Sam. I think we'll see it again."

"Wouldn't it be something if I could tell Frank we've seen it twice? What are we waiting for? Let's go. Ursula, this is some legend and we're living it."

CHAPTER 8

We retraced our tracks back towards the teahouse even though that would put us off the path to the side of the island where the rocks were. We did this to keep the Cuzco Four from following us, since I felt certain they would and Ursula agreed. She'd abandoned her previous admonishment for me to ignore them. If we did find gold, she didn't want them around any more than I did.

We'd walked these paths enough times that we knew which paths went where. Our pace was more rapid than usual, so both of us were breathing harder and faster, me more so than Ursula.

"Ursula, you said no one you spoke with earlier has ever seen the flowing gold we saw at the sacrificial stone. Did they know of someone who has, besides Frank, that is?"

"No, but it doesn't keep them from watching and hoping. They said that if you see the flowing gold, God has found you in favor."

Odd that Ursula and I had seen something these people had been seeking all their lives, as had Frank, if he really was the pilot.

"I feel like I've cheated the Peruvians," I said. "To them, seeing the gold is a divine gift. They live on and work their land. Any one of them earned the right, but I didn't."

"Do you really feel as badly about this as you sound, Sam?"

I stopped, looked squarely at Ursula then started walking again without answering. Neither of us spoke until we reached the stones.

We spotted where the group was standing and positioned ourselves where they couldn't see us.

"Damn, look at the size of those stones," I said. "Just yesterday, they were covered with water. Where did the water go?

51

There must be a dam somewhere. The stones look like a wall, don't they? Maybe it's an old Inca ruin. And look at the size of the frogs. The place is covered with them; and today, they've gathered only on the flat rocks. Weird."

We stood there for about an hour and watched and waited. The anticipation of seeing something spectacular was more than the actual event. The most activity we saw was the frogs jumping into the water—the rocks must have gotten too hot—and swimming back in our direction.

"Sam, we'd better get back to the barn. You said you need warm clothing and the compass for your meeting with Frank."

"You're right. I have a little over an hour before I meet up with him. We'll have to look for the flowing gold another time. It must be the people come here in hopes of being favored by God and seeing it. We sure didn't see anything like that from here."

"Are you nervous about tonight?"

"No. Are you?"

"You're the one meeting Frank."

"No, I'm not nervous. Why should I be?"

"I… I just have a feeling. I can't tell if that's good or bad. Take a gun."

"I won't need it with Frank."

"Still…"

Back at the stone barn, I added long johns and an alpaca sweater to my garb. I decided to take my bedroll and backpack, which I'd stuffed some camping candy into, along with the knife and a pistol. I didn't decide to carry because of Frank. There were other contingencies to consider. Four specific ones came to mind.

Ursula had more than one bottle of Pisco in her backpack. That made me realize how heavy her bag had been until now. Her figure was terrific, and from our touching sessions, firm and soft in the right places; but she must have done some specific training before this trip. I was the only one ever really winded or affected by the altitude or climbs, no matter how steep.

My compass was on a lanyard that was made into a noose, and I hung it around my neck. I swapped my felt cowboy hat for a Peruvian knitted cap to keep my ears warm. The finishing touch was a pair of gloves without fingertips, characteristic of the region.

"Well?" I said as I stood modeling for her.

"Typical tourista for sure, Sam. Time for you to go. Don't want to be late meeting Frank."

In a romantic novel or movie, I would have swept Ursula into my arms and kissed her until she swooned. Life is full of *ifs* and *what-ifs*. I reached up, as is my habit, to tip my cowboy hat, which of course, I wasn't wearing. I pretended it was intentional and told her I'd see her in the morning.

It was still light, so I followed the path that led to Frank's rock without any problem. It wasn't too long after I reached the rock that I saw Frank come around the bend in his reed boat. He pulled up to one of the now exposed flat rocks. He was wearing normal-looking clothes.

"Find it interesting, Sam?"

"Who pulled the plug?"

He responded with a chuckle then, "Are you ready?"

"Ready as I'll ever be."

Frank was in the rear, holding onto the rock by placing his paddle on top of it. I threw my backpack and bedroll on board and with not as much finesse as I would have liked, got into the boat.

"Well, I'll be," I said. "She's steady as a rock." Frank started back-paddling to move us away from the rocks. "What time do you think we'll return, Frank?"

He didn't answer my question. Instead he said, "We have to race sundown before the Andes take away all the light. Here, Sam, take this paddle. You row on the right side and I'll make up for mistakes and steer." We spun around and faced away from the island. "We have to paddle hard and fast now."

Paddle hard, we did. We kept up this frantic competition that had no checkered flag waiting for us until finally the thin air took its toll on me. My heart was pounding.

"Frank, you just lost an engine. I'm completely out of breath."

"Sit back, Sam. Relax. The rest of the ride is on me."

The island was long gone, replaced by darkness. After what seemed like an hour, Frank stopped paddling and we slid silently along the lake's surface, neither of us speaking for a while.

"You brought the Pisco?" he asked, breaking the silence.

"Yup."

"Well, uncork it and take a slug. Unite with the surroundings."

Unite with the surroundings? What kind of comment was that? I followed his advice, opened the bottle, but passed it to him first. After he took a good swig, he passed it back to me and I took a turn at it.

We drifted quietly for a time until Frank spoke. "Sam, I'm going to tell you some things that may answer your questions. Any I don't, you can ask."

It was not so dark that I couldn't distinguish the mountain ranges; yet when I twisted around to face Frank, I could hardly make him out. I could see only his outline with the Andes as a backdrop.

"Frank, I don't feel the cold any more." I turned back around.

He asked for the bottle. I passed it to him over my head. The boat moved ever so slightly as Frank took it from my hand. I heard him take a good-size drink. If he was anything like me, he was enjoying what the Pisco was doing to his inner soul, as well as throughout his body.

"Here," he said.

I reached my hand over my head and took it back. I took a deep pull as I faced the bow. "The rocks were overrun with frogs earlier; but when you and I left, not one was in sight. Where did the frogs go?" I waited, but Frank didn't reply, so I twisted around. "Frank?" He looked like he was asleep. "Frank," I said louder. "Are you okay?"

I thought about nudging him with my paddle but then heard him breathe, and relaxed. Maybe he was exhausted; after all, he'd had to do most of the paddling. I realized we had plenty of time, all night if he needed it. Strange, though, how warm it had suddenly become, considering that nighttime was always cold. I reached over to feel the water.

"Don't do that," Frank warned.

I was startled to hear his voice. "I thought you were asleep."

"See how still the water is, Sam? You don't want to break the spell."

"What spell?"

"Still water is, itself, perfect silence…casts its own spell. I lived with the Uro Indians on their floating islands, and also in the Amazon, then on the Island of Tequile. I spent many years out on the lake seeking the knowledge of the Incas. I've come to appreciate the stillness of the water."

"Where does the water go, Frank?"

"That's a two-part story. One part is that its movement is quite natural. If rivers from the Andes are heavily laden with melting snow, the lake swells. The water then migrates from the lake down into the Amazon basin. If the basin is dry, it takes up the excess flow very easily. It's possible to see a tremendous drop in water level in as short a time as a day."

"What's the other part?"

"The other part goes back to the start of the Incas. Not the Incas the archeologists have been studying. No. The Incas I refer to existed way before anyone imagines. Just know there are no records, no proof, nothing to substantiate what I'm telling you. There are only legends passed on by primitive tribes of the Amazon.

"Most of the natives consider the Island of Tequile to be the beginning of the world. There was no lake here a long time ago, only a large valley with tall hills behind it that eventually became the basin.

"The lake tribes, even if very primitive, all had one thing in common: They had a religion. Plus, they lusted for gold so much they incorporated it into their religious beliefs. There are drawings of silo-type structures that, I've been told, were built to hide gold, mass quantities of it, with the entrances blocked by a stone door like the one that leads into the ruin of Machu Picchu.

"These tribes became the Incas. Their love and lust for gold was such, they spent their lives acquiring it to use at the large cities they built of stone. There used to be a city at the base of what's now called the Island of Tequile. It was built at that sight because a tunnel was there that led from the valley to the jungle where the gold was brought. For security reasons, they blocked the tunnel with a trapezoidal stone just like the ones that open into the gold-filled silos, but this stone was tremendous in size. It was balanced in such a way that it could only tilt forward towards the jungle. It covered a chasm that fell into the belly of the Earth. Passage was possible from either direction; but if the door at the other end was up, passage into the city couldn't be achieved unless someone lowered the other door from the side that faced the city. In this way, their safety was controlled. Reach your hand back towards me."

I did so and he placed an object in my palm. "What is it, Frank?"

"It's a one-time exchange. I give you my compass and you give me yours."

I could barely see Frank's compass, but it felt like an old railroad watch with a flip-open cover. I took my compass from around my neck and passed it over my head. Frank took hold of it.

"Why the exchange?"

"In time, you'll understand."

Frank's compass also had a lanyard on it, so I put it around my neck. "Here Frank," I passed the bottle back to him.

He took a good swallow of Pisco and gave the bottle back to me. This time, however, I stuck the cork back in and placed the bottle between my legs.

Frank continued, "The leaders here eventually got fat and lazy. Soon, they needed slaves to do the menial work while they indulged in the fine art of degradation. The gods had a son who had his work cut out for him. Sound familiar? Well, anyway, it soon became apparent that the son, who had great influence on the others, wanted to instill his religious beliefs on everyone. This put the tribal leaders in an awkward position. Doing nothing to further the good of the city and the masses was fine with them. They had the good life, even if it was at the suffering of others; so, they decided to kill this upstart.

"Legend says that it rained as never before when he was killed and did so for a long time. 'The gods were crying,' the shamans said. The basin filled with water and covered the city. The followers of the gods' son took refuge on the hill. Before it was too late, the non-followers fled with their gold through the trapezoidal door, never able to return using that route.

"As a reminder of what happened, it's said that the gods lower the lake by opening the trapezoidal door until the remains of the city are exposed. At the same time, the gods also fill the valleys of the Andes with the color of gold. Once this happens, the lake rises up over the ruins again until the next time.

"About the frogs…When descendants of the decadent ones die—as an added reminder of that time—their souls return as frogs to the lake. Only the inhabitants of what is now called the Island of Tequile are not included in that misery."

"Why do you spend the night on the lake?"

"Not just the night, most of my time. I've been searching for the door thinking if the lake lowered enough and I was in the right spot, who knows? Maybe, just maybe..."

"And your compass?"

"The answer to the compass will come in time."

"What will you do if you locate the door?"

"Circumstances have changed. It's too late for me, Sam. You have to find the door."

"Me?"

"Yes."

"Why me?"

"What did you hear about me?"

"If you're who I think you are, which doesn't entirely make sense, but if you are... I heard that after the war, you and a couple of war buddies became bush pilots seeking adventure and gold, and that you crashed in the jungle of the Urabamba Valley. They say that you were the only survivor and were befriended by a tribe in the Amazon. After a while, you took up residence on the Island of Tequile."

"That's almost true. After the war, we took jobs with the Peruvian government as spotters to find Inca ruins. I had extensive low-flying experience. The Urabamba was the main area of our search for ruins. One day after many flights through the valley, we saw the flowing gold in the Valley of the Gods. Until it happened to us, I was sure it was only a legend. We crashed not from seeing a legend come true, but from engine failure.

A tribe had seen us crash and took me, the only survivor, under their care thinking I was sent from the heavens. After my injuries healed, I searched for the gold I believed I'd seen.

"Years went by and I began to realize that the real wealth of the Andes was the people, and a sense of being part of a tribe. No matter which tribe I was with, I made an effort to learn their language and their stories. I began to realize that there was nothing for me back in the States. I took a wife who bore two children, a daughter and a son. At first, being with her was more about meeting a variety of needs. I was surprised when I realized I'd come to love her. That connection grew even stronger when I realized she was carrying our child. The following year after our daughter was born, she was carrying our son. Sadly, I… Sorry, Sam, I think I'll hold off on telling you that part of the story for now.

"I went to the island in the middle of 'the lake of the gods' tears.' I went because a shaman told stories of what had happened to the people who lived there. He told of the rising and lowering of the lake water, and of a door at the bottom of the lake that controlled the flooding."

"What about the flowing gold? What causes that effect?"

"It's not time for me to share everything I know about that just yet either."

"Damn it, Frank. You said you were going to answer my questions and the ones you didn't answer, I could ask. I'm asking."

"You thought I was going to tell you precisely how to find the gold, didn't you?"

"Well...yes."

"In a way I have." He held up his hand to stop me when I started to speak. "It wasn't fair of me to say that I'd answer any question. You're going to have to trust me. Can you do that, Sam?"

"Yeah, I can do that; but it kinda blows." If I was disappointed, I could only imagine what Ursula would have to say. Frank seemed to give me a few moments to calm down before he spoke again.

"I decided that if I could find the great wealth lost in the Andes, it would be possible to protect my children and the tribe, as well."

"How?"

"I would have been able to buy vast tracks of land and save them from civilization. Now, civilization is killing them."

"You're telling me you never found the gold?"

Frank stopped speaking, and I sensed I should stay quiet.

We didn't have an anchor down, but I noticed we drifted very little. Neither did the boat create a stir on the adhesion of the water as we rested on it. Everything was still until I felt it was time to talk.

"Frank, I've seen the flowing gold."

"I know. I also know a lot more than you do about why you're really in Peru."

"What do you mean by that?"

"A local shaman repeated a dream he had of a man and woman at the top of a great stone of sacrifice. He said that while the woman was in a death-like state, the man saw the flowing gold through her eyes. He also said this man would seek me out, but not to wait for that to happen, that I had to hurry to him because there were four from one tribe who would bring him to death's door. That's why you and I are out here. I needed to find out what you really want and I had to tell you what I want. However, those two wants may not follow the same path."

"What do you want, Frank?"

"I want you to help my adopted people. Society, industry, and the greedy are bent on destroying the Amazon and everything and everyone in it. When that's accomplished, these annihilators will pack up and go home. My people, those who survive, will be abandoned with no place to go. They're jungle people. It's all they know. They won't fit into what we call civilization. Their stories will be gone and soon they'll become more mythical than real, like the Incas. History will repeat itself."

"What can I do? And, what prevents you from joining me?" I'd barely finished speaking when I thought of my four French *friends*, four from one tribe. "Damn, Frank! There are four people on the island right now from one tribe, if you want to call it that. And, Ursula is there, pretty much unprotected while I'm out here, since it would be four against one. I should paddle my butt back there immediately. If your shaman saw all this, what else does he know? What else do I need to know, Frank?"

"The jungle is where you will and must go to find the gold, Sam."

"How do I do that?"

"Ursula will lead you there."

"Ursula?"

Frank offered no more warnings or information, but added, "As I am now, so shall ye be." It was barely audible when he said it.

I'd heard him, but still said, "What?"

Once again Frank uttered the statement. Suddenly, I was struck with fear. Frank fell silent. I put a hand into the water and let my fingertips sink in up to the knuckles, deliberate about not creating a disturbance in the surface. The water and the air, which had both been a comfortable temperature, suddenly got cold. I yanked my hand out and dried it.

"Frank, what's going on?" I twisted around and found only a pile of clothing at the back of the boat where moments ago, Frank had been. I was alone. The hair on the back of my neck stood up. There had been no splash, no shifting in the boat's stillness. Frank had simply and silently disappeared.

I looked at the water around me; it seemed to have changed. I hadn't felt movement before, but now I could feel the boat gently rocking, as boats usually do on water. There was something about Frank that put me at ease. I wanted that back.

The lake was no longer the placid place it had been to me moments ago. Its depth carried with it Frank's tale of the city which was now covered by "the gods' tears. I became aware that I didn't actually know how deep the lake was. My fear of being alone, rational or not, was gaining intensity. *Easy*, I said to myself. *Deep is good.* For a brief moment, I imagined the shallows to be unsafe, filled with things unknown to me, creatures unseen by me in the darkness of the night and the shallow water that could get to me easily. Yet, the depths could carry its leviathans.

Calm down. Think. Which way should I head to go back to the island? Frank had been with me, so I hadn't paid attention. *Stupid!*

Double stupid. I took out Frank's compass and strained to read it in the dark. I could see it well enough to know it didn't work. Had he deliberately swapped his broken compass for mine? For what reason…unless he wanted me to have a challenge getting back. I didn't know Frank, but it didn't seem like something he'd do. Disappearing as he had didn't seem like something anyone could do.

I needed a drink. I picked up the bottle of Pisco. It was half-full, enough to flood some warmth back into my body and maybe calm me down.

"So Frank," I said aloud, "you left me with a great, but incomplete story and even some Pisco. What more can a man want?" I laughed the laugh of a baffled and fearful man. Then I made a toast, "To you, Frank, and your Amazonian people. And, to the gold that flows." With that I took a drink and then poured some Pisco into the lake.

I looked down into the shadowy depths. "How am I supposed to find your damn door?" I shouted.

The silence that surrounded me made me wonder if I wasn't actually dead. My fears were that of a child, which surprised me. I'd been a soldier, damn it. I'd lived the life of the homeless who slept with rats. Even the company of rats would be welcome now. I was alone. I'd never actually been alone like this before.

It was quiet and the cold penetrated me at deeper levels than it should have. All I could think to do in the dark was open my bedroll, climb into it, and stare up at the stars.

CHAPTER 9

"This is turning into one big bullshit story, Sam," Harry says to me. "You should leave the booze alone."

"Harry, I know how this sounds; but if you think what I just told you sounds like bullshit, just wait, it gets even better."

"I'll need boots, Sam."

The next thing I heard was a scratching sound. I'd fallen asleep and hadn't realized it. The reed boat was rubbing up and down against some of the large rocks of the island. With no effort on my part, I'd returned from my journey, right back where I'd started, and without Frank.

I threw my backpack and bedroll onto the rocks and jammed the boat between the large boulders so it couldn't move. This allowed me to scramble out of the boat; but by doing so, the boat became lighter and rose higher, freeing up from the rocks. I tried to grab hold of it, but it quickly floated out of reach. As it drifted away, I saw the bundle of Frank's clothing still resting where he'd sat at the back. For a moment, I wished I'd taken them with me.

It wasn't easy for me to walk. My body had become stiff from being in one position in the cold for what had to have been over ten hours. I'd gotten used to Ursula's warmth when I slept. The sun was starting to come up over the Andes, and I had quite a story to tell her.

As I reached the top of the hill, I looked down at the rocks and located the boat, still moving away, seemingly, on its own. The lake seemed more turbulent than I remembered it being before. Glare struck my eyes, and I held my hand to my brows to block it a bit. The sunrays created fluttering specks of light on small wave crests; and the boat, still drifting farther away, was now barely visible.

I had to get back to Ursula. In a near run, I made my way back to the barn. I reached the door and called out her name. Ursula slowly emerged from a shadowed corner.

"Welcome back, Sam."

I was never so happy to see another human being. Ursula, despite her predictable unpredictability, felt like a soothing balm that I needed. I started to walk towards her, but as I did so, the room felt like it had started to spin. *Too much running, too little oxygen in too thin air,* I thought. For a moment, I believed I was back in the boat, back in the dark, had fallen into the water, and was now sinking into the terrifying depths.

"Sam! Sam!" I heard Ursula shout.

"How did I get on the floor? I must have passed out, but I'm okay now. The run up the hill must have eaten up all my oxygen; but, I have too much to tell you. I'll rest later."

"What are you talking about, Sam. What do you have to tell me?"

"About Frank, of course, and my night out on the lake. He filled me in on a lot. Left out a lot, too."

"Who's Frank?"

"Frank! Ursula, are you all right?"

"I'm fine, but you're not. Why do you keep mentioning someone called Frank?"

"Cut it out, Ursula. It's not funny. We rowed for what seemed like at least an hour. I had to stop, but he just kept going."

"He?"

"For Christ's sake! Are you sure you're okay?"

"I told you I'm fine, but you…"

"The thin air had no effect on him. He just kept up his rowing pace. I wouldn't have believed that weird looking craft could move so quickly, but as fast as he…"

"Frank?"

"Ursula, I don't know what's going on with you, but try a little harder to keep up. Anyway, he stopped paddling and we coasted straight as an arrow, ever so slowly. There must have been some kind of current pulling us along. The locals probably know about it. As if on cue, the boat came to a rest. Never saw anything like it. No anchor, we just stopped.

"First, there was stillness, no motion of any kind. There was a sense of illusion like we were floating on air instead of water. I know it sounds crazy, but it was incredible. I felt a warmth come over me. I thought it was kind of odd at the time. You know how cold nighttime is here. Funny, everything I'm describing to you about what it was like out there didn't seem as important then it does now. Anyway..."

I rambled on and on until I'd finally brought Ursula up to speed with my experience, including Frank's disappearance.

"So, what do you think?"

Ursula was wearing a sad expression. "Sam, none of that happened. After we came onto the island and were led into this barn, you passed out."

"I know, but you came back that evening and told me what you'd heard about the pilot—Frank—from the Cuzco Four."

"Sam, the last thing that happened was that you and I had one of the most delicious kisses I've ever had and then you passed out cold. I became frightened and ran to find help. Our hosts weren't home so I ran to one of the paths. At the top of the hill, I came upon a crowd of locals. Your Cuzco Four were with them. I told them about you. One of the women said she was a nurse and came back with me. She checked your vital signs, said you were all right. Said Pisco mixed with the thin air and altitude wasn't a good idea if you weren't used to it. She said all you needed was a good night's sleep."

"What are you talking about, Ursula? What about our walks on the paths? The really bad meal we had at the tearoom? We were both with the Four and the crowd. We followed them when we left the tearoom. You know that. What I'd like to know is what they were doing with the crowd at the top of the hill? As you know, I wouldn't trust the Cuzco Four any farther than I could throw them, as a group or individually."

"They were watching the sunset. Sam, we never walked the island together. We never did any of the things you just mentioned. You must have overheard me..."

"Cut the crap, Ursula. If we never walked the island together, how is it that I know all the paths lead to the center of town, that there's a church there, an old dilapidated one? And, you know as well as I do it was noon, not sundown."

"I don't have an explanation for you, Sam, other than you had an extraordinary dream while you were out. All I know is you've been unconscious and barely moved since you collapsed."

"One of us is out of their mind; I'm just not sure which." I stared at Ursula. She looked away. "You said you had one of the women check me out. Did she or any of the other three happen to say why they're on the island?"

"Yes. She did."

"Wait! Let me tell you what she said."

"Go ahead, Sam." Ursula looked more exasperated than curious.

"She said they work for the church, the Church of the Christ."

Ursula stared at me for longer than just a few moments. Speaking slowly, as though I might need her to, she said, "Though I don't recall exactly when, maybe we talked about it while she was here and you heard us while semi-conscious, just as you must have heard...."

"I'm telling you... Look, at this point, I'm not sure what happened. I need some time by myself. I'm going to walk around the island."

"Only if you feel strong enough. Maybe moving around, getting your circulation going will help. Just go slowly, Sam. Walk slowly. The air is so thin."

"I'll be fine." I grabbed my cowboy hat and stuck it on my head. I recalled reaching to tip my hat to her last night when I left to meet Frank. Or was Ursula right, I'd been unconscious and dreamed the whole thing?

I left the barn and took the path that went towards the edge of the island to the rocks, and in particular, Frank's rock, by the large round stones. "Everyone who lives here gets his own," Frank had said.

The lake was high now. The flat stones lay out of sight, hidden in the depths of the water. I turned away and continued along the path that brought me to the teahouse. Another path put me at the side of the church. I walked around back and saw a small cemetery. The path took a sharp turn to the left and went up a little hill. I stopped for a moment so I could catch my breath then continued to climb up a ways.

I sat down on the ground and stared at the cemetery. Gradually, a shape got my attention and came into focus. It was obviously one of the headstones, but for some inexplicable reason, it stood out from the rest, though didn't look all that different. My legs felt rubbery as I lifted myself from the hard, cold ground. I had to go look, but was I going to like what I saw?

I began to work my way around the other headstones until I stood directly in front of the one I couldn't pull my eyes from. Maybe Ursula was telling the truth. Maybe, in spite of cacao tea which was supposed to help, this altitude was wrecking my brain. I took a deep breath and read what was carved into the stone...

FRANK BUERO
1926 - 1966
AS I AM NOW, SO SHALL YE BE

According to this, Frank had been dead almost twenty years. What the hell was happening?

Underneath the saying, a small slot was cut into the stone. For all of a few seconds, I thought everything was an illusion, or rather, a delusion—until I remembered a couple of specific things. The first was the fact I knew his name. No one who'd talked about the pilot had mentioned a name. The second thing made me reach inside my shirt and grab the lanyard that hung around my neck. When I pulled it out from under my shirt, it was Frank's compass not mine. I wasn't sure what was going on, but I knew that my time with Frank on the water could not have been anything but real.

The compass and the slot seemed about the same size. When I tried to slide the compass in, it was a little too thick. I pressed the button to pop open the case then placed the compass into the opening. A perfect fit. I pulled it out. The needle started to spin at an unbelievable speed, so fast it spun off its pivot. Last night, it hadn't moved.

Was Frank's headstone a doorway? As far as I could tell, nothing around me opened, shifted, or creaked. This had to be at least one thing Frank meant for me to discover; but why? That the compass fit into the slot verified a match. It also proved he was real. But he was dead, a ghost, a Pisco-drinking specter running around naked in the Andes or wherever. I felt like laughing and did. Nothing about this made sense.

I turned to go back to the barn to show Ursula the compass and prove I wasn't delusional. She'd seen my compass, so would realize this wasn't it. She knew every possession I'd packed since she'd bought each one. Even if she tried to argue that I'd gotten it when I said I was meeting Frank, I'd remind her that she'd said none of it happened, so when could I have gotten it. We wouldn't have been apart, according to her, except for when I was supposed to be unconscious. She was a bullshitter and manipulator, but this was too much. I wanted her to tell me what the fuck kind of game she thought she was playing. If I had to, I'd take half the money and leave her beautiful but irritating ass in Peru and head home.

I stopped dead in my tracks when I noticed up the hill, with the blue sky as a backdrop, four shapes facing my direction. Even though I couldn't see their faces, it was easy enough for me to recognize the Cuzco Four. Then another shape came into view, one I definitely knew.

Ursula joined them where they stood in perfect formation, almost at attention. The shock of what I'd just seen at Frank's tombstone didn't affect me as much as the sight of the five of them standing together looking in my direction. Slowly, one by one, they started to turn and leave. When the Cuzco Four were gone, Ursula stood watching me for a while; then, she also turned and left.

I decided to go to the teahouse before returning to the barn. Ursula was sitting alone, looking out at the lake. The smart thing to do was confront her about what I'd seen on the hill, but I was pretty sure I wouldn't like what she had to say. And the fact Frank said Ursula would lead me to the gold made me decide to keep my mouth shut. I might be full of piss and vinegar about this stunt she was trying to pull, but if Frank was right, I wasn't going anywhere until I found some treasure. It's not a good idea to stir up a hornet's nest if you plan to stick around.

"Do you know what I found out?" I asked.

She didn't seem to care to hear about it. "Sam, I have the money sewed into my bedroll as I said I would, and I'm as good as gone. Money is important to me right now."

"What the fuck?! Where's this coming from?"

"You're acting really odd, Sam, and it makes me uncomfortable."

"I'm acting odd?!" I took a couple of deep breaths so I could get a grip on my mouth and not say more than I should. "Look, Ursula, I need you. Frank told me you would show me the way to help him and find the…flowing gold. Hide the money or bury it, if you need to; but, there are things I need to do and I need you to tell me where I go from here."

"I told you, it was just a dream, a delusion, that's all it was. Nothing else."

I started to pull the compass out from under my shirt, maybe even drag her back to the cemetery, but something inside me put on the brakes.

"It wasn't a dream or hallucination," was all I said.

"Sam, listen carefully. I'm leaving you behind if you don't come to your senses. I don't intend to stick my neck out for a dream. Maybe we were both dreaming. The altitude makes you walk around in a daze until you get used to it; and, look at all the cacao tea we've had. Who knows what that's done to our ability to think clearly; but I do know one thing for sure, we have a lot of money. So, I say we leave your dream behind on this island and head back to Cuzco. We'll go to Lima, check into the best hotel, take hot showers, eat good food, and let our minds clear up. After a few days, if you still think there was a Frank and that you should become a crusader of sorts, then you get some guides and head back to the Amazon on your own."

I stared at Ursula for some time; she starred at the lake again. This was not the Ursula who'd been hell-bent on finding gold. And, what about her uncle? I hadn't brought him up because I knew there was no lost uncle. If I mentioned him as the reason for this trip, she'd give me some answer that had nothing to do with the truth. She might feel differently about staying here, but now so did I. It was my turn to have a purpose or cause, even if I had no clue what hers really was. Sure, I wanted the gold, but I owed it to Frank to help him, too. I decided to play along. If worse came to worse, I'd make her give me some of the money, enough to keep me going, then, she could go wherever she wished.

"Okay," I agreed, "let's head back. But my gut feeling is that it won't be too long before we return to the Amazon. Whether we like it or not, fate carries our destiny."

"Bullshit," she said. She stood up and walked out of the teahouse without waiting for me.

"Well, you'd know all about bullshit," I muttered to myself.

Unless I was mentally shifting between delusion and reality, the compass was real. That it had fit into the slot on Frank's headstone was real, as well. If this wasn't a dream or some kind of cacao-induced fantasy, we would soon be headed into the Amazon jungle; and everything Frank had said would happen, would.

It was what he hadn't said that concerned me.

CHAPTER 10

"Personally, Sam," Harry says as he leans back in his chair, "I think Ursula, if there ever was such a person, was right. Bullshit. This is complete crap. You heard me say I'd pay for a story, and you're really giving me one."

"Harry, you're welcome to leave any time. Go join your woman over there; or get your woman, your case of Peckerwood, and your pecker out of here. You're also welcome to keep listening. So, partner, which is it?"

"Shit, Sam. As the saying goes, 'In for a pence, in for a pound.' "

"I'll save time by telling you that we arrived back in Puño. That part of our journey went off without a hitch."

In Puño we boarded a bus with six other passengers also returning to Cuzco, but ran into a little bad luck in the form of a mudslide. The driver told us this unfortunate incident would put us behind schedule, at best, by one day. This is otherwise known as a South American time warp.

The driver tried, with great effort, to turn the bus around on the mountain pass. Of course, all the passengers had gotten out and stood a distance away. I would have been impressed had he actually been able to do it considering the size of the bus and the width of the road. After a lot of gear grinding and brake squealing, he sat still and stared straight ahead, with a large portion of the bus hanging precariously over the edge.

He sighed deeply, like a man resigned, got off the bus and stood for several moments seeming to make a quick evaluation of his predicament. He gestured and spoke first to the mudslide and then to his now useless bus, using hand gestures complemented by an assortment of carefully chosen Spanish and English phrases.

Satisfied that he'd treated us to a theatrical display worthy of an academy award, he took a bow, turned about-face, and started to walk away without another word to us. Other passengers appeared to be anxious. I felt right there with them. The driver kept his fast pace, kicking stones and sand in all directions from the road under his feet. I surmised he'd decided to walk back to town to find a very large bottle of Pisco.

It had begun to shift from dusk to dark as we stood on the road wondering if we should follow the driver or cross over the mudslide. I didn't feel we had a lot of time to decide since once the sun goes down the night shift of dangerous creatures seems even more hostile due to being mostly unseen in the absence of light. At least, that was my concern.

Ursula didn't share this concern, or seem to, since she picked up her backpack and bedroll and said, "Let's go."

"Where to?"

"I'm not sure, but we're stuck on the Puño side of the mudslide. There's a chance someone is stuck on the other side, and they might be able to turn around and head back towards Cuzco."

"The mudslide is Frank's way of leading us to the Amazon."

"Sam, it will take more than a mudslide to make me think Frank is giving us signs. I keep telling you it was just a dream brought on by a combination of things. Nothing actually happened. Look, we heard tales about a pilot back in Cuzco. Now, add the hallucination you had about the flowing gold at the lake with all the other hallucinations you had while unconscious, and there you have it. They were great dreams; but, it's time to wake up. I hold the passports and the money; and by the way, the airline tickets back home. So, I suggest you give in to the fact that we're heading back to the States."

Ursula had started to walk as she made her statement and was a good ten yards away from me. She was moving quickly over the fallen boulders and debris brought down by the slide.

Male pride made me stay rooted while my passport, ticket, and the money left with her. I turned back towards the bus and saw the other passengers following after the bus driver. Ursula was determined to head in the direction of Cuzco, and everyone else was going back to Puño or wherever. And, of course, with the arrival of darkness, the damn jungle had come alive.

I decided I'd better catch up to Ursula, but couldn't see her. At one point, I yelled out, "Ursula, where are you?" No answer. She scared the shit out of me when she stepped out from behind a tree.

"Christ, Ursula. What are you doing?"

"Answering the call of nature. Glad you decided to join me on this side of the mudslide."

"You could have answered *my* call. You had to have heard me."

"I did, but I also figured you'd come find me and I wanted a little privacy."

We walked for several minutes in silence until we rounded a bend in the road. Ahead, we saw shadows going back and forth in what looked like headlights. As we got closer, we saw a truck stopped on the road. The shadows were people moving around in the headlight beams and doing a lot of yelling. Another truck had been in the path of the mudslide that had come down this portion of the mountain, and had been pushed over the mountainside, plunging down at least six hundred feet. Someone said the truck had been headed for a town called Paucartambo and that it might have been loaded with men, women, and children.

There was no way to reach anyone down there without lights or equipment. I thought Ursula would want to keep going, but we mutually decided to stay and help. When the sun came up, we'd climb down and try to reach the wreck. Since it was not a straight drop, it was possible that people had been thrown or jumped out close to the upper road; and there was just a chance, even if a small one, that some of them may have survived. I was just as affected as the others seemed to be at the fact we didn't hear any voices calling up to us. In fact, we didn't hear any human sounds at all.

It was going to be a long night. Large bonfires were lit on the road both to give warmth and act as a light to guide any person down below who might try to make their way up. Men took turns yelling that help would soon be on the way; soon being relative, of course. These shouts of cold comfort went on—always unanswered—throughout the entire night.

Ursula and I sat next to each other and leaned against one of the truck's tires for warmth. The owner of the truck had turned off the lights to save the battery. It didn't take long before we both fell asleep, using our bedrolls as pillows.

It wasn't that I was used to jungle noises, but I knew to expect them, which is why the sound of stillness woke me. I'd woken several times during the night when the men would call to those below; but I suppose even they had to rest.

Light was starting to trickle through the thick growth of trees. I nudged Ursula awake and recommended we get up. We dragged our belongings behind us as we approached the crowd of spectators at the edge of the road where the truck had gone over. A fog hung over the tops of the trees that were at least two hundred feet below us. As we watched the fog slowly start to lift, the outline of the truck appeared. It was like looking down on a scale model vehicle. It had landed right-side-up and was wedged between some trees, giving the illusion as though it were on a road below us. There were neither people to be seen, nor signs of any mayhem. No one near us said a word.

My thoughts were broken by a voice from below. Someone in the crowd shouted back. This went on for quite a while.

"Ursula, what's going on?"

"I don't know. It's not really Spanish they're speaking."

Then, as if someone threw a switch, everyone around us started to laugh. Ursula asked one of the locals what was up. He told her the driver was okay and that he had one passenger who was also uninjured. Now, they were trying to catch the cargo they'd been carrying—pigs. The pigs must have scattered, because they're usually noisy and we hadn't heard one squeal since we'd arrived on the scene.

The laughing became infectious. Everyone was relieved after an anxious night worrying about what we could expect with the arrival of morning light. We watched the activity below for a while. Ursula suggested that we still might be able to grab a truck heading back to Cuzco. So, off we went, again, Ursula scooting ahead with me covering the rear.

"Easy, lady. Maybe this is all a sign," I reminded her again.

"No more, please."

"I have to try every chance I get."

"Not while I hold all the cards."

About a quarter of a mile down the road, we found a large truck at the end of the line of vehicles that had been stopped on the road, which meant the driver would be the first to turn around and leave once he realized he still couldn't pass because of the mudslide. The road could be blocked for days. The only thing for him to do would be to head back the way he'd come. Ursula approached the driver, discussed this with him, and made a deal for our passage back to Cuzco.

We tossed our gear into the rear end of the truck then got on board. We were sharing the back of the truck with about ten people, a combination of men, women, and children. Ursula and I sat next to each other on the left and just inside the truck next to the tailgate. I looked across from us, and forward, and saw the young drug dealer who had been pulled off the train staring straight at me. He smiled, showing me a mouth full of gold, every tooth gleaming.

I gently elbowed Ursula. "Look who's here."

"You thought they shot him," she whispered.

"Doesn't look like their aim was too good. Aw, fuck. Look who's near the front of the truck."

"Shit! It's Carlos. Sam, where are the guns?"

"Mine wasn't in my backpack, so you must have them in yours, but are you fucking kidding? You can't sit here holding a gun. Listen, if we have to, we'll make a deal."

"Reach into my backpack and give me a fucking gun. No deals. Carlos should..." Ursula cut off her sentence. I didn't ask why.

"Aw, damn," I said when Carlos glanced our way. "We're going to die or, worse yet, get hurt bad, and with the nearest medical help days away."

"Not if we act first."

"You're serious, aren't you?"

"You bet your ass I am."

The truck lurched to a start and got underway, shaking and bouncing over the dirt road. Ursula didn't move to jump off, so I figured we were going to stay put and take our chances. Most of the people in the truck started to nod off, including Carlos and the young drug dealer. When Ursula saw that, she groped through her backpack to get a gun. I thought she'd abandoned the idea.

"Ursula, think. There are a lot of people on the truck. Let's just get the hell off when we get the chance." My heart was pounding so hard that I thought everyone near me could hear it.

"Take it easy, Sam."

Ursula was telling *me* to take it easy. She did, however, let go of her idea to pull out a gun which made me feel it was okay to breathe again.

Several hours passed before the truck finally came to a stop. Between worrying about how bad this could turn and the jostling from the road, I was so tense you could open a bottle with my butt. The driver came to the back of the truck and said something.

"You make out any of what he said?" I asked Ursula.

"Sounds like the truck is at a crossroad. To the right is Cuzco. To the left is Paucartambo. He's heading to Cuzco."

Everybody got up and left the truck, except for our two friends and us.

"Out. Now," Ursula whispered.

"I thought you wanted to go to Cuzco?"

"Move!"

I grabbed my gear and was about to get out.

"Señor," Carlos said, "you have forgotten one of your bedrolls."

I picked up Ursula's bedroll and vaulted off the tailgate. The drug dealer was standing alongside Carlos in the truck, both of them wearing shit-eating grins. I waved.

"What are you doing?" Ursula questioned. "Are you crazy?"

"I'm not the crazy one. You almost left your treasure behind."

"No, I didn't. I switched bedrolls this morning. Do you think I want to get caught with the money?"

What the hell was with her? The bedrolls were identical, and apparently she'd switched them after they were rolled up; otherwise, I would have noticed I was carrying the one with the cash.

"You know, Ursula, I'm almost used to the fact that you change with the wind. I may not like it, but it is what it is. But, even a little more information so that I'm minimally kept in the loop would be appreciated."

"Let's go," she insisted. "That truck up ahead must be going to Paucartambo and don't say it. Frank has nothing to do with this. I just want to stay away from those two in the truck. Come on."

The road to Paucartambo was so narrow traffic heading there could only use the road on Monday, Wednesday, and Friday. Traffic headed towards Cuzco had the road on Tuesday, Thursday, Saturday, and Sunday.

Our trek to the town of Paucartambo was uneventful. This town also had neither electricity, nor toilets that flushed. At this point, I'd be more surprised if I saw a typical toilet. I'd probably head straight for it like a male dog seeing its first tree in days after running across the Sahara.

We'd arrived in time for the Festival of Paucartambo. We walked around town to see what was available in the way of transportation and ended up meeting the town mayor, an attractive woman whose bloodline was half-Peruvian and half-Venezuelan. She seemed highly-educated and told us she spoke four languages fluently.

The mayor walked with us and explained that Peruvian families had brought the wares they'd made over the past year to sell. During the festival, the town became a gigantic flea market.

"These few days of festival are very important to the Peruvians as it is a way for them to get money to see them through the following year," she told us.

I leaned over and whispered to Ursula, "Now I see why the men knit non-stop."

All around us were round faces and high cheekbones of the locals. Like the other Peruvians I'd seen, these were also short in stature. Many of the children had runny noses, just like the children I'd seen before. Though I wasn't sure at what age it happened, adults had the weathered look of those who live high up in the Andes, the freeze-dried effect, maybe. And, of course, nearly everyone we saw had a blackened mouth.

I think because we were American, the mayor invited us to stay at her hacienda while we waited for a ride back to Cuzco which wasn't possible, she told us, until the next day. The mayor escorted us to her home, which was simple, but nicer than most of the dwellings we saw on the way. Near her house was a waterfall that split into two rivers. One river moved towards the town of Paucartambo. The other lost itself in the jungle, most likely heading towards the Amazon basin.

She showed us to our room so we could drop off our gear, and asked what we'd like to do. We still had the rest of the day to ourselves, so decided to enjoy the festival along with the mayor, who insisted she be our guide.

We were getting ready to go back to town, so I picked up my backpack. Ursula told me we wouldn't need to carry anything with us. The mayor was watching this exchange. I was anxious about leaving everything there, but realized if I acted anything but casual, it would draw attention. More than likely, no one would dare anger the mayor by stealing from her guests. I put the backpack down and hoped this wasn't the last time I saw the bedroll.

There were real, live gauchos in town; and my guess was they'd traveled from Bolivia just to raise hell. They were great horsemen and rode at full-gallop around town, even on the cobblestone streets, chasing the men and women who ran ahead of them as part of the festivities. They created quite a sight as their full-length leather coats, still muddy from the long journey to Paucartambo, flowed wildly behind them.

Strangely-dressed men who seemed almost clown-like, but unlike typical American clowns, ran on foot; and as it seemed customary, also chased everyone. What was unique was the fact each man carried in his hands what appeared to be a penis with testicles attached. They took great pleasure in chasing the women around with their newly-acquired genitalia. I decided not to ask which animals were now singing some high Cs. At least, I hoped they came from animals.

Like most towns in South America, there was a plaza and a church at its center. The one here was beautiful; and, the mayor informed us, the people were very proud that this church, in particular, had a noted priest in its history.

"The priest was a famous orator," the mayor said as we climbed up the steps in front of the church and walked in through the front doors. "When he died, the people missed him so much they cut out his tongue and preserved it."

We reached the altar and the mayor gestured towards a large clear jar with what looked like a cow's tongue floating in liquid.

"And here he is," she bragged. Ursula took one look then quickly went in the opposite direction.

"As you see, the jar has been decorated in religious finery," the mayor said proudly.

"Good thing he wasn't known to be an excellent lover."

The mayor turned towards me, and in a most deliberate and careful way said, "Some have their tongues revered, others eaten." Then she turned and left.

Ursula was on the front steps, but had heard this exchange. "It's too bad your mouth moved before your brain had a chance to think."

"I couldn't let it pass by. It wouldn't seem right."

"We'd better head back to the hacienda and pack up. When the mayor walked by, she announced we wouldn't be sleeping there tonight. We'll find some place to stay or camp out. We can hitch a ride back to Cuzco tomorrow." From her tone, it was obvious Ursula was annoyed.

The mayor was standing off to the side of the church with a few monks. Seeing my hand move upwards, Ursula said, "Do not wave goodbye, Sam. She's unhappy enough."

"It's difficult, but I'll do my best."

We got back to the hacienda, hastily packed, and departed. We'd walked along the road for about fifteen minutes when we came to an abrupt halt as we faced down some tough-looking locals brandishing machetes.

"Sam, they look very angry about something."

"Try some Spanish."

Ursula rattled away for a few moments, but it had no effect. They kept their position and hostile expressions.

"Look behind the men," I said. "See the women holding the children? They look frightened. Something else is up. Step aside."

"What?"

"Step aside." As soon as we moved to the right of the path, they hurried past us. "We were blocking the way. Curious. I wonder how long they would have stood there waiting for us to move."

"Sam," Ursula said, "they had machetes. We don't play chicken with people holding machetes."

"Right."

We continued on the trail that followed alongside the dirt road and went back towards Paucartambo. We agreed that we might be able to bypass the town and after awhile, hitch a ride back to Cuzco. About twenty minutes later, as our path snaked closer to the road, a van pulled up to a dusty halt beside us, but aimed in the opposite direction.

"Buenos dias. Please let me give you a ride," the driver called out.

"Thanks, anyway," I said, "but you're heading in the wrong direction for us. We're aiming for Cuzco."

"No. I think you are going in the wrong direction," he replied.

"You sure? I thought Cuzco was past Paucartambo, heading back up the Andes," I said.

"It is, but that is not the direction that you want to go."

"Well, in what direction do we want to go?" Ursula asked.

"Why, the way I am going. It is the only way for you."

"Thanks, but no thanks," I said. "We're heading in this direction and we'll do just fine." In a whisper I told Ursula, "Take off. Something's going on."

He saw us moving away from him. "Stop!" he shouted.

"Keep moving, Ursula," I said. Then, as if we both had brakes, we stopped when we heard the persuasive sound of a gun, a big gun, and saw the small trees near us get blown away.

"Come back and join me, Sam and Ursula."

Ursula and I looked at each other.

"If he were going to kill us, he'd have done that already," I whispered to her.

"My pistol is in my jacket."

I paid no attention to her and started walking towards the van. "Sir," I said loudly, "if it's about that incident in the church…"

"Listen carefully, Sam," Ursula said catching up to me, "I don't think this is about a priest's tongue. I'm not giving up the money without a fight; and though my father taught me how to handle a gun, it's been a very long time since I shot one. When I do start shooting, you'd better watch your ass so you don't get shot along with this jerk in the van."

"Let's go. Both of you," he called out.

He got out of the van and stood there holding his shotgun down, but in our direction. He was my height and a bit more muscular. He was also around thirty-five, which made him about ten years younger. He did not look Peruvian; that was for sure.

"Who are you?" I asked.

"I am Juan Griego; and that is all you should need to know."

"What's the problem here, Juan?" I asked, "Is it coming from the mayor?"

"The mayor? Ah, yes. Not quite," he laughed. "No, amigo, from a much worse place."

"What do you want?" Ursula asked.

I noticed an interesting tone in her voice, but it wasn't the time to ask about it.

"I am the day manager at the hotel in Puño. I found Carlos in the back alley. He was alive, but just barely. Before he died, he mentioned there was money in a black bag. I found the black bag, but the only thing inside were sweaters and underwear. Whoever shot him must have taken the money. Since you two were the only guests that night, I would say you meant to kill him and that the money is with you."

"Okay, *Juan*," Ursula said. "There's no use trying to fool you; but first, let me tell you something that you obviously don't know. We didn't shoot him. Carlos is very much alive and he's hanging out with the guy who originally had the bag. We know this because we just saw them this morning. They appeared to be pretty friendly, so I think you have your trails crossed. When we saw them, they were on a truck headed towards Cuzco, and that is exactly where we should be heading. They're the ones you want. They have the money."

"They are both dead," he sneered. "Carlos died in front of me and so did that little shit." Juan began to laugh. Then in a low growl he said, "I want the money. Now climb in. You, Sam, get in the front seat. Ursula, get in the back, behind Sam."

We threw our gear in and sat ourselves in the van as he'd instructed. Juan placed the shotgun across his lap with the barrel facing me, shifted into gear and jerked forward, heading away from Paucartambo.

"How far are we going?" I asked.

"Not far, amigo. Just far enough."

Ursula and I made a few futile attempts to plead with his good sense, assuming he had some. We kept up our ruse about the money and repeatedly told him that we had only enough American dollars left for our trip back to the States. He ignored us.

"Yes, this is good," he said and stopped the van. "Get out, both of you."

We were in the middle of what could be considered an intersection in Peru. I'd gotten out and held my hand out for Ursula. He motioned for us to move away from the van. I went to the left. Ursula went in the same direction, but stood about seven feet apart from me.

"Isn't it dangerous to stop here?" I figured small talk might buy us some time.

"Money. Now!" He pointed the gun at my chest. "Where is it?"

"Look, Juan," I said, trying to appear more in control than I felt, "there is no money, or at least, we don't have it."

Juan cocked the gun and took aim at me. Ursula yelled, "I have it."

He spun to face Ursula; and as he did, I heard the report of Ursula's Beretta. Juan's arms fell to his side, mouth open, eyes registering complete surprise. The shotgun fell to the ground, and so did he.

"Get in the van and start driving," Ursula demanded. "Hurry!" she yelled.

I couldn't move. I was as motionless as Juan. Ursula shoved me hard. "Go! Now!"

"You shot him. Holy fuck!"

"What the fuck do you think he was going to do to us?" she screamed. With a complete change of demeanor, she said calmly, "Get a grip, Sam. You need to toss him down the hill. Nobody will ever find him down there."

"You want me to throw him down the hill?"

"We need to buy ourselves some time. We don't want anyone to find his body any time soon, or ever, if possible."

I walked to the edge of the road and looked into the thick jungle brush that grew to the river's edge and mumbled under my breath, "Just throw him down the hill. Nobody will ever find his body." I walked back to where he lay face up.

I was grateful there wasn't much blood; I'd seen enough for a lifetime in 'Nam. The bullet had gone into his chest, but hadn't come out. And, good aim must be like riding a bike to her. I hadn't shot a gun in a long time either, but I'd be willing to bet I wouldn't be that accurate without some target practice. Especially at the speed she'd aimed and fired with.

"Let's go, Sam. Push him over."

I grabbed Juan's arms and dragged him the five feet to the edge of the road and let go of him.

"What are you doing, Sam? Push the bastard down the hill!"

"Give me the gun," I said. Maybe it was my tone of voice. Ursula didn't argue, just handed it to me. "Look!" I pointed to an area behind her and when she turned, I aimed the pistol at Juan's chest and fired. Ursula jumped. I gave his body a strong push and sent him down into the thick growth. When he rolled over, he made a sound.

"Is he still alive?" Ursula asked.

"I can't imagine he would be. He probably just expelled some air when he rolled onto his stomach. Where to now? We can't just drive around in someone else's van. Someone might see us and report us."

"We have to go ahead," Ursula insisted.

I looked down the hill at where Juan had crashed through the dense undergrowth. If you didn't know he was there, it was impossible to see him. *Some animals will eat well tonight*, I thought.

Ursula walked to the edge of the road with Juan's shotgun in her hand. "Here," she said. "Send it down with him."

I took the shotgun and tossed it down so that it landed fairly close to where I knew Juan was. I turned towards Ursula and grabbed her by her arms, hard. I looked into her eyes then focused on her lips. She looked confused. I liked that. It was her turn. I bent my head down and took her mouth with mine, gently at first, then with heated emotion. It had been a while since I'd felt so strongly for her. She was a real ball buster, but she'd saved my life. Ursula wrapped her arms around me and returned my passion. When I lifted my lips from hers, tears flowed down both her cheeks.

"Good," I said. "I was afraid you…"

"Shut up. That was the last time, Sam. Now we can go the way you wanted, into the jungle."

I wondered if she meant this would be the last time she would kiss me, cry, or kill. There wasn't time for this, though. We needed to get going. Juan had conveniently left the keys in the van. I would not have enjoyed retrieving them from him.

"What made you change your mind about heading to the jungle?"

"Later. We need to move."

I put the van into gear and we drove ahead until darkness from the heavy jungle growth filled the rearview mirror. Ursula described this as though a dark green door had opened then swung shut behind us.

The scenery didn't change as the miles and hours went by. The only sure thing was that we were continuously going downhill. For a dirt road, it looked fairly well-traveled, though we never saw another vehicle or even anyone walking. Once in a while, the river would show itself through the trees on the right side of the road then be swallowed up again into the same deep green we were traveling through.

"Gas is getting low," I said as I checked the gauge. "I hope we hit a town pretty soon."

It wasn't too long before the road came to a fork. I stopped the van. "Well? What do you think; left or right?"

"Go right, Sam. Keep the river on your right." As I did this, Ursula asked, "Why did you shoot him?"

"His death hangs on both of our heads now."

She was quiet for a moment then said, "I'm hungry."

I don't know what I thought she'd come back with, but that wasn't even in the ballpark. I thought she'd appreciate how fucking noble I'd been and all she commented on was her stomach being empty.

The road and bad shocks bounced us around for about another hour until we came across a short line of trucks that blocked our way. We had come to the end of the line—at least, for now.

CHAPTER 11

We grabbed our gear, left the van on the side of the road, and made our way to the lead truck. I walked to the front of the truck and saw we were at a small town. The few buildings there were made of wood, every one of them covered with rusty tin roofs. The jungle was pressed, literally, against the back of most of the structures. The road and dirt areas were desert dry. Packs of dogs, skinny as rails, barked and carried on as if they were on speed, raising dust clouds as they scrambled around.

Maybe the town's inhabitants were indoors because nobody was in sight. The sun was setting, so we needed to find a room and some food. At the center of this outpost was a bar. We went inside, and movies about saloons in the Old West flashed back to me.

There was only one lantern lit. Most of the room was dark corners and shadowed areas. Four men were seated on two benches on either side of a wooden table. Probably the drivers of the trucks we'd seen lined up at the edge of town.

"Buenos dias," I said using the extent of my Spanish. "Does anyone here speak English?" No one responded, just stared.

Ursula walked around the one table in the place. I stayed were I was and watched the heads of the men turn to follow her. Naturally, they'd be curious, but their expressions were damn curious.

She walked over to a woman who stood in the shadows and said something to her. It was barely audible, but I could tell they weren't speaking Spanish or English. The air was full of smoke from the thin brown cigarettes and cigars the men puffed on, and I strained my eyes to see across the table to the far end of the room where Ursula was still talking with the woman. Both of them had moved into the shadows, so when one of them moved, at first I thought it was Ursula, but it was the other woman, dressed in khaki military attire. When the lantern light hit the woman's face, I was startled to see how closely she and Ursula resembled each other.

Ursula walked over to me. "Follow me outside and don't say anything."

I fell in sharply behind her and we walked out into the street. Ursula stopped, turned, and said something to the woman who had followed us out, but stayed about eight feet behind us. I recognized the language now that I could hear it–German. The woman walked closer and came to a military-like halt. I felt like I needed to stand at attention for inspection. I looked at Ursula; she never took her eyes off the woman.

"Well?" Ursula said.

"Yes…Yes," the woman replied, "Now, let us have a toast." She reeled around and walked smartly back into the bar.

Ursula was about to follow when I grabbed her arm. "What the fuck's going on here? I thought we just happened on this place, but that's not how it looks now. What's with the inspection, the German, and her attire; and, how about the simple courtesy of an introduction? And why the hell when I look at her is it almost like looking at you?"

"Get inside, Sam. I'll explain everything later. Meanwhile, she and I are going to speak in German most of the time. You just smile or at least stay quiet while that's happening. And when the toast is made, act happy about whatever you hear."

"Just how many languages do you speak, Ursula?" She ignored me and went inside.

The men who'd been in the bar must have left out a back way. The woman placed a lantern at the center of the table then took a seat. She motioned for Ursula and me to sit across from her. Before another word was spoken the woman put a match to the oily wick and placed the chimney back. Black smoke filled the glass and spiraled upwards, and I watched until it brushed against the inside of the exposed tin roof, already thick with black soot. She adjusted the flame and a warm glow covered the room.

Ursula and the woman spoke in rapid German while I busied my mind with other things, like the fact that most of my time with Ursula meant I stayed pretty clueless about what she was really up to. A short man came into our lantern light from the back of the bar. I hadn't seen him earlier and he hadn't been with the other men. Ursula and the woman stopped talking long enough to acknowledge him.

"This is Marcos," the woman said.

I was about to extend my hand to shake, especially because I saw his right hand, which had been behind him move in my direction. He placed a bottle of Pisco on the table with one hand and three tin cups down with the other, took two steps back, and stood there with his eyes fixed on me.

"Please, Sam, will you do the honors," the woman said, and then added, "My name is Sonya." A broad smile played across her face; and again, I was struck at how similar she and Ursula were. It's said that everyone has a doppelganger. Either this was the case here, or Ursula had a lot of explaining to do. My bet was on the latter.

I pulled the cork from the bottle, filled the cups, and handed one each to Sonya and Ursula, then picked up my own.

Sonya raised her cup, "To our health and successful result."

I felt Ursula looking at me. Act happy, she'd said. I tapped my cup against Sonya's. "To our successful result," I mirrored as though I knew what the fuck I was talking about.

It was all I could do to bite my tongue and not ask what the hell was going on. I was as much in the dark as the jungle outside. Every time their cups emptied, I'd fill them with Pisco hoping to loosen them up enough to say more than they intended. It didn't work.

Sonya and Ursula slipped back into German while Marcos stood like a stone pillar in the shadows.

We continued like this until Sonya said, "In the jungle, we sleep when the dark comes and we get up with the light. Please let me show you where you will sleep." As she stood up, she said something in a language that sounded a lot like Spanish.

Marcos walked to the table and promptly put the cork back in the bottle. Without a word Ursula got up, picked up her gear, and followed behind Sonya. There was nothing for me to do but go with them.

We were led down a narrow, dark corridor. The only light was the fading illumination cast from the two lanterns in the bar. Sonya took us to a room barely eight-feet square. I could just make out two army cots. As my eyes started to adjust, Marcos came in with a lantern and I got a look at our room.

On the wall opposite the door, there was one glassless window covered with heavy wire mesh. The door was made from the same corrugated tin that covered the roof. There was no lock or latch, or for that matter, a doorknob or handle.

Marcos placed the lantern in the center of the floor then made a hasty but silent exit. Sonya bade us goodnight then started to leave. She stopped, turned back towards us, and said, "As soon as possible, you should put the lantern out. Otherwise, it will attract the flying predators waiting and circling us at the edge of the jungle." She closed the door behind her.

Ursula and I faced each other, and I allowed a few moments to pass so Sonya wouldn't overhear before I said, "I want answers as to what the fuck is going on."

She walked to the door, cracked it open a bit to peer into the hallway, then pushed the tin sheet back in place and walked towards me until just inches away. "Give me until morning, Sam. It's important no one overhears what I'm going to tell you. I need your help, badly."

"Ursula, it's one mystery or agenda after another with you. God damn it! All right, I'll wait until morning. Just tell me one thing, are we safe here?"

"You've never been so safe. In the morning, Sam, I promise. Sonya was right about the light. Look at the size of the bugs gathering at the window."

I'd thought Sonya's use of the word *predators* was dramatic, but considering the bugs on the mesh, it wasn't that far off.

We followed our practice or habit of staying in our clothes to sleep. It finally felt warm, which made me believe we must be getting closer to the Amazon basin.

Ursula pushed the two cots together, opened my bedroll—the one she was now carrying since she'd switched them on me, and placed it over both cots. The blankets went over this.

"It's warmer here. This'll work better," was her explanation. I watched her get settled onto a cot. "Take care of the lantern, Sam."

A slow twist of the lantern's knob lowered the wick until the flame went out and the room filled with instant blackness. I managed to make it to the cot without stumbling too badly. As we lay there, I stared at the window as my eyes adjusted to the dark. Ursula was supposed to finally offer an explanation in the morning. I could lay awake all night making a mental list of a thousand things she might tell me, and I still could be wrong. And, how much of it would be true could be anybody's guess.

The nighttime sounds seem amplified. Dogs yapped constantly. Even without the lantern light, large bugs encrusted the wire mesh covering the window. Several times, I saw bats swoop down for an easy meal, using the mesh as a backstop.

Back in the States, the act of eating is sanitized for most of us. Food comes prepped and packaged; most of us don't have to hunt it down. We might occasionally see a cat catch a mouse or insect; but in the jungle, different rules apply. I could identify with the bugs. They probably never saw the bat coming in to consume them. I'd felt that way often since I'd been in Peru.

Rising from my cot, I walked closer to this eerie slaughter and peered at the wire mesh until my focus went beyond it to the edge of the jungle. Something was in a small clearing. I couldn't make out what it was, but knew it didn't belong there. I leaned as close as I dared towards the window.

"What are you looking at, Sam?" Considering how fast Ursula falls asleep, it surprised me that she was awake. She got up and stood at my side.

"In the clearing…a shape; you can barely make it out."

"It's just a tree stump."

"Maybe." Maybe it was my eyes playing tricks on me; but it bothered me that the shape seemed familiar, and out of place.

Ursula turned and got back on her cot. "Get some rest, Sam. I told you, we're safe."

I didn't say anything, just climbed back onto my cot. In the morning, I'd take a better look. A bat hit the wire mesh and dogs started a frenzied barking. I listened in case something was actually going on outside, but everything went quiet. Well, as quiet as a usual night in a jungle can get. I don't recall another thought. I fell fast asleep.

CHAPTER 12

Morning hit me like a slap across the face. I opened my eyes and didn't feel so much like greeting the new day as yelling at it. I'd slept, but it was a restless sleep, full of dreams where I was constantly on the move, fleeing from something or someone. The night sounds were gone, as were the many creatures that had been on the screen mesh. They'd been replaced with beautiful prismatic-winged butterflies, safe for now in the daylight from things that go bump or feed in the night.

I walked to the window and looked at where the mysterious shape had been; there was no tree stump as Ursula had suggested. In fact, there wasn't anything there that resembled what I'd seen. A chill went across my shoulders. My mother used to say that meant a cat had walked across the ground where I'd be buried. Good thing I'd had that sensation numerous times before, or I might have had extra cause to worry.

Ursula was still asleep. At rest, her face was serene, almost innocent except for the obvious sensuality that never left her. We'd been on quite an adventure so far, and it wasn't over yet. This woman I hardly knew had become a part of my life, even if in a bizarre way. Ironic what we can become accustomed to.

Ursula, the enigma. Ursula, the woman of secrets. Why did she feel a need for such secrecy with me? In New York, we'd spent a lot of time together going through the books she'd asked me to read, planning the trip, getting to know each other or so I'd thought. She'd behaved pretty normally then. What had I missed about her?

I heard her breathing shift. Eyes still closed, Ursula stretched her arms and legs in that feline way she did—except I was the one who felt like purring as I watched.

"Good morning," I said. "Welcome to the jungle, or at least the threshold to it."

"Coffee," she moaned. "I need coffee." Then she raised herself off the cot and walked over to where I stood at the window and kissed me. It wasn't a kiss like I'd given her on the road after we took care of hiding Juan's body, but it would do for now.

"You know, there's a lot you have to explain to me," I reminded her.

"I have to have my coffee first. I made a specific request to Sonya last night for coffee instead of cacao tea."

She got up from the cot, finger-combed her hair, and without another word started to walk out.

"What about the bedroll?" I asked.

"Leave it."

That was uncharacteristic of her, but maybe she was right. There were only two ways into the room, the window and past us through the main room. I hadn't seen where or how the four men exited the night before, but it wasn't anywhere near our room. The mesh on the window was secured to the wall from the inside. If anyone tried to remove it to get in, we'd hear the racket. I glanced at the bedroll then followed her out.

Marcos was sitting at the bar with a pot of coffee in front of him. Except for him, we were the only ones in the place. Sonya was nowhere in sight. We sat at the table rather than at the bar with Marcos.

He came over and motioned as though to ask if we would like some coffee. Ursula and I nodded. He brought us the same tin cups we'd used for the Pisco the night before; I recognized a dent in one of them. As he poured the coffee, he stared at me not unlike the way Sonya had during her *inspection*.

I found myself smiling at Marcos, it was hard not to. He had that kind of a face…friendly, not at all threatening, and a pair of what I considered unfortunate ears. His high cheekbones and deep set eyes gave him the appearance of a blend of Inca and Spanish-European heritage. There was something else I couldn't put my finger on, something almost familiar. I'd just reminded myself that looks can be deceiving when he smiled back at me, exposing a full set of teeth. No typical black mouth; but a good number of teeth were capped in gold.

The coffee was good. I held my face over the steaming brew and took in its aroma. It was a welcome change from cacao tea. Ursula obviously savored it, as well, because she either made a small sigh or moaning sound after every sip. Marcos brought us some rolls, oranges almost the size of grapefruits, a few bananas, and some fruit I had never seen before, all nestled in a basket made of leaves and flowers. I wondered if Marcos had arranged it or if someone else had. Didn't matter, it was the most appetizing food we'd had since we first arrived, if not our first jungle feast, though technically, we weren't yet in the real jungle.

Ursula must have been hungry because in no time, a roll and a banana disappeared into her. As she ate, she looked at me and then at Marcos who had stationed himself inside the frame of the opened door. I turned to look, as well. With the sun at his back, his face was dark, like he'd donned a mask. His features were almost indistinguishable. He wasn't tall, but the strength of his silhouette was obvious. *Our very own Tarzan of the Jungle*, I thought.

Ursula got up from the table and went towards Marcos. Marcos stepped aside. She never slowed as she walked towards him, as though she knew he'd get out of her way. Outside, she turned and called to me, "Let's walk, Sam."

She was leaving the bedroll.

"Ursula, maybe I should make a quick trip to the room for…"

"Come on, Sam."

I got up to follow her outside like a puppy on a leash. Marcos didn't move from the door. Instead, he blocked my way.

"Excuse me, Marcos," I said. No movement. He didn't even blink. I wasn't sure what to do next. We stood there and he seemed to size me up. Satisfied, I suppose, he moved aside. "Thank you" was the only thing I could think to say; he didn't respond.

This little bit of play must have meant something important to him because as soon as I'd passed him, he ran in front of me and blocked my way again. He took hold of the compass Frank had given me, which I hadn't noticed was outside of my shirt rather than in.

"Marcos," Ursula called out, "vamoose."

He let go of Frank's compass, gave her a look that scared me, especially when his hands knotted into fists. He turned and walked back into the bar. Typical of Ursula, she appeared unaffected. I slipped the compass back under my shirt.

Vamoose? That she told a jungle man to vamoose and he did was interesting. That she said it in English and he understood her was a lot more than just interesting. What the fuck was going on here? That question was quickly becoming my new mantra.

Ursula called out to Marcos. He came back to the door and she said something to him in Spanish. The only word I understood was *Sonya*. Marcos frowned, nodded, and turned away without a word.

She headed off in a direction different than the one we used to enter the village the day before. I sidled up to her and said, "Ursula, I want to discuss the money you sewed into your bedroll, which you previously chose to make your constant companion, and why *now* you've suddenly divorced yourself from it."

"Yes, the money… Well, it's no longer important."

"No longer important?! What the fuck is going on with you? Ursula, if you don't tell me…"

"Sam, what's important is that you… Ah! This is good. Let's go in here."

Here seemed to be a fair-sized clearing. Ursula sped up her pace until she was in a ways, away from the road. She turned and faced me then sat down and motioned for me to join her. "Time to tell you why you're really here."

"This ought to be good." She ignored my sarcasm.

"I had a friend," she started, "Jack Green, who was born in Venice. During the Second World War, he fought as a partisan at the foothills around Lake Garda, Italy. He was told that Hitler and Mussolini were expected to convene together at the lake and there was going to be a huge undertaking to rid the area of any troublemakers. Jack said that, usually, partisans were tolerated as mere nuisances; but measures were taken to round up as many of them as possible so there'd be the least amount of problems. Jack was captured by the Nazis and brought to one of the hotels at the lakeside where they locked him in a basement wine cellar with, as he used to say, "With myself and myself.""

"What does 'With myself and myself' mean?"

"Jack had a twin brother named Ethan who was also captured and brought to the hotel. They hadn't seen each other for six months prior to that time. Jack said Ethan's wife and daughter had been sent to a German death camp and he was afraid they were dead. He and his friends had tried to stop the train they were on, but he and many others had been either captured or killed in the attempt.

"Eventually, a Dr. Wasser and his young son showed up. Dr. Wasser had an obsession about twins, so Ethan and Jack were kept alive. The Fuehrer, himself, was behind the twins project and would soon after give the doctor both funds and his project carte blanche. After the meeting took place between Il Duce and Hitler, the hotel became a laboratory for Dr. Wasser.

"Jack said he and Ethan were separated after that first day, and it was the last time he saw his twin. Dr. Wasser took personal care of Jack; in fact, he made certain Jack was treated quite well, all things considered. They'd been exposed as Jews; and because of that, Ethan was subjected to horrible experiments."

"If they knew they were Jews, how is it they didn't treat Jack the same as Ethan?"

"Ethan had been born a few minutes before Jack, so he was the twin who got circumcised, not Jack. That's how they chose which one to physically experiment on. Jack was experimented on, but differently."

"If Jack never saw his brother again, how did he know he'd been tortured?"

"Jack explained this as something particularly acute between twins, especially identical ones—they feel each other's pain. They'd torture Ethan, but not before they'd wire Jack up to a machine that had a paper roll on it. The machine would read and chart his reactions during certain hours of the day, like one of those electrical brain wave monitors or lie-detector tests. Jack said that even if he thought all was well, the needle marking the paper would make large movements and he'd know Ethan was in pain. Many times, he'd feel pain though nothing was being done directly to him. One day, they left Jack by himself, strapped to an operating table for most of the day. Dr. Wasser and his son would go down at intervals to observe him, clipboards in hand. Jack witnessed their excitement at their findings.

"Jack told me, 'American forces soon started to move into Italy and everything sped up. I was sure that I knew exactly when my brother Ethan died; and the graph paper showed my reaction, as well. A short time later, Dr. Wasser and his son came down to my room, took the graph paper roll and left. Dr. Wasser's son bragged that he was the one who'd tortured and eventually killed Ethan. He also said they were leaving me alive, adding that torture is not only of the physical kind. It was fairly soon after that when Wasser disappeared with his son.

'The remaining guards were Italian Catholics, so they released me. I told the Americans about Dr. Wasser and his experiments, and that he was tutoring his son in those same experiments; but Dr. Wasser was never considered the horrendous murderer others were. This was mostly because the allies could find no records or, for that matter, any witnesses who could or would come forward, only me. Many Jews did not trust anyone when the war ended. It took years for concentration camp victims to speak up. By then, medical documents were locked in vaults by the allies for safe-keeping and were not available as evidence.' "

"Christ, Ursula. You hear stories, but…"

"Years later, after Jack had passed away, a woman approached me. She introduced herself as Salene and said, 'We had a mutual friend named Jack Green. I belong to an organization that hunts down Nazi war criminals still in hiding.' "

"Even after all these years?" I asked.

"Yes. She said that it was her life's work. I was fascinated by her story and her burning passion. She spoke not in an angry way, but with a desire to right a wrong. She talked and I listened.

"Soon, this led to even more meetings with others of her group. They asked me to help them, said they needed me; but that it could prove to be a dangerous undertaking. This was told to me one night by a short, stocky gentleman in his sixties. I was never told their names, other than Salene's; but, I recognized some of their faces. Sometimes, there were as few as three people at the meetings; at other times, there were as many as ten. The gentleman said, 'If we succeed, our greatest reward will be to know that we helped bring a monster to justice.' It didn't take long for me to give in to what they wanted me to do. They had all the facts. They believed in their cause. And, Sam, you know enough about me now to understand that another motivation for me was they were the most exciting people I'd ever met."

"Was Salene one of the first to start the hunt for Dr. Wasser?"

"Yes. Salene and her mother were taken by the Nazis. Salene's father was a partisan fighting in the Italian resistance. This jeopardized her mother and, of course, everyone else in the family. After her father was captured, the whole family was rounded up like animals and sent to concentration camps in Germany."

"Are you telling me Ethan Green was Salene's father?"

"Yes, this makes Jack her uncle. She told me that she and her mother, Dora, had been taken from the Jewish ghetto in Venice. They were forced like cattle on to a train, with only one destination—a death camp.

"Italian partisans, including Jack, made a daring attempt to stop the train by blocking its path. When they broke the locks on the sliding doors, the human cargo poured out, weak from thirst and starvation and being transported like cattle. It was years before Jack learned that Salene and Dora had been on the train.

"The people on the train tried to get away; but there was a small river between the train and a large field, and that prevented most of them from escaping the Nazi rifles. Shots were heard echoing through the fields. Each rifle crack meant death, even if not immediate death. If a person didn't die when shot, they weren't going to be given medical treatment. Dead and wounded were thrown back into the train cars along with the living since the Nazis couldn't leave the ground littered with bodies.

"It was early morning. A ground fog made the horror even more gruesome because as a body would fall down at the edge of the river, the weight of it would push the fog away for a moment. Then the fog would slowly fold back over the body and cause it to fade out of sight, as if nothing had happened.

"Those who surrendered were gathered, again like animals, and dragged, kicked, and electrically prodded back onto the train. Somehow, in that moment of human insanity, Dora seized an opportunity. She quickly stripped all the clothes off Salene, six-months old at the time, and placed her tiny body behind a rock in the ravine. The naked Salene looked just like one of the bleached river stones she was lain upon. Dora had stripped Salene so she could roll up her clothes and blanket to look like she still held her child.

"Dora boarded the train without waiting to be beaten aboard. She wanted to position herself at a little window that was barely large enough to get air through; but she could see Salene, just barely moving. She hardly heard her cries over the pitiful sounds of the soon-to-die and the beatings that were taking place as the victims were forced back onto the train.

"Salene lay on her back, her little hands opening and closing as if she were trying to reach for her mother. Dora's heart pounded and she held her breath when two soldiers stood like giants over her daughter's tiny body. One soldier motioned the other to shoot her then moved on to hunt others in the fog. For that one moment, Salene was quiet and raised her little hands up toward the Nazi as if she wanted him to pick her up. He lowered his rifle and took aim. Dora's voice failed and only a moan came from her throat. But instead of shooting Salene, he raised his rifle and fired it into the air, then moved on.

"The train lurched forward then started to move very, very slowly. Dora's eyes strained for one last look at her daughter. The stony landscape replaced her view of Salene. Dora looked up to heaven and prayed. When she looked back, a farmer came out from behind a nearby tree. He pointed first in the direction where Salene was then gestured to his heart, and with both hands made like he was rocking a baby in his arms.

"Dora thrust her two arms out the tiny window as far as she could reach and gestured with her palms up, fingers spread apart. She believed the farmer was an angel in a human body. Salene would be saved. She'd done the right thing. The distance and slowness of the train made it possible to see the farmer for some time, enough time to see him start walking towards Salene. Then the train picked up speed; and soon, the only thing Dora could see were fields filled with small sheep and goats.

"Dora thanked God and pulled her arms back into the train. She relinquished the little window to those needing the sparse air that flowed through and melded back into the throng only to face a woman holding a crying baby. The woman was terrified and weeping. Dora closed her eyes. She no longer had a future but she had hope, hope for her child, and that was enough.

"When Salene was old enough, and the war was many years behind them and information had been revealed, the farmer told her what her mother had done. 'I watched in horror,' the farmer said. 'I saw it all. The partisans tried to stop the train to save the people, but they were not able to do it and many died in the attempt. Unfortunately, the train had been stopped at the wrong place. A small river hindered their escape. Maybe the partisans thought the early morning fog that covered the river would help the captives to escape, but not many could get across the river. There were only several who were able to escape out of the hundreds on the train.

'Before the train was stopped, the river was clear; but after five minutes of slaughter, it ran red. In the pandemonium, I saw a woman, your mother, do something extraordinary. I watched her try to save you. When she climbed back onto the train, her face appeared at a tiny window and I followed her terrified gaze to where a German soldier was standing over you. He lifted and fired his rifle upward and left you there.

'People were forced to carry the dead back onto the train. No dead or dying were left for evidence so we Italians would see the Nazis for what they really were. But, I had seen, as had others. The Nazi's shots of death pierced the silence of our fields; but we could do nothing, which was even more torment for us. As the train slowly gained speed, puffs of heavy black smoke fell back on the cars. Then the smoke mixed with the fog and the train was gone.' "

Ursula paused and looked away before continuing. "Salene was told that the family had no trouble explaining her sudden appearance as most births took place at home. Though they felt they could trust most of their neighbors, especially the ones who'd witnessed the slaughter, it was wiser to not give anyone else reason to speak about Salene. Eventually, they tried to find out about Salene's real parents, and her real name, but all that they had to go on was Salene's tattoo number. That cataloging wasn't available at the time.

"When the war ended, an Israeli organization formed to document the atrocities, as well as to categorize the tattoo numbers. However, nothing showed up until some years ago. Salene received a call from the organization almost forty years after the war. It seemed that the organization had received documents of experiments that the Nazis had been conducting in one of the concentration camps. The Germans took pride in keeping good records as they were sure the world would belong to them. Through the files in Israel, and the use of computers to link what was known about victims with tattoo numbers based on records the Nazi's kept during the war, Salene's number came up and also her mother's number and name. However, Salene had earlier learned her mother's first name only, and in a spectacular way. But now, she was able to end the long mystery and misery of not knowing what had happened to her mother.

"The file with her mother's number was on a page, a list, with at least fifty other numbers. All the numbers had been given to Italian Jews. At the bottom of the page was Dr. Carl Wasser's name.

"How she learned her mother's first name was truly extraordinary. One of the passengers in the car with Dora survived death camp. When he was able, he returned to where the train had stopped and tracked down the farmer and Salene, and recounted what he could remember happened after the train resumed it bleak journey that day. He and Dora spoke on the way to the concentration camp, after the failed rescue, and she told him what she'd done and about the farmer. He only recalled her first name, though. In fact, Salene said that when he was telling this history to her, she asked and prayed and hoped that he knew her mother's name. When he told her it was Dora, she said that was the most beautiful word she'd ever heard. It wasn't until Salene had access to the list that she learned her full identity."

"What was the list for?"

"Dora was married to Ethan, but wasn't a twin herself. The list, it was learned, included people married to twins. Perhaps they wanted to track their children in case they were twins, as well. No one is exactly certain about that since there were no notations, but the file did say she was experimentally deceased. Can you imagine Salene finding that out? They had experimented on her mother and her father; and it looked like that bastard Wasser did his experiments only on Italian Jews."

"I wonder why?"

"I asked Salene that same question. The organization said it had to do with his obsession for using human guinea pigs from the same culture. There would be less mixed blood. Salene was also told that Wasser was still alive, so she offered her services to any organization going after war criminals. She was asked to move to the United States from Italy.

"Salene also told me about David Stivers who worked for National Geographic and was given a grant to find a hidden lake in Peru. Well, he did find something, but it had nothing to do with a lake. He found Carl Wasser and his son. David also belonged to one of the organizations that hunted Nazi war criminals. There was never a grant and there was no National Geographic assignment; that was his cover."

"This is a tragic story, Ursula, but what has it got to do with me?"

"When you were living in the subway, you were spotted one time after you'd been cleaned up, and a photo was taken. You see, Sam, you look just like Dr. Wasser's son."

"I don't like the sound of this. Nor do I imagine I'm going to like where this might go."

"I thought you might react like this. But..."

"Besides, how would they know that? From what you told me, the son was still quite young when he left Germany."

"Though they couldn't get to him, people have seen him. This person said the son and you could be twins."

"And this means...?"

"They want me to locate and meet with the son. I need your help because you so closely resemble him. We believe it will come in...handy in getting him to meet with me. Without you, I don't know if I have a chance."

"Ursula, why the hell didn't you tell me what was going on? It would have made it so much easier on everyone, especially me. Were they afraid I'd say no?"

"I had nothing to do with that decision. I told them all along that you should be informed, but they had a file on you and based on their findings, decided to keep you in the dark until absolutely necessary, which is now. Because of that incident back on the road, I'm afraid everything may be coming apart. I just don't know."

"What file? What's coming apart?"

"Are you really certain you want to know?"

"Damn right. You're telling me about a bunch of people I don't know making decisions about me and my life. Except for you, I don't give a fuck about any of them. And I really don't appreciate that they didn't think enough of me to inform me from the beginning. They want me to risk my life without proper information? Fuck them! By the way, why didn't they just come here and kill him? Before you answer that, I want to know about my file."

"They said they have you figured out; know exactly how you react to certain situations based on notes in your military file; what your political views are; and even how far you would go if you learned what we were up to. They used the words, 'collectable survivor with a common intellect' to describe you."

"What the hell does that mean?"

"The short, stocky man I mentioned summed it up this way, 'Ursula, Sam needs direction and strength; and we need you to get him to Peru. We need him to have a reason stronger than what our reasons are because we know he will not be willing to do this for our cause alone. He needs something else as a motivator; money may do it.' "

"I like money as much as the next guy, but they were wrong."

"There was no way to know that then. I know it now."

"That makes me suspicious about how many other things they may get wrong. You said you're to find and meet the son. There's got to be more to it than that. Exactly what assignment did you accept? I want to know, right now, what the fuck is it. So I look like his son. What good is that? Why should that make him want to meet with you?"

"The organization sent a team here two years ago, and they've never been seen or heard from again. Because they failed to get the father and he found out about their attempt to get him, Wasser left Peru and went into hiding. They think he went to Brazil and now, maybe Berlin. But the good news is he left his son here."

"Why did he leave his son?"

"The organization thinks the Wassers have been conducting new tests on certain tribes—business as usual—which means the son would not leave so easily. We know he's committed to his father and that he *enjoys* his work.

"So you know more, the first contingent sent to Peru to find Wasser had orders to assassinate him instead of taking him to a tribunal in Israel. This was because it would be nearly impossible to get him out of Peru. Lima has a large anti-Semitic population and the military is in power there. They wouldn't tolerate Jews taking a German in hiding out of the country, especially when they had, in actuality, granted sanctuary. Eliminating Wasser was the only other choice. Unfortunately, the organization hadn't taken into account how large a following Wasser had in both the Amazon and Lima. All our resources were spent in finding out his exact whereabouts, but to no avail. But, we found the son, Sigmund."

"Where do I come in?"

"You're to exchange places with Sigmund so we can get at him and get him away from his protective layers."

"Oh, really; and how are you going to convince him to do that?"

"Don't worry. He's already convinced. He believes his father's people have sent help to get him out of the country and unite him with Carl in Germany. The organization worked on the details, but first they had to make sure that you would go along with them or, rather, me. The organization was able to intercept communications between father and son; and in doing so, they coordinated this plan. They soon had Sigmund thinking he was dealing with his father's people."

"I don't see why he just doesn't leave on his own."

"He can't leave, Sam. He knows that if he leaves the safety of Peru as himself, he could jeopardize his father, as well as the money that now supports them both. That devotion has made him stay until something could be worked out."

"Ursula, he knows the organization was after his father and not him, so what was his concern?"

"The organization made it known that if they couldn't get Wasser, his son was to be killed, sort of a lesser form of justice, but one that might cause Wasser to expose his whereabouts. With that information leaked to the father's people, it was easy to intercept Wasser's messenger sent to warn Sigmund. Our replacement messenger gave Sigmund the plan for how he's to get out of the jungle."

"So, where do I come in?"

"Sigmund will leave with your passport and head straight into the arms of the people who will use him to get at his father."

"What happens to me?"

"This is where trust comes in, hard as that may be for you after all that's happened. The plan is for you to stay hidden for a few days. Then you'll come out of the jungle and get taken back to the American Embassy in Cuzco. By then, people at the Embassy will have been told of what transpired and of your complete ignorance in the affair. Now I'm going to tell you about Juan. The man who told us he was Juan Griego wasn't the agent who was supposed to meet us."

"I thought there was something going on there, but Jesus, Ursula. You keep... I'd appreciate no more hidden agendas or withheld information from now on. You said he wasn't the right person. How do you know that?"

"Juan Griego is not the real agent's name. When we were to meet, he would have used his real one, Rudolpho. Only those he made contact with in Sigmund's camp would have known him as Juan Griego. Anyone not with us who knew that name was on the wrong side. It was the only true way of telling who was who. The man we met somehow knew we were to meet Rudolpho on the outskirts of Paucartambo, and that we would have the money with us. He was a crook, and he probably killed our agent. Now, Sonya will deal with him."

"Sonya? And while we're on the subject of her, why don't you explain why *you* two could be twins."

"I promise to tell you more, but another time. There are more important matters to deal with now. One of them is I told Marcos what happened and that I sent Sonya to find the body and bury it."

"She'll never find him."

"Yes, she will. I noted enough landmarks between there and the bar. And, there aren't that many intersections between here and there. Just reverse tracks and there's Juan, or whoever he is."

"Why did you tell Sonya anything about him? Wouldn't it have been better to just let him rot or be eaten?"

"I had to tell Sonya. She has to know everything that goes on."

"Are you sure you can trust her? She looks like a Nazi."

"That's part of her cover. She's one of us. I told Marcos that I was sure this so-called Juan was not on our side because he said you were to die first; that was a dead giveaway. Anyone involved with us knows to do whatever is necessary to keep you alive. Too bad about Rudolpho, though. He'll never see Wasser brought to trial."

"What makes you think Sigmund will let me live after he leaves Peru? He could easily have me killed, you know."

"He wouldn't harm his cousin."

"Hold on. You're saying he'll think I'm his cousin? Why would he buy that?"

"Oh, he'll buy it. He already has. You told me you thought you were Lithuanian, at least that's what your mother told you. And what happened when you had the urge to find your roots? A cousin you found living in Wyoming told you she was making up a family tree, and you asked her when your parents had come to the United States from Lithuania. She told you they didn't come from Lithuania, they came from Germany and settled in Johnstown, Pennsylvania, and that both were born in a small town near the Black Forest. You said your mother told you the Lithuanian story because of the war with Germany. She must have been afraid of reprisals in the States. It wasn't easy for the American Germans or Germans who came to America during that time, I would think."

"Ursula, my Mom was a Jew."

"I know, Sam, but she may have found it easier to hide the fact that she and her husband were German as well as Jews. Mistrust had become a way of life for Jews at the time. And, even Americans didn't fully embrace Jews during those years, despite what was happening to them. Many didn't actually believe the stories when they started to come out. They were simply too horrible to accept as truth. Self-protection and survival came before heritage, at least until a level of acceptance changed. Being Lithuanian was no problem since most people didn't even know what that meant."

"And my father went along with the charade."

"Sure. You told me how much your mother said they were in love; but when your father died of tuberculosis at the age of twenty-five, and you were only four at the time, why should she bother changing the story?"

"And why does this make Sigmund believe I'm his cousin?"

"Guess where Wasser comes from? A small town near the Black Forest. There was so much confusion during that time, it was easy to lose track of relatives.

"Carl went along with anything that kept him in high esteem with that fucking mustached maniac in control. But for some reason, he kept a low profile as far as his torture chambers went. He was very clever with his vocation and with keeping it secret.

What he couldn't know then was that some of his work would become popular forty-five years later. A few years ago, some of his documents started to show up in South America and then in the United States. Even Israel was able to acquire copies. Now all medical torture chambers keep copies of Wasser's work on their shelves. It wasn't long before Wasser became known as the Doctor of Pain. So you see, from being the least wanted criminal, he now became the most wanted; but different groups want him for different reasons."

"You know, Ursula, we should get our asses out of here right now, before anything bad happens to the two of us."

"After what I just told you, you just want to leave? You said you understood. And, what about *your* Frank; have you forgotten about him?"

"Are you saying that now you think he was more than a delusion?"

"I don't know what happened to you, Sam; but some of what you told me was accurate. Let's just say I'm keeping an open mind."

This was my second-best moment to show her Frank's compass and tell her about his headstone, but that strong feeling not to do it came back. I decided to pay attention to it. I also thought about seeing her with the Four. Again, I had a feeling to leave it alone.

The two of us stood up. My butt was numb and my head ached. What Ursula was asking could get us killed, but there was a good chance the scheme could work. And if it did, who knows? I might be able to get rich, save a country, maybe even write a best-selling book.

CHAPTER 13

After we got back to the main road, a jeep approached us from the direction of town. Dust kicked up from all around it so that it was impossible to see who was driving. As it neared, Ursula said, "I think it must be Sonya."

It was if Sonya had grown a beard overnight. The jeep stopped about twenty feet in front of us. The sole occupant, a male, sat motionless for a moment. Then he slowly opened his door and stepped out. He looked to be my height and was very slim. He also had a slim, but very large rifle in his hand. He started walking towards us and said something in Spanish. All I could make out was Rudolpho."

Ursula left my side and met him half-way. He laid the gun down to hug her then picked it back up before they both walked towards me.

"Hello, Sam," he said as he extended his hand for me to shake. "I'm Rudolpho; but around others outside of our little group here, you will only know me as Juan Griego." I shook his hand and nodded.

"I thought you'd been killed," Ursula said.

"Well, that should have been the case; but the man that you disposed of, Sam, never was a good shot."

"I disposed of him," Ursula contradicted. Rudolpho nodded, but looked grim. "Did you see Sonya?" she continued. "I sent her looking for the other Juan's body."

"She found him. His real name was Tinko, Sonya's husband."

"Her husband?!"

With all we'd been through, this was the first time I'd ever seen Ursula go pale.

"Sonya's husband," she said quietly. "She knows we killed him."

"Oh, now it's *we*." I said. "What happened to just you?"

"Don't worry," Rudolpho interrupted. "She will not be coming back."

"You killed her?" I asked.

I glanced at Ursula to see how she took this. She blinked once, but her even paler face wore no expression.

"I had to, Sam. Since I no longer had my van, I was on foot until I got this jeep. As I walked, I heard someone weeping in the brush on the side of the road. I approached the edge and looked down and was surprised to see Sonya climbing up carrying Tinko's shotgun. When she saw me, she aimed the gun at me and screamed, 'They killed my Tinko! I should have killed them both last night, but I *will* kill them after I kill you.'

"I told her not to fire the gun, not for my sake but for hers. I could see that she had used the gun as a staff to help pull her up the hill. She was so enraged she didn't realize that mud and grass had packed the barrel of the gun. She began to laugh and then pulled the trigger. There was a violent recoil when she fired that forced the barrel upward, and sent her tumbling back down. I was deciding whether or not to look for her when she started up again. This time, she had a sidearm in her hand. I knew she could use it very effectively, so I sent her back down for good. I had to do it. If she killed me, you two would have been next. The mission would have failed.

"So, here I am. Sonya was unfortunate to make certain assumptions about Marcos. He works for me, under Sigmund's instructions. When she saw you two enter town, she had to know Tinko had failed to kill you or had missed finding you. And as I said, he missed his chance to kill me."

"I never knew she was married and certainly not that she was working against us," Ursula said.

"You can't feel guilty about what you didn't know," Rudolpho said. "As for me, I was negligent. Tinko rode with me in the van when I was coming to meet both of you, at least he asked for a ride as far as the town. He carried his shotgun, but that wasn't unexpected or anything I thought I needed to be concerned about with him.

"About an hour's ride from town, he said he had to piss. When he got out, I did the same, but to stretch. As I left the van, he pulled out the shotgun, aimed it at me, and pulled the trigger. As I said, he was always a bad shot. Anyway, I didn't wait for him to try again. I jumped off the side of the road and ran into the thick brush. Luckily, he didn't follow me. He fired some shots in my direction; but if he had hit me, it would have been shear luck. I soon heard him start the engine. When I heard the van leave, I climbed up to the road and headed towards town.

"When I arrived after dark, I found Marcos. He told me you were asleep in the spare room at the bar. I kept watch of your room from a clearing at the jungle's edge. Today, I had to negotiate for this jeep. I was walking to get it when I found Sonya. Even though I knew where to find the van, I thought you might not be happy to see it approaching you again."

"I knew I saw something or someone last night. I even wondered if it was Frank," I said.

Rudolpho wore a quizzical expression and looked over at Ursula who remained quiet. "Everything is still on for the swap to take place," he said. "Now I have to find a way to tell Sigmund that Sonya and Tinko were shot by you, Ursula. It won't work if I tell him the truth. Don't make me explain, Sam," he said when I started to interrupt.

"Okay, but why just Ursula?" I asked. What was I thinking to ask that?

"The best story I can think of at the moment is to tell Sigmund that Tinko duped you both to accept a ride in the van to an area were he and Sonya had prearranged to meet. After he pulled a gun on both of you, he waited for Sonya to show up. When she arrived, they went through your backpacks, but didn't find the money they knew you were carrying. They decided to force Ursula to tell them where the money was by threatening to shoot you, Sam. Of course, they never expected Ursula to be carrying a gun or at least not to use it on them. In order to save the mission, Ursula had to shoot them both. Well, what do you think?"

"It should work," Ursula said.

"How is it that everyone seems to know we have the money?" I asked. "I mean, a few people, yes; but..."

"Let me interrupt you," Rudolpho said. "In fact, let me let Ursula answer your questions and maybe it will give you more confidence in the mission and us."

Ursula started, "The drug dealer we met on the train was actually supposed to deliver the money to the hotel in Puño where Carlos was going to take the bag and have it delivered to Sigmund. However, the police had been tipped off, by us, that there would be drugs on the train. They showed up and it forced the drug dealer to try to unload the money. When he saw you sitting on the train, it was natural for him to want to give it to you because he thought you were Sigmund. When you refused to let him put the bag by your feet, he became confused. So he went to the bathroom and put it behind the door, thinking you, as Sigmund, were paying attention. You weren't, but I was; and it's what we hoped would happen, that is, that he would leave it somewhere on the train. I watched him enter the bathroom with the bag and exit without it. I kept an eye out to make sure no one went in there before I could.

"When the police took him off the train, I went to the bathroom, found the bag, and came back and told you about it. You responded perfectly. I hoped you would take it along once you looked inside. I never imagined you wouldn't look. Anyway, even if you hadn't taken it, I would have."

"I realize," I said, "that some of what's happened could be coordinated ahead of time, but it seems you always have something arranged no matter how things change. Except for rare occasions, like the night I went with Frank, you're never out of my sight. How…"

"We used the fact that you don't speak anything but English," Ursula said. "Many times, when you thought I was asking questions of total strangers, I was communicating with messengers. Other times, I got messages from people who seemed to engage in conversations that anyone might overhear. I know you're frustrated that you're not fully informed at all times, but it's for your protection. If something significant changes, the less you know, the better."

"How did you know the young smuggler was the one with the money?"

"We knew it was to be delivered by a drug dealer then learned it was him, thanks to Rudolpho, who got word to me of where we had to be and when so you and I could to be on the same train and in the same car. Things got tricky when we got to Puño because Carlos knew who was supposed to deliver the money. It was quite a surprise to him when he saw us with the bag. He thought there'd been a change of couriers and no one informed him of it. Plus, you look so much like Sigmund it confused him, so he didn't know what to do. The only thing he knew for sure was that he had to get the bag and have it delivered as he'd been instructed, no matter what was different. That would be the smart thing to do."

"How do you know this?"

"I did talk to him when I went downstairs. I lied to him about what was going on; told him to leave the hotel. I told him that's what you wanted him to do. He still wasn't sure if you were Sigmund or not and knew better than to ask; so he did what he was told."

"I thought you'd shot him. I could've sworn I heard a shot or a car backfiring."

"You did; but it didn't have anything to do with us, so I wasn't concerned."

"And then you lied to me...again. What about Tinko's story about Carlos being killed in the alley? Did that happen?"

Rudolpho jumped in. "Tinko *had* hit Carlos on the head and fled with the bag, but was in for a rude awakening when he checked the contents. I know this because word got around fast."

"And going to the Island of Tequile? Was that part of the plan?"

"Not originally, then it had to be," Ursula said. "I had to convince you I was obsessed with finding the pilot. I had to let you believe we were following a new plan. Anyway, I was able to handle all the problems that confronted us; at least, I was until you became even more obsessed about Frank than I pretended to be. Then I had to become a little creative.

"Next on the agenda was to make sure we reached Paucartambo, though I told you our destination was Cuzco. The mudslide almost fouled us up; and then we got into the truck with Carlos and the drug dealer. My nerves became frazzled. Though, meeting up with them on the truck helped me get us where we needed to go without my having to think of a reason for a change of plans."

"I thought I was going to have to sit on you so you wouldn't grab a gun and start shooting."

"I didn't know what Carlos or the drug dealer knew at this point. I would have been forced to explain something to them that might make sense while at the same time, you would have been wondering what was up. I don't think it would have been a good scene."

I had a mind full of stories and what I thought were facts, which sometimes were and sometime weren't. Facts, such as they were, seemed to change on a dime around Ursula. This was a tapestry with lots of loose strings. I just wasn't sure which one, if pulled, would unravel the whole thing and, possibly, me along with it.

"Who's Frank?" Rudolpho asked.

CHAPTER 14

B efore Ursula or I could respond to Rudolpho's question, we heard a voice call out his name. Rudolpho picked up his rifle and walked towards Marcos who was running in our direction. The two of them spoke at a distance, which was far enough from us it was impossible to hear their conversation. Rudolpho returned and Marcos headed back to town.

"Marcos was concerned for my safety. Now I would like to hear about who Frank is but I'm afraid we must first go back to town."

"I'll tell you about that later," Ursula said. "What happens now?"

"You'll drive into the jungle with Marcos as your guide and travel until daylight, where you'll reach a small town. Marcos will leave and you will drive the rest of the way to meet up with him again. After you pass through this town, there will be a large bulletin board at its far edge. You must write your names and passport numbers on paper—you must bring your own pen and paper—and attach the paper to the clipboard kept inside the wooden box that is nailed to the board. Then you can continue on your way."

"What's with the names and passport numbers?" I asked.

"It must be done. You will be watched from a distance and photographed. Once you do this you can continue on."

"Sorry, Rudolpho, but you didn't exactly answer my question."

"It's a Peruvian formality, a way of knowing who has entered the jungle. When you come out, it is necessary to repeat the process. Of course, it will be Sigmund using your name when he leaves. Once you go past the bulletin board, there are no more towns for you to travel through; only a river will block your way. Marcos will take over from there."

"And you?"

"Sigmund is sending me ahead to Cuzco, then on to Lima. I will be clearing the way for Ursula and him; he is a very cautious man."

"Wait a minute. Ursula leaves with Sigmund?"

"Yes, she must. It must look like you and Ursula leave the jungle together, as you arrived. Otherwise it will trigger a search and that would not be good. And since you traveled to Peru together, it must appear you leave the country together."

"Ursula explained I was to wait a few days, then get to the Embassy; but how am I supposed to get out of the jungle?"

"You'll know more about that when it's time. We should go back to town now."

We climbed into the jeep. Instead of getting in back, Ursula sat on my lap. The engine sprang to life and we headed towards town. I glanced at Rudolpho's face often enough to study it the whole way back. Something bothered me. Of course, the whole damn business bothered me, but something wasn't right. I just didn't know what the hell it could be.

"Earlier, when I drove towards you," Rudolpho said, "I was not too sure who was standing there. At first I thought I was seeing Sigmund, and you looked a lot like Sonya, even though I knew where she was. This is good. Everything should be fine."

Ursula kept quiet, but I felt her body stiffen when he said Sonya's name.

He pulled the jeep to a sharp stop in front of the bar. The dirt street was filled with dust-coated children playing with several dogs. We got out of the jeep and walked towards the bar. Marcos appeared in the doorway. I thought for a moment he might try to block me as he'd done before, but he stepped aside.

It was dark inside. I quickly looked around and saw it was also empty, just as Rudolpho said it would be. Marcos took a position behind the bar while Ursula walked to the table and sat down. Rudolpho sat opposite Ursula and laid his rifle across the table. I walked over to the bar to where Marcos was and saw he was wearing a smile.

"Pisco, please, Señor Marcos," I said smiling back. He didn't respond, just stared past me towards the table.

"Pisco, Señor?" I said again. This time he reached down and came up with a bottle. I reached across and grasped the neck of the bottle. Marcos held fast to the bottom and we had a brief macho tug of war. He smiled. When I smiled back, he let go.

I leaned back against the bar and rested my elbows on it. The room was dark with the exception of shafts of sunlight that streamed through the windows. Inside the rays of light, dust rose and floated towards the edge of darkness. I pulled the cork from the bottle with my teeth and spit it out on the floor.

"What a shame. That cork'll be too dirty to use now," I said. "Guess we'll have to finish the bottle."

I took a long drink, turned towards Marcos and handed him the bottle, motioning for him to take a drink. Without hesitation, he mimicked my pull on the bottle and handed it back me. I turned and tossed it to Rudolpho who made a good catch. He wasn't afraid to drink down a good amount of Cuzco gold either.

When he put the bottle on the table, Ursula picked it up and placed the bottle to her lips. She tilted her head back and scanned us with her eyes—first Rudolpho, then Marcos, then me. As she drank, I reflected on what had happened to us since she and I had become a team, even if I had to use the word loosely since I'd been mostly uninformed or misinformed as it were; but it all seemed trivial compared to what lay ahead.

The Pisco overflowed Ursula's mouth. She let it run over her chin and down the front of her blouse, soaking her. Her exposed skin glistened, and my blood started to warm up for more reasons than alcohol. She held the three of us in a trance, deliberately demonstrating her control over us.

I knew Ursula could take care of herself. My mind started to imagine what it would be like to personally take care of her, meaning finally take her, and my head was off to the races. My heart started to beat like crazy. Once that happens, common sense usually heads out the door. I told myself to slow up, but not before Ursula caught how I was looking at her.

There was another current of excitement in the room that couldn't be missed. Sitting in that tin-covered shack so near the Amazon Jungle, I looked around and realized we were about to pull off the most daring kidnapping ever and for the best reason. Plus, I hadn't forgotten Frank said there was gold at this end of this rainbow. After feeling like the odd man out most of the time

I was in Peru, I believed the four of us were bonding together as a team. It was almost like a pulse. I started to laugh without explanation. The others joined me, as though if there had been any doubt in our minds before, we now knew for sure this plan was going to happen. We were the good guys who had come to town to take on the bad guys at any cost. The ghosts of the past would have their revenge. Sigmund was in trouble. And, I'd feel like Midas since Frank had said Ursula would lead me to the gold.

"Maybe it would be best if we hit the road," I said. "Standing around and waiting to leave is making me antsy. As it is, I'm starting to have booze balls."

"Booze balls, Sam?" Ursula said. Rudolpho and Marcos turned their heads to look at me, so I was the only one who saw the teasing smile in her eyes.

"Ask me later," I replied.

"Okay, then," Rudolpho said, slapping a hand on the tabletop. "This is where I say goodbye. I will leave immediately. Marcos will take over, so listen to whatever he says. He knows his way around the jungle."

One thing still bothered me. Well, more than one thing. I called out, "Hey, Rudolpho. I'll walk you out. I need air." I knew no one would believe that, but it was the best I could come up with at the moment.

He followed me out onto the dirt road that had emptied of people. Even the dogs had disappeared. I turned and faced him. "What's with Marcos? I know you said he works for you, but what's with his attitude towards me?"

"He's not in on the entire story, Sam, so don't discuss it with him. Let Ursula do the talking. He worships Sigmund and he wants to see him safely away from danger and back with his father. He's lived with them since he was born, almost like one of the family. They were his source of education; his life, too, if you know the whole story.

"As someone from the jungle who has never left it, Marcos is considered well-educated. He is a Yanomami, also Peba-Yaguan; but his ties are more Yanomami. He can speak English and some Quechua, and of course his own language which is called Yagua. He can neither read nor write any of the languages he can speak. The Wassers kept that from him because they were afraid he would learn too much about them. Anyway, he feels he owes his very existence to both of them. Without them, he would probably be at the bottom of a gold mining pit, facing a very short life."

"What gold mine?"

"Forget I said that. Marcos believes you are here to save Sigmund, that's all. He's very jungle smart, which is what's needed by us and you. Now, Sam, I must get going."

"Ursula! Marcos!" he shouted, "I leave now. Bye, Sam. Know that what you are doing is great. It is an opportunity to serve mankind; a beast more deadly than any that inhabits the jungle will be brought to justice. Keep that in your mind and your heart. I forgot to mention that among his many other accomplishments, Marcos also speaks German, of course."

With that, Rudolpho started walking in the direction of Cuzco. Ursula came out from the bar and stood at my side. He looked back and gave us a wave. We returned it.

"Well, Sam," Ursula said, "there he goes."

"Are we going to meet up with him again?"

"Maybe, but I don't really think we will."

I took a moment to collect my thoughts. I really wasn't certain what to think of Rudolpho. Back at the bar, I'd had that moment where I felt part of the brotherhood, so-to-speak. But I was back to feeling bothered...because I couldn't shake the feeling something was wrong. Ursula had made it a point not to explain Frank to him, nor could I imagine what she might have said since she thought he was nothing more than a hallucination of mine, though she'd admitted to doubts.

I put my arm around Ursula's shoulder as we walked back to the bar. Marcos had once again taken his favorite stance to block the door.

"Yes, Marcos, what is it?" Ursula asked.

"Sam, Ursula, I want you both to know that from now on I will no longer vamoose."

He put out his hand to shake hands with me, but instead of offering him my hand, an impulse I didn't understand made me reach under my shirt and lift the lanyard that held Frank's compass, over my head. I moved forward to slip it over his head.

"Let me do that," Ursula said. She took it from me, stood in front of Marcos, and put it on him. It was a little tricky to get it past his ears. Once it was on, it was kind of a tighter fit since his neck, what little there was of it, was a lot thicker than mine.

Marcos stepped back into the bar and fingered the compass. He looked at us and smiled ear-to-ear. Without another word, he walked down the corridor.

I waited for Ursula to comment that the compass wasn't mine, but she didn't. Maybe she hadn't paid attention or maybe she thought one compass looked like another, even though mine didn't have a cover.

I went behind the bar, reached down into a small tub of water, and took out another bottle of Pisco. "Join me?" I asked Ursula.

"Sure, why not?"

"Ursula, did you notice that the town seems suddenly empty?"

"I did," she replied. "Sigmund's power has no bounds. Rudolpho told me that from now on, Sigmund wants to make sure nothing happens to us. The original plan was for it to look like we were tourists with a guide who would actually be an armed bodyguard; but everyone was concerned that might call too much attention to us, so they let us work our way here pretty much on our own. Besides, we couldn't find a better guard or guide than Marcos."

I walked over to the table and picked up Rudolpho's rifle. He'd left it behind. "Nice gun," I remarked. "Double-barrel. I had one of these when I was a kid."

"Watch how you handle that gun, gringo," a voice speaking perfect English shot into the bar from outside. Two scruffs walked in. So much for Sigmund's protection. They looked like they hadn't showered in years. Smelled that way, too.

"A gun like that needs a man to hold it," the man said.

"Well, gentlemen, this gun has all the man it can handle." As I made that comment, I prayed it was loaded.

They walked towards the bar where Ursula was standing. These two were going to be trouble. "Come over here, Ursula," I said, keeping my eyes on the men.

"No, gringo, she stays with us." His hand had moved to inside his jacket and returned holding a large pistol. His comrade walked to the other side of Ursula. He displayed no gun, and that was a good sign; but with both of them standing on either side of her, it made the rifle too dangerous to use and they knew it.

Fear-tinged sweat dripped into my eyes. It stung and I had trouble keeping my eyes open. I tried to make my squint look intimidating. "What's up with you two?" I demanded.

"The money; we want the money and we go away. Nobody gets hurt. What do you say, gringo?"

The fucking money again. "Sure; but we mostly have traveler's checks. Not much help to you out here."

"Hey, stupid, we want the money from Puño."

I stared at Ursula who faintly shook her head from side-to-side.

"Look guys. We had the money, but somebody already beat you to it back near Paucartambo."

"No good, gringo. We know better."

I looked at Ursula, then back at the one with the big mouth. "We don't have any idea what you're talking about."

"Sure you do. We were panning for gold in the river by the road. We found a man who had been shot. Before he died, he told us about you two and some story that made no sense about a German in the jungle. He said we should kill you both and the money would be ours."

"We never shot anyone," I said. "Look, we did have the money once, but that man stole it from us. Maybe whoever did shoot him took it."

"You shouldn't mind if we have a look at your bags then, should you?" He said to his friend, "Go to their room and bring back their bags."

"Yes, I would mind," I said. I swung the rifle up and aimed it at Big Mouth. "In fact, it's time to end this bullshit, boys."

"You fire that thing and the woman gets hit," Big Mouth said as he positioned Ursula in front of him.

"I wouldn't have taken you for a coward who hides behind a woman," I said. He didn't take the bait.

Sweat was streaming down my face. He jammed the gun into Ursula's side and she winced. I thought she must be scared because, for once, she wasn't trying to talk our way out of a situation.

"It's your move, gringo. Put the rifle down," he demanded.

"No way, jerk. Your buddy doesn't have a gun, so I plan to shoot you first, then him."

"Go ahead and shoot him now!" Ursula called out louder than she needed to. The unarmed guy looked at her in surprise. "Shoot now," she said in a very calm voice.

I pulled back the two hammers without lowering my aim. I said to Ursula, "Let's give them the money, get the fuck out of here, and head back to the States."

"If we give them the money, we're dead anyway," Ursula said, acting very composed. "I *said* to shoot now."

"See," said Big Mouth, "there is money."

Those were the last words that asshole ever spoke. He fell forward on his face and by the time his buddy could react, Marcos appeared from the darkened corridor with a blowgun in one hand and a very large knife in the other. He tossed the blowgun into the air. It hit the tin roof and distracted everyone. Marcos covered the distance of the room to where the second man was, grabbed him by the wrist and twisted. I heard the snap followed by the man's cry of pain.

"Look to the door, Ursula," Marcos commanded. She turned away and he shoved the knife into the man's chest, moved it clockwise, and yanked it out. Marcos used the knife handle to hit the side of the man's head, and that was that. Considering the hole in the man's chest, the hit to the head seemed like overkill to me; but, I wasn't about to comment.

I reached down and picked up the pistol that had fallen from Big Mouth's unmoving hand and stuck it in my pants waist as I'd seen cowboys do in the movies.

"Ursula," I said, "we need to get our gear. Now."

We got everything together in record time and rejoined Marcos in the bar.

"We go," Marcos insisted and pushed Ursula towards the door.

Ursula moved faster than I'd ever seen her move. "Are they dead?" she asked.

Marcos didn't speak, just walked out the door. He turned quickly, and gave us his biggest gold-toothed smile and said, "Now we all vamoose, amigos."

We walked onto the street without looking back. Marcos got to the jeep ahead of us. Ursula and I stopped walking when two men approached Marcos. He said something in what sounded like Spanish. The two men went into the bar.

Marcos said, "The River claims many lives. Those dead men will soon become part of the jungle," and he started to laugh. "Jungle mush." He kept the laughing up and I thought he was a lot more entertained by this than I was.

Marcos turned the key in the ignition and the jeep engine sprang to life. He said loudly, "The River claims many lives, some good some bad. It doesn't care which. It turns them all into mush. What a word! Try to teach a native what *mush* means." The word must have really amused him because he didn't say it without laughing.

Ursula fitted herself sideways in the back jump seat and I took the passenger seat. The jeep lurched forward when Marcos shifted gears.

"Ursula," I said, "a lot of people are dying around us, for one reason or another. How many more?"

"As many as it takes, Sam. As many as it takes."

I didn't have a ready response, so kept quiet.

CHAPTER 15

Marcos kept the jeep as steady as he could on the road that had changed from just rutted dirt to rocky. As far as I could look up, I saw green. It looked like we were headed into the depths of what might as well have been an ocean of green; but instead of riding on the surface, we were in it like a submarine. How the jungle below the tremendous growth above could flourish was beyond me. The deeper we went into the jungle, the heavier the humidity became. The overall effect was that even though we kept moving forward without a stop, time seemed to stand still.

The jungle canopy let enough light through that it created a strobe-like effect. This flickering made Marcos, Ursula, and me part of a kaleidoscopic show. I was trying to be obtuse about staring at Marcos, but something must have shown on my face.

"What?" Ursula said sharply.

"Nothing," I replied. "I was just keeping myself amused."

She tried to say something but at that moment, the jeep hit a hole and we all got jostled around. I heard "you" as air was forced from her chest. "Fuck you," probably, but I wouldn't swear to that on a bible.

The river remained on our right as we traveled. Not only did we not cross over any bridges, I never saw any to cross. This gave me something of a sense of security because I felt I could navigate our way back to Paucartambo, if I needed to do so.

Whenever we were engaged in moving from one place to another or running for our lives, which seemed to be most of the time, I didn't give a lot of thought to my situation. Now that we'd been traveling for hours and had more to go, I had lots of time to think. Maybe that wasn't such a good idea because all that reflection made me suddenly fearful for my life.

I knew Ursula still needed to be watched. Her story about why we were here, and our roles, was compelling; but she was just a bit too comfortable about people being killed. And she'd been clear that if it took more killings, so be it.

Since Puño, I'd been in something of a fog, like I was most of the time in my drugged-out days. All my life it seemed I'd been willing to travel along, accept my fate, whatever it was. No denying I'd indulged in too much booze that led to too many hangovers; but for once, my head was clearing. Some of my recent fate had been designed for me by others, and I didn't feel reassured that they had my best interest in mind.

There were also the other aspects to consider: Meeting Frank, and how mostly inexplicable yet intriguing that was; the thought of finding a wealth of gold; and of course the money we'd been carrying around. Each had seemed to cast a spell on me. Or, maybe I was a few quarts low on perspective.

At first, Ursula's fluctuating attitude about the money confused me. I guess as players and circumstances changed, and since I hadn't been in the bigger loop until lately, confusing me didn't concern her. In fact, it probably was part of the plan, that or she just liked to play with me like a cat does with a mouse. Only, we know how often the cat lets the mouse go…never. The mouse is usually found with its head missing.

Then there was the killing. Killing meant nothing, at least, not to the people I kept meeting up with here. They didn't seem to give a shit. Jesus! Here I was up to my lower lip in a pool of piss, hoping no one would jump in and make a wave. *Jump out and head back now*, I thought. *Keep the river on the left and you'll be back in Paucartambo in no time*. Then all I would need was a truck ride back to Cuzco…and money, my passport, and my ticket home.

We stopped to take a bathroom break. As I stood there watering a bush, I looked back down the road. Marcos noticed and said "With me along or by yourself?"

"What?

"You're thinking of taking off. Daytime is a better time to do this. You walk and make lots of noise. With luck, you can make it through one night; but the second night, you will be followed by the meat-eaters. With no fire, you will die. Even if you have a gun, you will never see what you will be feeding."

"Thanks."

"Second thoughts, Sam?" Ursula asked when I got back into the jeep.

"Just aiming to stay safe."

"*Safe* is what waits ahead for both of us."

I'd believe that when I was back in New York in the nice apartment I'd rent or buy with my share of the spoils.

Our bodies were pounded for hours by the jagged road, but Marcos was relentless about getting to our destination. I would, from time to time, peer at his eyes. From my point of view, they seemed like large black marbles. Sometimes, a smile would play across his lips. Maybe because he knew I was looking at him, or maybe it was his own thoughts of anticipation, or even something I would never imagine or want to.

Night was taking over. It would soon be pitch black with only our headlights to lead the way. We still had hours of travel ahead of us based on what Rudolpho had said.

Marcos stopped the jeep suddenly, shut off the engine, and stood up. He faced the direction we'd just come from.

"What's up?" I asked. "Are we stopping? I thought we were driving through the night."

"We are not stopping." He restarted the engine and popped the clutch a little clumsily, which he hadn't done before. The way he focused straight ahead seemed to have more intensity; and he seemed angry.

"At dawn," he said after several silent minutes, "we will reach the town. From there you will drive on without me until the river blocks your way."

"Marcos," Ursula asked, "are we being followed?"

Marcos smiled, but I couldn't get a read on him. He braked and shut off the engine. "Stand up and be very quiet."

All three of us stood. I could see Ursula was listening hard, just as I was. "I don't hear anything, Marcos," I said.

"Same for me," Ursula added.

"Quiet. Smell anything?" Marcos asked.

"Our hot jeep and something else, but I'm not sure what," Ursula replied.

"I don't smell anything," I said, "other than what she said. Is it flowers?"

"The flowers close at night. When that happens, their scent stays inside the bloom. That's why human scents or odors become more noticeable. The same is true about the animals if you know what to smell for. The breeze carries the talking and the body odors to us, and also to the night feeders. That is how they find their prey. As I told you before, Sam, the night has many eyes that don't have to see to find and kill us. The animals will not bother us as long as we are moving. The noise and smell of the jeep keep them away."

"Great lesson, Marcos; but, you didn't answer Ursula's question. Are we being followed?"

"Yes."

"How close?" Ursula asked.

"They are very close, but they have stopped for the night."

"They?" Ursula asked.

"More than one, yes."

"Right. You want us to believe you can *smell* they've pitched tent or whatever they're doing," I said.

"I smell them *and* I hear them, Sam. I understand why this seems strange to you, but I am from the jungle. I know when something is different and what is different."

Marcos leapt from the jeep and started to run back the way we'd come. He was silent as a panther, even at the speed he was moving. Ursula and I watched him disappear into the darkness; but before he faded from view, I saw his blowgun in his hand. I noticed he'd left his knife on his seat.

"I wonder if he's going to use that thing," I said. Ursula was staring at me intently. "What?"

"Understand something, Sam, about the people who've been killed by us or because of us. Each of them was going to kill *us*. I don't think we should lose any sleep over them."

"I get that, Ursula. I was in 'Nam, remember? Kill or be killed; but, I don't have to feel good about it. Frank never said anything about a need for people to die."

"Fucking Frank, again."

"You'd like me to forget about Frank, and the flowing gold, and just focus on your goal. It's not going to happen."

"When are you going to get it, Sam? Frank was just a delusion and the flowing gold is a myth, a legend based on nothing more than a trick of the light. Where's Frank, Sam? Have you seen him anymore? No. Well, guess what? You won't see him and you won't find the flowing gold either. Neither one are real."

"You still think I'm delusional when it comes to those things. Let me remind you that Frank said you'd lead me into the jungle and that's exactly what you've done."

Ursula went quiet for a moment. "What else did Frank say?"

"He asked me to help save his people."

"Fuck him *and* his people. I remember what you told me and delusion or not, let the Peruvian government do their job. I have a job of my own to do and I intend to do it. And, Sam, be very, very clear… Nothing and no one is going to stop me."

CHAPTER 16

"Ursula, everything that's happened since you found me has moved between a dream and a nightmare. What Frank told me," I put up my hand to stop her from interrupting, "is happening. It also ties in with what you're here to do. Whether there's conflict or agreement about certain details doesn't matter in the big picture. We're still heading in the same direction. I've had some rough times in my life, but I always thought of myself as civilized. When we got here, we slammed the door shut behind us on the civilized world. We became a part of the world that exists here when we killed Tinko and, indirectly, others.

"Sometimes, I want to find Frank and tell him to go fuck him himself, his mission, and his flowing gold, and then make my way back to the States, even if that means taking up space in a box again."

I waited for Ursula to say something, but it wasn't her voice I heard. It was Marcos, who'd returned. Instead of approaching us from the road, he emerged from the brush nearby. I hadn't heard so much as a twig snap.

"What do you know of the flowing gold?" he asked staring hard at me.

"Damn, Marcos, you scared the shit out of me," I said.

"What do you know about the flowing gold, Sam?" he repeated.

"What were you doing? Hiding and listening to us?"

"They could hear you in Lima, as loud as the two of you were talking. The gold?"

I sensed Ursula tensing next to me, caught on, and lied. "Nothing, Marcos. I was just repeating a story we heard in a bar in Cuzco."

"What about the people behind us?" Ursula asked.

He glanced over at her. "It was a collectivo…a driver, two men, two women, speaking fast in a language I don't know."

"The Cuzco Four," I said.

"What did you do about them, Marcos?" she asked.

"I made sure they had set up camp for the night. Enough talk," he said. "Sit down. We have lost enough time."

Ursula appeared to relax when she heard his answer.

Marcos took up his post again behind the wheel, his expression stone-like. He started the engine and jammed down on the accelerator before Ursula and I got fully settled in. Neither Ursula nor I attempted to learn anything more from him since he made it obvious small-talk, or any talk, was out of the question.

I was way past exhausted, which meant that even on the rugged road, I managed to fall asleep. Ursula didn't need exhaustion for motivation. Her ability to sleep anywhere, any time was annoying. I'd wake now and then and glance over at Marcos. He never seemed to be fading from tiredness, just intent on his task.

He drove through the night; and by the time dawn appeared, we had pulled into a clearing and, soon after, into a little village. On our left, was a small building. I thought it must be a school because I could hear children's voices even though it was still early. On the right was a gas station, if you could call it that. A pump was attached directly to a motor. Behind it, a large fuel tank rested heavily on steel stilts. Next to the station, also on stilts, was an official-looking building, though it seemed it would, at most, have only one or two rooms or offices. Marcos stopped the jeep, got out, and started to fill the gas tank, as well as the two gas cans hanging at the back of the jeep.

"Marcos, what's that building?" I asked pointing to the official-looking one.

"That," he said nodding his head toward the building, "is a postal office, the only one in all of the Amazon's upper basin."

None of us spoke as he finished his task. He put the nozzle back on its hanger and said, "I leave you, now. Continue on the road until the river stops you. Leave the keys in the jeep. Carry your gear to the river's edge and wait for me there. I will come from down-river in a dugout. Give me the gun you took from the man. Keep the other guns you have easy to reach; but don't worry, no one will bother you."

"What about animals?" I asked, handing him Big Mouth's gun.

"There will be no animals where you stop. The sun will be up; and there will be only beautiful butterflies."

Marcos picked up his knife which was still on his seat. I watched him walk around the side of the post office then moved over to the driver's seat. Ursula climbed into the passenger seat.

"I'm ready when you are, Sam."

I put my hand on the keys to turn the engine over, then stopped and looked at her. "Do you know something that I should about the Cuzco Four? Anything at all you want to tell me about them?"

"Start driving Sam. Just drive."

I could have argued, but what was the point.

We'd lost our protective jungle cover once we entered the village and the sun started to beat down on us. I kept my cowboy hat on to dampen the sunlight in my eyes. I didn't bother to wipe away the rivulets of sweat streaming down my face. Ursula didn't appear bothered by the sun or humidity. Ursula didn't usually appear bothered by much very often, with the exception of whatever was next on her agenda. And, of course, Sonya, whatever that mystery was about.

Several miles down the road, I saw a large sheet of plywood nailed to a post. As we pulled up to it, I noted the faded painting of a skull and crossbones on the wood; a warning of what lay ahead, I imagined. The box with a rusted lock, no doubt with the clipboard inside as Rudolpho had said, was attached to the bottom of the post. Crude lettering was painted onto the plywood as well. Even though it was in Spanish, it was obviously a request for name, passport number, and the time and date.

"Do we do what it says?" I asked.

"We have to. You know that, Sam. Here, you'll need this."

Ursula took a piece of paper out of a pocket. She took a pen out of another and I watched her write the date and time on it. She already had the other information written down, though I'd never seen her do it. I walked over and did what was required then got back into the jeep.

"Well, that puts us officially in the Amazon Jungle," I said.

"How about a toast before we enter?"

Ursula had both feet rested on the dashboard with the rifle across her lap. She was holding a bottle of Pisco, put it to her lips, and took a deep drink. I took the bottle from her, placed it to my mouth, and tilted my head back. I felt something solid touch my groin. She had the barrel of the rifle pressed against my privates.

"Scared?" she asked.

"Stop fucking around, Ursula. If that gun goes off, I'll have to find work standing guard outside a harem. More likely, I'd die and you'd be in deep shit with a lot of people." I moved the barrel to the side and took a healthy swig of Pisco. "Aim that damn thing outside the jeep." Let her think what she'd just done didn't bother me, which it so fucking did.

I handed Ursula the bottle, cranked up the jeep, and started forward. It turned out to be only an hour's drive to the river. At the end of the road was a small wooden sign that read *Rio Madre de Dios*—Mother of God River.

The riverbank was surprisingly wide here, about three hundred yards wide, in fact. I didn't know if this was a flood zone or if the width was manmade. Instead of the expected dirt or mud, it was covered with perfectly round stones. Most of them were at least four inches in diameter.

Marcos was right about the butterflies. There were thousands of them, twirling skyward like small tornados. Some were so large they could have been mistaken for small birds. We watched the butterflies engage in a ritual or dance that started from where they piled into a circular heap that looked to be fifteen-feet in circumference and four feet high. They'd stay in the heap with only the slightest fluttering of their wings, until as though a conductor had given a downbeat with his baton, they would break loose. This happened in layers, starting at the top, and continued until each of them was headed skyward where they'd dance on the wind until their descent to earth repeated this pattern over again.

"Ursula," I said, "I don't know about you, but I'm bone-tired."

"I'm tired, too, Sam, and filthy. We both are. A hot bath or shower with lots of soap would do both of us good."

Here I was in an exotic, primitive locale with an unpredictable woman, danger all around me, and moving around in a foreign territory mostly at the mercy of others. But the beauty of the place could still take me over at certain times. The only other country I'd been to was Vietnam. Initially, I'd felt affected by the lushness of that landscape, as well; but imminent death from almost day one took care of eliminating any fascination with the scenery.

"There's a funny thing about the Amazon," I said. "We've come through hells and highs; but no matter what happens here, the beauty always gets to me. It's mysterious, even majestic."

"What's with you?"

"That seems to be a constant question in my mind: What, and even who, is with me," I said looking directly into her eyes.

Ursula looked away. "Marcos said to get to the edge of the water. We should do that."

The keys stayed in the jeep's ignition as Marcos had instructed. We grabbed our gear. Ursula held on to the rifle. I reached into the outer pocket of my backpack to make sure the gun was still there, along with the knife. Ursula had the other gun in her pocket. We wobbled over the stones until we were right at the edge of the river. The butterflies scattered. Our intrusion had disturbed them. I kept glancing back, watching for them to resume their ritual, but they didn't.

Ursula sat on the ground, so I sat next to her to wait for Marcos.

"The river current is fast, but it looks like we could walk across," I told her.

"You don't want to do that, Sam. This is an Amazonian river. Things live in there you don't want to meet up with."

"Just think, Ursula. Right there, on the other side of the Madre de Dios, is the Amazon Jungle."

"Yeah," she said then went quiet, her attention focused down-river.

I stared across the river to the sea of green on the other side. The city of New York is called a jungle; and it has its own music, its own beat, its own dangers. The music of the Amazon jungle during the day had a nearly silent beauty. Nighttime erupted into a level of treachery, danger, and racket. Once we entered and moved into the jungle, I imagined this would only get worse.

As we sat on the riverbank on alert for Marcos, I noticed the way the sunlight on her hair and face highlighted how beautiful she was. Ursula had behaved one way in New York City and another once we'd landed in Peru; and, even almost like a normal woman the first night we spent in the tent. The deeper we got into her conspiracy, the more unpredictable or sporadic she became. Her explanations, when she bothered with them, seemed plausible; at least until they were proven to be lies. And, of course, she'd justify them with more pieces of the puzzle like a carrot dangled in front of a horse to make it walk. This led me to believe the deeper we went into the jungle, the deeper the bullshit and lies might become. A part of me wanted to stick it out just so I could finally learn what the *real* truth was.

Well, jungle, I thought, *let me introduce you to Ursula-the-Terrible. It's a good name for her, keeps everything in order. Expect the worst from her and don't let her fool you.*

It might not be easy to do, but it was time for me to abandon any assumptions I might have about her. Ursula seemed to constantly push the limits of our relationship, whatever that was. If I could get her to be honest with me for once and ask what she's really about or who she actually is, I bet she'd say, "You really don't want to know."

"Listen," Ursula said. "Do you hear that sound? Look over there."

A good-sized dugout canoe came into view as it rounded the bend from down-river. It was traveling against the current, as well as dodging large boulders in the water, so seemed to inch its way towards us. At intervals, its forward movement slowed almost to a stop then it would lunge ahead and gain tremendous ground. Marcos was at the helm, but he wasn't alone. He'd failed to mention others would join our party. He was steering the boat and driving it hard as he could with a loud engine mounted on the stern.

The boat pulled up to us and I got a good look at the propeller which was at the end of an eight-foot long shaft. It doubled as the tiller. Too much downward pressure on it by the operator and the propeller would lift right out of the water. The dugout inched up and around the rocks, and white plumes of spray were thrown high up and back over the passengers.

A white man wearing what looked like a khaki-colored uniform stood perfectly erect at the bow. He focused straight ahead and pointed as though showing Marcos how to navigate. Behind him were three natives, heads moving from side-to-side, keeping an eye on how good a job Marcos did to get the boat close to the riverbank.

Marcos shut off the engine, looked at me and Ursula and smiled. The sun hit his gold teeth and I had to look away.

The three natives jumped from the dugout and pulled it further up the rocky embankment. They wore no clothing to speak of and were barefoot. A lifetime of shoeless existence in the Amazon had formed calluses about an inch thick on the soles of their feet. I also noticed a nasty-looking white fungus covered their toes.

Their *clothing* was actually long, coarse grass spun together like rope and tied around the waist, though I couldn't readily see a knot. Another grass rope was attached at the waist in the back and curved to the front between their legs. Rather than that end tying to the waist, it was tied to a gold ring that pierced their uncircumcised penises. Another piece of grass rope was attached to the top of the ring. That segment was tied tightly to the rope at the waist and made it look like the penis was always erect. Their testicles were left free to hang in the breeze. A specific part of my anatomy thought about retreating like a turtle into its shell when I imagined what the piercing and moving around must be like.

The man in uniform climbed out of the dugout. I fixated on him because we looked a good deal alike, but I was heavier by at least ten pounds. He was careful not to step into the river. His spit-shined boots looked like those from old English aviator movies, with laces tied high up on the leg to just below the knee.

A few large steps forward placed him right in front of where Ursula and I stood. He gave me an inspection-like once-over much like Sonya had, and signaled his acceptance with a wide smile. Ursula stayed motionless. The smile left his face when he looked her. His expression was blank, as was hers.

Considering his imposing presence and dramatic arrival, I was surprised when he addressed us with a soft rather than booming voice. His German accent was heavy. "Welcome to Amazonia. I am Sigmund Wasser."

I started to speak but Sigmund broke in. "You are obviously Sam. This is, of course, Ursula."

"Sigmund," Ursula said at last.

He stepped forward and reached out both hands towards her. She put her hand out to shake his. Wasser clasped Ursula's hand in both of his and pulled her forward. They were face-to-face, only inches apart. After a few seconds, he muttered something in German. This is when I had the thought that Ursula had found her lost *uncle*, the doctor, since Sigmund was who she'd been looking for all along; and if I applied the term loosely, he could be considered a medical man of the worst kind, though his father had the degree.

A noise behind me caused me to spin around. It was Marcos. The three natives had vanished. I turned back around to face Wasser. He'd let go of Ursula and she came over to my side. She stood at attention, still silent.

"What happened to the others," I asked no one in particular.

"Yanomamis," Wasser said. "They don't trust strangers. They will watch us from the woods and come when I call them. They can be quite harmless and child-like. So, Sam, we finally meet."

"Finally," I said, and said it as though I'd been in on the plan since the beginning instead of how it really happened. "I feel like I'm looking into a mirror, Sigmund."

"I should hope so." he said.

CHAPTER 17

We stood there looking at each other. No one spoke until Ursula said, "Marcos es el capitán," wearing her biggest smile. Marcos stood tall when she said this. That was an odd comment and made me suspicious.

"Marcos is also a good companion," Sigmund said. "Now, we must make our way on the river before it starts to rise."

"Rise?" I questioned. "Is it tidal?"

"No, not tidal," Sigmund responded. "It is worse than that, it is not predictable. I will tell you about the danger of this river of the Amazon at the camp."

Wasser motioned towards the woods with a swoop of his arm and brought his hand in an arc so that he gestured toward the far bank. The natives came out of three separate parts of the jungle, running at full speed on the gravel stones.

I commented under my breath to Ursula, "That's got to hurt."

"You know what they say about pleasure and pain, Sam."

All things considered regarding Ursula, I wasn't going to touch that one.

"Into the Amazon," Sigmund said. He walked straight into the river to climb aboard the dugout. The spit-shined boots must have mattered only as a first impression. Marcos followed Sigmund and we fell in behind them.

We tossed our gear into the boat and climbed on board. I sat in front of Marcos; Ursula sat directly in front of me. The three Yanomamis pushed the dugout into the river and jumped in to take up their positions in front of Ursula and behind Sigmund who was at the bow of the boat.

Marcos fired up the engine and we motored off heading upstream for about half an hour. Then we took a sharp left and then some right and left turns up smaller rivers and waterways. I became completely disoriented.

"Camp Uricka is ahead," Sigmund said. "We have to pick up more natives then we will go back to the main river and down to our Camp Sonya."

"Camp Sonya?" I said into Ursula's ear. She didn't respond.

Except for an occasional bump by the dugout on some rocks under the water, the trip was like most boat rides. My neck got a workout as I tried to look at everything on both sides of the rivers and waterways we traveled.

Camp Uricka wasn't more than a clearing with a couple of wood huts built on very high, thin poles. We barely stopped the dugout so two natives could hop on board. These two wore bathing trunks, but were shirtless and wore flip-flops on their feet. One got in front of me and the other behind me. The dugout, with its complement of nine mixed nuts, aimed its way back to the river and deeper into the jungle.

About an hour later, a camp came into view. Ursula turned her head to the side and I saw she was smiling. I wondered what she was thinking.

Camp Sonya was on the opposite side of the shore from which we'd departed, if I had my bearings right. As we approached the small wooden dock, I looked around to make sure Marcos and the native behind me were looking elsewhere and carefully slipped the pistol out of my backpack and into my pants pocket. As soon as we docked, the Yanomamis took our gear.

The camp had four barrack-style buildings perched atop the high riverbank. Even though elevated, these buildings rested on very high stilts and were surrounded by a complex boardwalk. This infrastructure carried itself not only the apparent route to each building, but snaked its way into the green womb of the jungle.

Sigmund, with Marcos behind him, led us to the barrack on the far right. This was the only one with a large veranda. We followed Sigmund and Marcos inside while the five natives stood outside with our gear.

"Please relax," Sigmund said. "Marcos will get us something refreshing to drink. It is quite safe here. You won't need your weapons. Please put them on the table over there."

Ursula moved forward and without a word or glance back, added the rifle to the table already covered with a variety of weapons. She got her pistol from her jacket pocket and placed it down, as well. I didn't move.

"All of them, please," Sigmund said looking me straight in the eyes. There was nothing else to do. I walked to the table, removed the gun from my pocket, and reluctantly added it to the pile. I waited to see if anyone would mention the knife in my backpack. No one did. I decided it was best if I avoided looking at Ursula.

Marcos entered carrying a large, heavy-looking jug and a small basket with several tin cups inside. He poured each of us a full glass of thick, sweet-smelling liquid.

"Tonight," Sigmund said, "there will be a party to welcome your safe arrival. However, there are some things that you should know before then. Marcos will have the pleasure of giving you that information later. Although they are a long way from their home region, these natives have become quite used to the area and insist on doing the cooking, which you should find very interesting, to say the least. Drink up."

"If the food is as good as this drink, I'm sure we're in for a wonderful feast," Ursula said. Marcos flashed her with another golden smile.

"Marcos," Sigmund said, "please take Ursula and Sam to their lodgings. You both should take some time to rest up. Jungle parties last as long as someone can still stand up."

Ursula put her cup down and followed Marcos out the door. I started to follow her, but Sigmund grabbed my arm and said in a low voice, "We will talk alone at a later time. You must tell me all about yourself and of your trip so far; it is the jungle way. Storytelling is the most important communication here."

I knew what he meant, but thought to myself that since I'd met Ursula, stories were pretty much all I'd been told. "And what about you, Sigmund?" I replied. He gave me an odd look and I immediately wished I'd kept my mouth shut.

"Later, I will explain all you must know. Now catch up to Marcos and Ursula."

I found them waiting several yards away. They stopped talking when they saw me. Marcos started walking and we followed. He led us to the furthest barrack from the one we'd just been in. Ours was one large room with two army cots set up in the center. Instead of a tin door, this was a heavily-wired screen door. There were two windows—one at the front, the other on the opposite wall at the back. Both were covered with the same wire mesh used as a door. No lights, no toilet, and no water. When—if—I got back to civilization I was going to kiss the first real toilet I saw. Marcos motioned for the natives to leave our gear by the cots. He said something to them in their language and they left.

"Are you from the same tribe?" I asked him.

"No. This tribe is all hunters, not farmers like my tribe is now. Before that, my tribe was hunters, fishermen, and tree eaters with no permanent village as now. 'Travelers of waters' my tribe was called."

"What does that mean?" Ursula asked

"They would build huts near a river and stay sometimes for a year, then would burn everything and move. Sometimes they would move up river, and at other times they would move down river. It didn't matter which way they went; but now, they stay in one place."

"Sigmund said you'd explain more about what happens tonight," I interrupted.

"Tonight, there will be a medicine man called a shaman among the visitors. Never stare at him, even if his back is turned, because he will know. He may slap you or spit on you; that is, if he likes you. He won't want to hurt Sigmund's feelings, so expect that it will happen. Whatever you do, don't spit or slap back. Only another shaman is allowed that privilege. He will also try to cure you of your ills, even the ones that you don't know you have. This shaman has been known to cure even fatal diseases. Sigmund's father, Carl, learned a lot from him. Eat or drink whatever he gives you; and don't make him mad, or he will prod you with a sharp stick each time he's annoyed. Shamans treat us all like children, because they are the wise ones. Respect is what they demand; it is how they make a living. Shamans give us healing. We give them free lodging, food, and women."

"Essentially, a freeloader," I said, but Marcos didn't seem to understand me, which was probably a good thing. "Marcos, how is it you speak English and speak it so well?" Rudolpho had explained this to me, but I wanted Marcos to give me his version.

"When Dr. Wasser, Sigmund's father, came here to study jungle medicine, the men that came with him got sick. It didn't take the doctor very long to see that the jungle air was no good for them. He said that breathing the thick air with the death of a thousand years of animal and plant decay was deadly to most. Once a man became ill, he would have to go back to Cuzco until he got better.

"He was always looking for a cure for this. Then, from some missionary monks, he heard about a man they called 'a gringo from the clouds.' The monks had also had the same problem of this sickness. This man from the clouds had lived with the Yanomamis for years, but never got the sickness. Dr. Wasser believed maybe this man had an answer.

"The doctor traveled very far to meet with this man and just by chance, happened to find my village. We had just been attacked by another tribe and needed medical help, but we could not send for the gringo because he was gone. When Dr. Wasser asked where he might find this other man, he was told the gringo had gone back to the clouds and the gods where he had come from.

"The shaman who had helped the gringo was the one who really helped with the disease; so, the doctor brought him back to Camp Sonya. That is the shaman you will meet tonight. Dr. Wasser also brought back many others with him, including my sister and my mother who was pregnant with me. Much later, I was told my father had been killed in the attack. I was born here at the camp. When my mother died soon after, the doctor raised me and my sister as his own family."

That Marcos had a sister was news to me, not that it was unusual he should have one; but she was obviously not at Camp Sonya. I hesitated to ask him about her, and it really didn't seem relevant.

Marcos believed Carl Wasser came here to study jungle medicine. Would he feel the same about the doctor and Sigmund if he knew the truth? The story Marcos told reminded me of Frank. He'd said Ursula would lead me into the jungle, which had happened, and that there would be four from one tribe involved. I'd thought it had to be the Cuzco Four, but now there was another possibility. Marcos and the three other natives made four from one tribe, even if not exactly the same tribe. It was possible a different bigger picture was coming together.

"Why don't we go outside and look around," Ursula suggested.

"Ladies first," I motioned and followed as she left. Marcos took up the rear and continued his story as we walked slowly along the boardwalks.

"The doctor used the knowledge of the shaman to help him with the cure so that the long, hard work he had done here wouldn't stop. He, too, would get the sickness and had to leave every year or so. He employed some of the tribes from deep in the jungle. In many ways, they became his family also. The elders said that when he arrived, he was a hard man; but, his new family cured him of this hardness."

I caught Ursula's eye. She held my gaze, but never changed her expression.

"Marcos," I said, "when you say this man from the sky went back to the clouds and the gods, does that mean he was killed and returned to the heavens or, specifically, heaven?"

"We don't send people up to your heaven, so I don't really know what it means. The shaman said he went back to an island in the sky."

Since I believed he had to be talking about Frank, I said, "Maybe he meant the Island of Tequile. You're familiar with it?"

"Yes. Do you think he went back there and not the clouds?"

"It is at a higher elevation, and that *is* where the flowing gold is said to be."

"Ah, the flowing gold," Marcos said. "You said you learned of it in Cuzco."

"It's only a myth, though, Marcos. Isn't it?" Ursula asked. I'd been wondering when she'd join the conversation; and she said this with such a straight face, I might have believed her myself.

"It is customary, here, to share our stories, or myths, if you wish. It is our way of communicating information from the old to the young. All must learn to tell of battles lost and won, and of enchantments of the jungle and all its lore. It is how we keep our history. I have never seen the flowing gold, but many say it is real.

"We have a while before the party begins. Soon, the river will have dugouts coming. It is a custom to greet natives coming to your camp. These are friendly farmers, but they will look unfriendly. You will soon get used to them. Gatherings like this allow them to bring back some of their past. It is something I am sure you have never seen. And, tomorrow, you will see the real Amazon."

Marcos looked away sharply. I followed the direction of his eyes and saw Sigmund motion for Marcos to join him back at the main barrack.

I waited until we were alone to speak. "Does Frank sound a little less like a delusion to you now, Ursula? Leading me to believe you wanted to find the pilot who knew about the gold may have started out as a ploy, but I found him, or rather he found me. It's okay, you can admit it if you're ready to believe me."

"I... All right, I admit I'm not certain anymore. The stories and what you say you experienced seem to suggest that Frank is the pilot, though I maintain it didn't happen the way you think it did. Still... Some of it just doesn't make sense, is all. And..."

"And, what?"

"I don't know. It's just... I imagined things going differently once we got here."

"Ursula, are you saying for once on this trip, you don't know what's next? That our boy, Sigmund, actually surprised *you* for a change? And getting back to Frank, I told you he said you'd lead me into..."

"Okay! You don't have to tell me that again. So, I've led you here, into the jungle as you insist Frank said. What now? Is my mission more important, or is yours? What if it all turns out the same in the end? I'm going for a swim."

"Ursula, you're gorgeous when you're angry and trying not to eat crow."

"Fuck you, Sam. You have no idea what I'm eating. Stay out here while I change."

I also had no idea what was suddenly eating at her, but something was.

Ursula went inside and came out a few minutes later wearing a white cotton dress. I went with her and sat on the riverbank. Ursula waded into the river, but stayed close to the side. When the water almost reached her knees, she sat so that the water level was just past her waist. She leaned all the way back until fully submerged. Rising from the water, she smoothed her hair back. The cotton fabric soaked up water and clung tightly against her skin, and she looked pretty damn good. We'd never seen each other unclothed. I'd been able to tell she had a terrific body, but now I could see how full-bodied she actually was.

"Ursula," Sigmund called out as he walked towards us, "no urinating in the water. These rivers are full of microorganisms that are attracted to a stream of urine. They follow it like salmon going upstream to lay eggs. They enter the urethra and you end up with problems forever. Ah! Here come our other guests."

Sigmund hadn't given Ursula a second-glance. I wondered if he had a different sexual preference or was non-sexual. I could barely keep my eyes off of her, but did follow where his eyes were aimed.

Two dugouts approached us. We hadn't heard them because these didn't have engines, but were propelled gracefully by natives using staffs like oars. They rowed in unison until they reached the embankment near where Ursula was. She stood up and I felt my pulse quicken at the sight of the nearly transparent cotton clinging to her. She looked at me, smiled like a woman who knows what she's doing to a man then pulled the fabric so it hung more as it should.

I cleared my throat, as though that might make a difference, and turned to follow Sigmund as he went to greet his new guests. The original three natives who'd traveled with us came down to the river, as well, and were waving and making cheering sounds. Sigmund told us it was expected for us to do the same, so we did.

Each of the dugouts carried at least fifteen men, all adorned in native splendor. Some had painted their legs and arms red, while others covered their entire bodies with what looked like white clay. Their faces were also painted; no two alike.

As they came ashore, I whispered to Ursula, "So far, I haven't seen natives other than our three wearing cock rings." She shushed me.

"What a sight. What an adventure," Sigmund said. "This area is not even visited by the botanists. They stay where the roads can deliver goods or the rivers are more forgiving. No, this area is for the true adventurer. What you are witnessing here is hardly ever seen by a white man."

"You mean that as close as we seem to be to civilization, no white explorers come here?" I asked.

"Oh, they come, Sam; but for the last three decades, we have controlled where they go and what they see. We know everyone's movements as soon as they leave Paucartambo, sometimes even as they leave Cuzco depending on who they are. In fact, four have been working their way toward us. But soon they will be deterred, at least until our party is over."

"Deterred?" I asked.

We will have them wait for a dugout one extra day, and then they will be able to travel up-river. Marcos will see to that. He went to intercept them at the place where we picked up you and Ursula. He will promise them a dugout tomorrow. Our native friends joining us tonight are very shy. There is no reason to ruin a good party, right, Sam?" He laughed and slapped me on the back as he said this.

"Won't Marcos join us tonight?" Ursula asked.

"You do not need to concern yourselves about Marcos. While you are here, there are other things you should know for your safety. When a man moves through the jungle, if he stops and lingers too long, this can mean only two things: The first is that he may be dying or will die soon if the jungle has its way. The second is that he is tired. If he stops to rest, he should do so only in a clearing, an area that has been burned for farming, never by the river. This river rises sometimes as much as fourteen feet in just a few hours at nightfall due to the melting of the snowcaps in the Andes. Traveling this close to the beginning of the flow down to the Amazon basin could prove fatal."

"Are there any warnings the river's going to rise?" I asked.

"The giant moths and butterflies like the warm stones. If the river is going to rise, they will fly further down-river. This, too, happens very quickly. The jungle always warns you. I will miss this place, my…"

Sigmund didn't finish his statement. He turned and walked towards some natives grouped together near the river. "Sam. Ursula. Please join me. I would like you to meet my medicine man, my shaman."

I hastily reminded Ursula not to stare, nor to slap or spit back if the shaman graced us with such a *privilege*."

"Not the woman, Sam."

"Not the woman, what?"

"He doesn't slap or spit on women," she answered.

"How do you know that?"

She didn't answer because Sigmund and the shaman approached us, along with the others. It was easy to see which man the shaman was from his finery. Trying not to stare, I quickly caught a glimpse of a wild man with pitch-black eyes, better described as black holes that compelled a person to stare into them. I concentrated on Sigmund.

"Here is my savior, my jungle mentor," Sigmund said. "Without this man, this healer, we would not have been able to survive in this environment. I present Philipe."

Old habits die hard. I had to make eye contact now, even if just for a moment. I thought surely Sigmund would warn me if I was about to make a serious mistake. Maybe the key was the word *staring.*

"Philipe, this is Sam and Ursula, friends of mine from another land." No hand shakes, no spit or slaps, just a nod. Philipe turned abruptly and went up the hill. Everyone, including Sigmund, followed after him so we joined them.

"Philipe," I said so only Ursula could hear. "That's some name for a medicine man."

"Did you see his eyes, Sam?"

"I saw them. Kind of unfair to have eyes that practically insist you stare at them and be forbidden to do it."

Back at the camp, large logs about twenty-feet long and at least sixteen inches in diameter had been placed at the center of the clearing. Natives scurried about, hauling large woven baskets laden with fruits, vegetables, and God knows what else into each of the barracks. These food items were a relief since I didn't know what jungle natives might consider fine dining.

Ursula and I wandered around. The feeling of excitement was palpable. Watching the natives fulfill their duties was like watching ants, each ant clear about what its role is and carrying it out without a thought of stopping. I noticed a group near the water's edge painting the bottom of their legs from the knees down with what looked like red paint.

"Look at those three," I said to Ursula. "I hope that's not blood they're using."

"Not the way it dries," she said calmly. "It's probably a root, or mud."

"Do you wonder what this is about?" Sigmund asked as he walked towards us. "It is a ritual that we will have the privilege to see. Tonight, Sam, Philipe is going to cleanse your body of any ills."

"Does he think I need to be cleansed?"

"It is his way of pleasing me, a harmless gesture. Tonight as the party progresses, he may poke and slap you, even spit at you. Don't worry, Sam, by the time the drinks have flowed, you will not feel a thing. And anyway, he is quite old so the strength is not what it once was."

"Marcos explained the home-field advantage."

Sigmund paused for a moment before he started to laugh. "You Americans. Always the funny sayings."

Sigmund went off to do whatever it was he did there, and Ursula and I watched as the preparations continued. We could've offered to help, I suppose, but Ursula didn't seem to concern herself with this so I left it alone.

Once the sun started to set, things really began to stir. The night sounds were kicking into gear, and since we were in the Amazon jungle, this seemed intensified as I'd expected.

A native came to us and motioned us to follow him. We were led to our barrack to gorge ourselves on food and drink. All of it seemed edible, so I enjoyed myself. About twenty minutes later, we heard yelling and went to the door in time to see the logs burst into flames. Sparks flew high into the sky, but nobody seemed worried the jungle would ignite. After a few more high-powered fruit drinks, I wouldn't care, either. Ursula and I went down to join the festivities.

As the party went on, the red-legged natives chanted and hopped up and down to a staccato beat for hours on end. Sigmund had pointed out this dance was another privilege few white men have seen. I had to admit it was impressive, especially their endurance.

I was engrossed in the spectacle, so didn't notice when Ursula left my side until I turned to say something to her. I gave a quick look around and saw her sitting with Sigmund on the veranda of his barrack. *Fuck them*, I thought.

Grabbing hold of my jug of jungle juice, I bounced from group to group of natives, stumbling with them, letting everyone watch me make a damn fool myself. Or at least, that's what I wanted them to see. I'd learned during my military service how to maintain control in a situation like this—appear to drink a lot, but spill most of it. Still, I had been sipping and was feeling some effects. The night and party wore on, and body after stone-drunk body hit the dirt.

The natives with the red legs chanted so loudly now, they overwhelmed the roar of the fire. I put the fire between myself and the barracks. Through voids in the flames, I kept tabs on Ursula and Sigmund. As far as I could tell, they weren't engaged in serious conversation.

The hair on the back of my neck prickled. I made an about-face and found Philipe behind me. His eyes bore into mine. When we'd met earlier, he'd seemed smaller. He appeared imposing now, powerful. I tried to pull my gaze away, but couldn't. He said nothing, made no sound. I remembered his face being more round. Now his cheeks were hollow, as though skin was sucked tight against bone.

I didn't see the slap coming. It was hard enough to draw tears that streamed down my face. Without missing a beat, Philipe spit in my face. He was staring intently into my eyes. The voice of reason told me to look away, but I didn't. Philipe shut his eyes and lowered his head. Not sure what he was doing, I didn't move. I did notice the sounds that had been so loud, were muffled. "Sam," he said. I heard him say something else, but didn't hear him clearly.

"What did you say, Philipe?"

Philipe's head came up and he slowly opened his eyes. The intense expression he'd been wearing was placid. "Sam, beware of the four."

Maybe his slap had been harder than I could feel after sipping jungle juice for hours, but I could've sworn I heard Frank's voice. The cliché, Stranger things have happened, would've fit here, except that pretty much everything here was stranger than anything I was used to.

"Sam," he said again.

"Frank, is it you?"

"The four from one tribe, they will try to destroy you. Save my people, Sam. Save my children. Ursula must complete her task."

"Frank, who are our real enemies here? Is Ursula an enemy or friend? What about Marcos?"

Philipe's head lowered, and came back up suddenly. It was obviously the shaman back in front of me once more. He turned and left. I didn't see him again that evening.

I decided my partying was over for the night, and I started towards Sigmund's barrack to join him and Ursula.

It felt like things were coming to a head, though I didn't know what that meant. Even the air felt different. I walked around the blazing logs up towards the barrack where Ursula and Sigmund still sat watching what was going on below them. They reminded me of Romans at the coliseum.

"Sam, what do you think of my natives?"

"Sigmund, I wouldn't have wanted to miss it." Neither of them mentioned what had just happened with Philipe, so I said nothing about it.

"Tomorrow," Sigmund continued, "I have decided to show you and Ursula something that we have found—the hidden ruin of Taquile, perhaps a greater find than Machu Picchu. And then, Sam, we begin the real adventure. Ursula has said you enjoy adventures."

"Ursula tends to enjoy adventures, as well. Don't you Ursula?" I said.

Sigmund stood and walked behind Ursula. He placed his hands on her shoulders. "Marcos will join us at dawn, which gives us only a few hours of rest. I must say goodnight, but you are welcome to stay and celebrate as long as you like."

"Ursula, let's walk," I said after Sigmund left.

"Sure, Sam, where would you like to walk?"

"How about we head down to the river?"

We followed the boardwalk that led down to the clearing in front of the barracks. Neither of us spoke until we were near the water.

"Something's gone wrong, Sam. Sigmund told me I may have to get rid of the four people waiting for Marcos, our Cuzco Four. He said it like if he were ordering a coffee in a donut shop. He even wanted my opinion, said, 'I would like to know what you think, Ursula? We must do everything necessary so that I leave without drawing attention. Death in the jungle is absolute if there are no witnesses. No documents that later show up, nothing.' I responded the only way I could and said, 'We must do whatever it takes to make sure you are united with your father.' "

"Do you think he was testing you?"

"I think Sigmund is foremost trying to save his own ass. He even asked me how I would feel if anything happened to you."

"What did you say?"

"What else? I told him I would be deeply sorrowed, but could learn to live with it."

"Thanks a lot."

"What else could I say?"

"I told you he might consider me expendable."

"Maybe you're right. Or, maybe he's testing my loyalty; and if not, then we have an idea of what he's thinking. Could be he's decided to alter the plan for his own reasons."

I didn't ask Ursula how she'd feel if Sigmund was serious about killing the Cuzco Four, just as I hadn't asked her how she felt about Rudolpho killing Sonya, or who Sonya really was. I didn't ask because I knew she'd lie and it would be a waste of breath. She'd acted as though she met the Four for the first time when I did; but her standing next to them atop the hill on the Island of Tequile proved that to be incorrect, or at least an inaccurate measure of the truth. Because I never mentioned it, she probably thought they'd been too far away for me to recognize her.

"Look at that," she said.

I turned to face the barracks area. An entire tree, stripped of its branches, was ablaze. Dark-skinned shapes jumped back and forth, up and down. The tempo was faster now, mesmerizing. For the first time in days, I felt dizzy.

"Ursula, I'm done for the night. Walk back with me, at least to the fire if you want to stay up."

"I'm ready to sleep, too, Sam."

"I've done my share of hard partying and hard living."

"I know," she said, looking at me more tenderly than she had in what seemed like a long while.

For a brief moment when I saw her slowly raise her hand, I anticipated the touch of her fingers on my face. Maybe she was going to do that and changed her mind because she moved her hair behind one ear. I took her hand and linked her arm through mine. We made our way back to our barrack and went to sleep in silence.

CHAPTER 18

Morning and the worst hangover I'd ever had arrived much too soon, and my teeth felt as though they were wearing sweaters. I didn't want to sit up, but did. Ursula was lying on her side, watching me.

"Hey," I said, "is it just my head banging or is there a new jungle sound?"

Ursula was able to rise up from her cot without difficulty and go to the window, a feat I would find formidable at best. Nothing in the room seemed solid yet, except that damn sound. I knew it was familiar, but my brain was too affected and pained to focus on it.

"C'mon, Sam. Get up."

"Easier said than done."

From outside, came, "Ursula! Good, you are up." It was Sigmund. "Please, join me for breakfast."

Ursula turned towards me. "You heard him."

"He said *you*. I'm passing out. Now." And that's what I did. If Ursula made any noise as she got ready to meet up with Sigmund, I didn't hear it.

Weird dreams made me toss and turn. So many sounds…loud swishing, lots of shouting, then silence. I woke when I realized the sounds were real. It was painful, but I staggered to the window. Getting a face full of sunlight was excruciating. Ursula stood next to Sigmund, and both of them were near a large red helicopter, its engine blades rotating slowly. Natives carried large burlap bags to the opening on the side of the helicopter. I stumbled outside to see what was going on.

"Sam, come join us," Sigmund called out.

It took a few minutes, but I did just that. "What did I miss?"

"Just the landing," Sigmund said. "We leave as soon as the provisions are loaded. Come, have some breakfast first."

"Actually, Sigmund, I don't know if food is a good idea at the moment," I replied.

"How's the head?" he asked, laughing.

"Awful."

"Marcos will join us soon. He will have a remedy for your hangover."

"As long as it's not the hair of what bit me, Sigmund."

"A saying I have not heard in years."

We started toward the main barrack.

"You know," he said, "it won't take long before this land falls prey to the vultures."

"What vultures?" Ursula asked.

"The vultures of the civilized world…scientists, doctors, museum collectors, those who would change all this though they claim to be preserving it. We spent many years keeping them out through politics, even violence; but now with my father away and me soon to follow, that will change."

Every deranged individual who ever sought control or power, those we considered evil, always seemed to have a soft spot somewhere inside them about something. Sigmund's concern for the tribes and the jungle, even if for his own agenda was not something I'd expected. I'd also noted his tone of voice as he spoke. He was more than concerned, he was consumed, obsessed. That's when I realized that in his mind, any death he deemed necessary for any reason, would happen, including mine.

While they ate and I tried not to watch, Sigmund continued, "Even the Peruvians will swoop down on their fellow man, like those vultures that fly high over the Andes. Many carcasses will overflow the landfills in the name of change. How many will have to die? Just as the Nazis who, like my father, killed their own people for the sake of change."

Ursula was sitting across from me at the table, so it was easy for our eyes to make contact.

"Made you uncomfortable, yes?" he said. "Sometimes, I like to play with emotions. It is something my father taught me to do. It keeps the edge going. At first, it was amusing; then it became a habit."

Ursula managed a small smile. I couldn't pretend such graciousness. His words brought me back to reality. Sigmund could not be trusted about anything. I'd have to really be on guard from this moment on.

Marcos walked in carrying a tin cup and said, "Sam, drink this."

"What is it?"

"A shaman's remedy, mostly coffee."

I glanced at Ursula and Sigmund. Both nodded their approval. I downed the concoction as quickly as possible. It was thick as honey but bitter. I waited for the usual barfing that followed other such cures I'd tried in the past, but it never came. In seconds, my headache was gone. Within minutes, as Ursula and Sigmund conversed in German, which meant I sat there in silence, the rest of my hangover followed.

"I'm cured. This is great stuff. We should market it."

"No good," Sigmund said. "There are ingredients in that mixture known only to a handful of people. Even I am not aware of the formula, is that not so Marcos?"

"Yes, Sigmund. It is the only secret I keep from you."

"You do have another, though, don't you Marcos?"

"No." Marcos, for the first time, looked less than his usual confident self.

"Perhaps, I used the wrong word, Marcos. The people up river… You have not given me a report."

"They wait at the river for me to come with a dugout."

"Good, then we will leave right away," Sigmund said as he stood. He nodded at Marcos who made a hasty departure.

"Should we carry any of our gear with us?" I asked Ursula.

"All that you came here with is on the helicopter," Sigmund replied.

I thought we were only supposed to visit the ruin he'd found. If all our gear was stowed on the helicopter, there was a new plan I wasn't in on. Again. He'd said *all*, I wondered if that included the weapons we'd arrived with?

We left the barrack and headed to the helicopter. Ursula spoke German to Sigmund as we climbed aboard, which was starting to piss me off. It was just another way of leaving me out of the loop.

Sigmund entered first, followed by Ursula, then me. There was just enough room to walk to the cockpit. Inside, it was packed solid with the burlap bags, the ones I saw the natives loading earlier, and our gear. Unless it was someplace else or buried under the bags, or inside the bags, I didn't see any gear for Sigmund, which didn't make sense.

It surprised me that Marcos hadn't come to see us off. One of the natives swung straps across the door opening and secured them. Sigmund took the controls. He indicated Ursula and I were to sit behind him. When everyone was strapped in, Sigmund made the beast come to life and we lifted away from the ground. He brought us straight up and when I looked down, I saw the layout of the barracks and boardwalks were configured like a swastika, something apparent only from the air. You can take the Nazi out of Germany, but you can't take the Nazi out of the man.

We hovered for a moment then took off at a dizzying speed. Sigmund followed the river below as much as possible. When the twists and turns prevented this, he'd cut across the jungle and pick up the river later on. Seeing the jungle close up is one thing. Seeing it from the air is another.

"Good thing Marcos took care of my hangover," I shouted to Ursula over the rotor and engine sounds.

"I find it exciting," she yelled back.

"Like that's a surprise," I shouted back. She shot me the finger.

"Now we head due west and look for our turn," Sigmund called back to us.

"How do you know when to make a turn? It all looks the same to me," I yelled forward.

"Good, that is what I hope will always happen."

Did he mean me or the people he feared would come to destroy the jungle?

I checked the time. Fifteen minutes later, Sigmund started a slow descent. At first, it looked like we were going to land on the jungle canopy; but at the last moment, an opening appeared in front of us.

I shouted to Sigmund, "What's that green hole? Is that where we're going?" I barely got the words out before we plunged down towards its center.

"That's the worst of it," he shouted back. "I call it a window because it appears to open only as the sun hits the canopy at the correct angle."

We slowly lowered into the center of the opening. Mist shot up past our windows and blocked visibility. There was a small jolt as we touched down, followed by Sigmund shutting the engine off. We sat silent and motionless. Gradually, the condensation on the windows slid down and we could see. We were in the middle of a pond that was maybe fifty yards wide.

Ursula grabbed me, "Look! Over there at the edge."

A low wall circumnavigated the pond. The wall was similarly constructed like the ones we'd seen in Cuzco, only these were covered with mosaic tiles. Ahead of us, just beyond the wall, was a trapezoidal door that looked like an entrance to a cave, except it was attached to a cylinder-shaped structure.

"We've landed on top a large stone surrounded by water," Ursula added.

Sigmund said, "Help me, Sam."

We opened the straps that acted as a door. Sigmund tossed a package into the pond, holding onto a lanyard.

"Raft?" I asked.

"Yes." He gave a yank on the line and a hissing sound was followed by the inflation of the raft.

"Ursula, you go first," Sigmund said.

Ursula climbed in and I followed. He grabbed two small oars and handed them to me before he joined us. We paddled until we reached ground, and pulled the raft out of the water onto the grass.

"What is this? The water's so clear. Was it used as a pool?" I asked.

"Maybe. There are steps that go to the bottom. We never found any signs of it being used for anything sacrificial. It is perhaps twenty-feet deep and that is always constant. It is clear, fresh water. No fish, no weeds. But, this you must see. Come."

I followed Sigmund through the trapezoidal door which was hinged at two sides, about four-feet tall, and kept open with a thick log. The door opened upward and inward like some garage doors.

Ursula followed a few moments later. She'd gone to look at the wall that encircled the pond. Catching up, she said, "You should see the tiles."

"Later, Ursula," Sigmund said. "We must see what is ahead."

On the other side of the door was a small circular courtyard, maybe twenty feet across. The 360-degree wall had a surface as smooth as marble that went up at least 50 feet and was open at the top. It reminded me of a grain silo. Frank had mentioned drawings of silos. At the moment, I couldn't recall exactly what he'd said.

I ran my hand over the wall surface. "What is this, granite?"

"No, look closer," Ursula said as she approached the wall. She smiled at me. "Blocks of stone placed so close together, it's hard to tell where one leaves off and the other starts." Then lowering her voice, "But, Sam, notice…"

"There are many of these around Peru," Sigmund interrupted, "for grain storage I think. Join me here in the center of the courtyard." He kept glancing at his watch and began to tell a story I was all too familiar with.

"The flowing gold," he started, "was thought to be just a legend, My father spent some time searching for it; but after a while, he soon put this search, as well as his other passion, aside."

"The ability to make a perfect race," I uttered.

Sigmund, checking the time again said, "So, it is finally out in the open. It doesn't matter. My father was successful for a while with twins; but then there appeared some genetic defects. We were forced to leave our homeland and take refuge here. When age began to move heavy on my father, he found something else, a different field, one which proved to be much more rewarding.

"The other gold of the Andes was more valuable than we ever realized, and right under our noses. This is a pun, of course—cocaine. We became the drug lords of the white gold. From our little outpost and with our many connections, we controlled the world market until our coffers overflowed. An army of mountain renegades protected us and still do. They are known as The Shining Path. Also, money protects us. But even all such protection could not stop us from making enemies in powerful places.

"It started with politicians in the United States who had been making large profits from a drug that was, at first, society's social joke. Then the lowest part of society wanted a share of what the uppers had, but they needed a cheaper drug. We were asked to come up with an alternative and we did. Crack was the result. It is something that can be derived in the United States.

"We were free to come and go in Peru until an Israeli organization full of zealots suddenly became interested in my father. They wanted to bring him back to Israel for trial. Their support came from within the United States from the same politicians we made rich and powerful. We threatened to expose many top officials to buy us time, but we became trapped in our own way in the Amazon. In many ways, it became our prison as well as our protection.

"Word reached us that the Berlin wall is to come down. With this information, we saw a new future. Soon, Germany will be ripe for us. My father made it out of Peru and is now well entrenched there. The Marada has since been waiting for me to lead them to him. Until you were found, Sam, my fate was in doubt; but now… Marcos."

A dripping Marcos came through the door with his blowgun up to his mouth. He must have hidden behind the burlap bags on the helicopter. I felt a sting on the side of my neck. I never got to say a word as I fell to the ground.

"He's still conscious," Ursula said.

"Marco assures me that Sam will sleep well. It is time for us to go."

My eyes were still open, but I couldn't move them. I was flat on my back, looking up at the sky. Ursula's face came into view. She leaned over and whispered, "The tiles…look at the tiles on the wall." She kissed me then disappeared from my view.

"His eyes are open," she said.

"In a moment, they will close," Marcos responded.

"We must go. All is as we planned," Sigmund commanded. "Look! It is time."

The interior of the silo started to glow until it expanded into the dazzling color of gold.

"As the sun moves directly overhead," Sigmund explained, "it radiates around the surface creating this golden spectacle. I believe this may be how the flowing gold myth started. If they did this here, maybe it was done many other places, and is why so many in other areas believe the myth is real. And for what purpose was it designed? What else? The great lust for gold, the same gold that you, Sam, now seek. Am I right? By the way, Sam, there has been a change of plans. Ursula and I will be starting our trip from here. As for you, let us just say your trip ends here. But we wait for just a few moments."

I don't know how long the few moments were, but Sigmund said something to Marcos in German and I heard some shuffling about then quiet. No one said a word as they left. There was a loud thud, then silence. My breathing became slower as a feeling of warmth swept down from my neck over my entire body. My eyes watered from not being able to blink and tears ran out the sides of my eyes. The gold light had faded, and so did my consciousness as my eyes finally began to close.

I wasn't actually dizzy, but it was as though I was spinning. I seemed to lift high above the ground. Glancing down, I saw my body lying there, until I felt I was being swept along on a river of gold. I met up with Frank and talked without meaning. Ursula and I danced. Sigmund laughed at me as I lay in a pool of gold that changed to blood. I dreamed a thousand dreams, some marvelous, some filled with horror.

CHAPTER 19

I slept the rest of the day and through the night. Morning brought me back to the reality that I'd been abandoned. I struggled to stand up then stopped. A stabbing pain in my neck made me reach my hand to the area. The dart was still there. I pulled it free and found a wad of cotton near the tip. The dart was not meant to penetrate deeply. This made me think Marcos had adjusted the dosage of whatever drug he'd used. He certainly didn't mean to kill me or I'd be dead; though I fully believed Sigmund intended the silo to be my tomb or my death chamber for sure. Why the silo? He could have thrown my unconscious body into the river so it looked like a drowning, if I wasn't lunch for whatever lives in those waters, that is.

The door was closed. That was the thud I'd heard. On hands and knees, I crawled to the door and recalled it swung inward. There were no finger grips, no levers or knobs. Pushing on every point and corner had no result. The silo was open at the top, but there was nothing to climb with.

I leaned my back against the door and closed my eyes. Sometimes a situation calls for the most basic solution to be tried first so I yelled *Help* several times as loud as I could. I realized my enclosure acted as though sound-proofed, not even an echo happened. Nothing outside fluttered or squawked, either.

There had to be a way out. I looked to the right and saw my gear across from me. Why did Sigmund leave it? Time to take inventory.

When I reached the backpack, I realized it was Ursula's, not mine. Surprise and relief flooded me when I found one of our loaded pistols and the knife in the front section. I put the knife into one of my pockets. Ursula's bedroll was there instead of mine, as well. I knew this because I gave it a squeeze and found the money was sewn inside. Why her gear and not mine?

I pulled everything out of the backpack and lined items up. Ursula had an inflatable mattress in there. There was enough dried food for seven days, if I had fresh water, which I didn't. Four cans of war surplus chocolate—I'd brought those along as a joke. Some fucking joke. There was also a folding shovel, a folding wood saw, and a good-sized bundle of thin nylon string, probably because the bulk of real rope would have drawn attention. Whoever had packed these items into Ursula's backpack had been deliberate about it.

The rest of the items included deodorant, an alpaca sweater, and two cotton dresses. Two items popped into mind that I wished were included: Pisco and toilet paper.

I repacked everything, stood up slowly, and wondered aloud, "What makes the gold color?" The walls were polished smooth, like a mirror. Was it reflective; and if so, what was it reflecting? And why design it that way?

The story I'd heard about the Valley of the Gods ritual said, "See the gold and die." I'd seen it twice, but was still alive. Was I fucked in a way I didn't know about yet but would soon find out? Of course the answer had to be a Yes, or Sigmund wouldn't have left me here.

This place definitely looked like a silo, but another memory tickled my brain—a small amphitheater. Sure, from the top, you could look down at what was going on below. Whoever the sacrificial lamb of the hour was would be trapped down here with that door swinging the wrong way. Starvation? No, that would take too long. Besides, the statement was you *saw* the gold and died. The sun comes in, the glow appears, and then death; but how?

Sigmund probably knew. The bastard planned all along for me to be a dead man. Maybe he didn't know what was in the backpack and bedroll. Or maybe he did, but left them for me as another one of his mind-fuck games. Let me wonder if I was going to have to defend myself, or believe I had a chance to get out and would need cash once I escaped. Odd that Sigmund never once mentioned the money everyone else seemed so interested in, especially since the story was he was the intended recipient.

Maybe whatever was supposed to kill me didn't have anything to do with defending myself. So, what could it be?

Whatever was supposed to do the job had had all night to do it. What was different from yesterday and now? My watch was working, but I hadn't looked at the time the glow had started the day before. Sigmund's comment was that the sun was "directly overhead." Was that noon when it was over the silo? When we'd seen the glow yesterday, the door was open, now it was closed. Was that it?

It was easy to see I wouldn't be crushed by the walls closing in since the structure was circular. That made the walls moving towards center physically impossible. What fucking time did the glow start yesterday, and how much time did I have before it happened again?

I looked back at Ursula's gear and wondered how and what she was doing now. My fantasy was that she was genuinely upset about Sigmund leaving me to die and had shot the bastard.

The mind jumps ahead sometimes, or maybe it was wishful thinking when I wondered which way to walk once I got out. *Get out first, fuck-head.* There's a time to think and a time to act.

I could use the shovel to dig my way under the door. That seemed my most logical way out. *Up yours, Sigmund; I'm getting outta here.* Unfolded shovel in hand, I knelt down in front of the door to get busy and got a surprise. The ground was damp, in fact, more than damp—wet. It had been bone-dry the last time I noticed and was getting wetter by the second.

I stood up and walked to the center of my circular prison. My heart started to race as I watched the water quickly rise an inch, then two, then three. The silo was filling up fast. That's when I noticed the gold color was back. It seemed it did matter whether the door was opened or closed. I didn't understand why being open kept the water out, aside from the obvious reason, but I was clear what happened with the door closed. I was supposed to drown.

In a matter of moments, I was up to my knees in water, then my waist. The gear was floating. I grabbed the backpack and pulled out the inflatable mattress, grateful it didn't require manual air because not only was I breathing rapidly, I would have had to blow it up while treading water. The mattress did a fast inflate and I climbed on top of it.

The water level went higher, which meant I went with it; and soon, I was within four feet of the top. I hadn't timed it, of course, but it seemed less than five minutes was all it took for the cylinder to fill. As I drifted around, I looked down. It looked like I was floating on liquid gold. The sun was, indeed, directly overhead.

The water was all the way to the top now, so I paddled to the three-foot wide ledge and pulled myself onto it and placed the air mattress on the ledge with me. The jungle was all around me, but nothing grew near the silo. No way to grab a branch or even leap for one; nothing there but a straight drop down. The view was, for the most part, solid jungle. I looked down to see where the water that filled the silo had come from. The contractor of this deathtrap had managed to keep that a mystery.

I walked to the opposite side and focused on the pool with the stone in the center. Naturally, the helicopter was long gone. From this perspective, I could see the stone's trapezoidal shape and this made me think of Frank's story about a door to a tunnel underground that connected Lake Titicaca to where the gold was stored. That's when I remembered he'd said the silos had been built to hide the gold.

A sound made me look back into the silo. The gold color was waning and the water was going down. Stay on the ledge or go back in? "Move, asshole!" I yelled as I grabbed the air mattress and dove in, and ended up with a mouth full of water. I realized I needed it and it tasted pretty good. I waited for a few seconds; and when I didn't die from drinking it, drank some more. Even if it caused dysentery, that was better than dying of dehydration sooner than later.

The water was going down fast, like someone pulled the stopper out. I started to spin around as the flow carried the mattress to the edge of the walls, then to the center. "Grab the ring, get an extra free ride," I yelled out.

I thought the bottom must be near and rolled off the mattress. Instead of my feet touching surface, I was swept along much more rapidly by the spiraling water. I hit the wall fairly hard and before I knew it, I was sucked through the door with the rest of the water. Spinning had kept me too occupied to notice the door had opened.

My body ached from the impact with the wall. I sat on the ground, soaked, and watched the last of the water pour out behind me and go straight into the pond. The heavy log that held the door open the day before was nearby. I jammed the door open with it as the last of the water came out.

I was outside. I'd escaped. Now what? In the city, gunshots cracked open the silence of the night or you saw threatening shapes lurking in doorways; but a true New Yorker learned to cope with these situations. I was in the Amazon, out of my element.

Where to start? Ursula's last words to me were to look at the tiles. She believed I'd get out. Maybe she'd packed the gear or conspired with Marcos on it. I walked to the pond. From this angle, the stone didn't look like Frank's door. Maybe I'd imagined it.

I went to the wall and bent down to study the tiles. A sound came from out of the jungle, from the far side of the pond. I stood and spun around. Nothing. Everything went quiet again. *Better get used to sounds, buddy.*

Back to the tiles. What did Ursula want me to see? Every tile had a figure of a frog on it. The tiles, themselves, appeared to be made with pottery clay, yet looked thin as paper. I looked closer and realized they were transparent.

"Ursula, you are some kind of woman," I said and laughed out loud. "And you, Sigmund, you ego-maniacal asshole, fuck you! You couldn't find your finger if it was stuck up your butt."

I used my knife to scrape an edge of the tile away to expose what was concealed—gold. I ran back into the silo, tripped on the air mattress, and ended up on my ass, sliding on the wet floor until the far wall stopped me. The smooth interior wall surface wasn't granite or any kind of stone. It was the same as the tiles, clay made to look like stone. Whoever had designed this was brilliant.

The shovel was still inside. I grabbed it and started to dig at the edge of the wall. I kept at this until I exposed a section below the ground. I was looking at gold. Whoever the builders were, they'd applied the surface camouflage only to the exposed part. I dug down about one foot. The entire silo seemed to be made of gold, and who knew how deep it went or how high.

I ran back out. The wall on the outside was real stone. If I wanted to know how thick the gold was, I'd have to chisel into the wall from the inside. This had to be the gold of the myth and what Frank was talking about. I went back inside and used my knife like a chisel and the folding shovel as a hammer to knock off different sized chunks of the gleaming treasure. I had plenty of pockets, and nuggets went into each one of them. I remembered that fancy pastry chefs put gold leaf on deserts, which doesn't harm the eater. A good number of smaller nuggets went down my gullet. I didn't know how long it would take before I could *retrieve* them, but I'd know where they were.

I figured I should gather up my gear. Most of it was outside the silo. Everything was soaked. I opened the bed roll so it and the money safely sewed inside could start to dry. I wondered if the gun would still work.

Ursula came to mind. She's a survivor. Unless Sigmund killed her, she'd do fine. In fact, it was possible he would discover he was the one in trouble, which according to what Ursula said the intended plan was, was ultimately the outcome for old *Seig Heil* Sigmund. I decided to abandon the idea that she was part of the plan to get rid of me. She wouldn't have told me to look at the tiles if she'd agreed to kill me. She had to believe I'd find a way out and had done everything she could to help me.

My mind was a whirlwind of conflicting thoughts. If I didn't get a grip, some native or explorer might find me and take me out of the jungle a raving fucking lunatic, but a rich lunatic if I had something to say about it.

First, I had to find my way out of the jungle. I remembered I'd given Frank's broken compass to Marcos and Frank now had mine that worked. I slapped at my chest in frustration and discovered something loose under my shirt. Ursula must have slipped it in there when she kissed me goodbye. I hadn't felt or seen her do it, probably because I was focused on being immobilized and trapped on my back like a bug. The sight of Frank's compass was a disappointment until I popped open the cover and saw it worked. I was feeling better about my situation. Not great, but better. I could tell because hunger hit me. The food items were drenched and probably destroyed. Maybe on nearby trees, I'd find fruit that wouldn't kill me or make me ill.

I turned around and saw I wasn't alone. Whether I'd been that focused or they were that stealthy didn't matter. My heart started to pound. Three natives wearing almost nothing were standing several feet behind me, weapons in hand. There was a similarity between their facial features and Marcos'.

I held out my hand to the one standing forward for a handshake. "Hello," I said looking him in the eyes.

He backed up so fast, he ran into the other two behind him. They ran to the edge of the jungle, then stopped and turned to face me. Not a good first impression. I'd forgotten that hand-shaking is not a universal gesture of greeting.

Humor usually breaks the tension. "Hey, guys, did you ever hear about the flasher who approached a Jewish woman on the street? He opened his rain coat to expose himself and asked, 'What do you think?' She replied, 'Nice lining.' " No reaction. Maybe I should have opened with a Catholic joke. This was a tough group.

The first guy I'd approached sat on the ground. The other two did the same. What the hell, I sat, too. After a few moments, guy number one got up, walked to the pond, and took a drink from it. He returned and sat again. I guessed it was my turn. I got up a little too fast, it seems, because they looked like they were ready to take flight. I slowed my movements and walked to the pond. This seemed to put them a little more at ease. I only meant to take one scoop of water as a gesture of whatever was going on here, but found I was really thirsty, so took several. As I did this, I nodded at them as though to say, *Yes, this is good. Thanks for sharing.*

I rejoined them and wondered what was next. They started to do what looked like social grooming of each other. Not sure what my role was here or if I wanted one, I did nothing but watch.

My stomach growled, loudly. They stopped their grooming and looked at me. "Hungry. I'm hungry," I said rubbing my stomach.

Can I clear a room or what? They were gone just like that. I was alone again. Not too bad for my first encounter. Nor had they indicated I was to be their next meal.

Gnawing hunger seemed to have replaced fear for the moment. I needed food. The trees nearest me didn't have anything more on them than giant ants, considered a food source for some, but not for me. I would have given anything for a pretzel from a street vendor, with mustard, of course.

I made a wish for the dried food to be okay. It needed water. It had gotten that, so maybe I had a meal waiting for me. I turned and was once again face-to-face with my three strangers.

"Guys, you can give a person heart failure doing that," I said. They said nothing.

Their weapons were in one hand, and each of them carried stalks of bananas in the other. The bananas were green, but they looked like steak to me. They placed the stalks on the ground and stepped back.

"My new friends, if this is an offering, I thank you from the bottom of my heart." I stepped over to the bananas and sat in front of them and motioned for the natives to join me. The one who seemed to take the lead came over and sat across from me. I decided to call him Number One. Numbers Two and Three stood and watched. I held out a banana to Number One.

"Please, you first," I said. No response.

I thrust my hand with the banana in it toward him again. He took the banana, but instead of eating it, mirrored my gesture. I smiled at him and took the banana back. Forget further formalities, it was time to eat. Even green, it was the best banana I'd ever eaten. My hand and mouth went into automatic mode and I ate bananas until I reached the point of wanting to gag.

Two and Three joined us. They'd waited until I'd had enough, before starting to eat. Their bananas were eaten at a much slower pace than mine had been. They started to speak to each other in whatever their language was. Not Spanish, maybe Quechua or Aymara, if I recalled correctly some of what I'd read in the books Ursula insisted upon me.

They chatted amongst themselves for what seemed like a long time. Now and then, they'd stop, stare at me, smile and continue. I wondered if this was the tribe that Marcos came from. The features appeared too similar for some relation not to exist.

The light started to shift. Critters I couldn't see were making a meal out of me. Something got me right about where my kidney was. I yelped and got up, walking very quickly, almost in circles to fight off the now agonizing pain. I put my hand behind me and found whatever bit me was still lodged to my skin, all the way through my shirt. It hurt like a son-of-a-bitch.

Two and Three took hold of my arms and dragged me toward one of trees that had large ants carrying leaves down from it. Three went into the woods and quickly returned with a handful of what looked like berries. He put them in his mouth and chewed until syrup flowed from his mouth.

By now, the pain was unbelievable. My whole body felt as if it were on fire. Three knelt down level with my back and sprayed me with the thick liquid he'd made in his mouth. Two and One turned me around so that my back was facing the tree. All three held me close to the tree trunk. Ants immediately climbed on my back mostly in the area of my bite. Great, I thought, after all this, they're going to feed me to the ants.

I could feel the ants doing something. The pain subsided almost immediately. The natives yanked me away from the tree, rushed me over to the pond, and pushed me in. As I sank into the water, l realized the pain was gone. I rose to the surface to three smiling faces.

I got out of the pond and they gingerly pushed me toward the tree to show me a cluster of ants devouring what looked like an orange caterpillar. With a stick, One wrestled it free from the ants to show me a set of pinchers at the front, and at the rear, a large stinger resembling that of a scorpion's.

He squeezed the caterpillar by holding it with a leaf, and a yellow substance came out of the stinger. Two collected the substance on another leaf, folded the leaf, and stuck it into a pouch made from the body of a small rodent. The little feet were still attached, but the head was gone. He used the tail to tie the pouch onto the grass rope around his waist.

I said, "Thank you," but wasn't sure they'd understand me, so added a little bow at the waist. "Now, my friends, let's see which of my belongings are salvageable."

They watched while I picked through the items. Every now and then, I held up an item, no matter what it was, and asked for approval. They seemed to enjoy this. These antics brought on a lot of talking and laughter. Sam Paris, court jester of the Amazon.

After I was through sorting what was usable in one pile and what had to be ditched in another, I sat down. I gestured over the pile of items useless to me and said, "Here, friends, take what you want from here." No movement from them. "Guys, this is yours for the taking."

I pushed an assortment of clothes and the cans of chocolate toward them. They caught on and went through the items with a great deal of excitement. One motioned at the usable pile, particularly the saw. What was I going to do? What else could I do? As far as I was concerned, they'd saved me. They could certainly take the saw away from me if they really wanted to.

"Smart choice, Number One," I said as I handed it to him. "What about you, Numbers Two and Three?" I held out the mostly dry and now warped packets of food to them, which made them happy. "You know, this stuff is full of chemicals. Be glad civilization hasn't gotten here yet."

I kept on with my organizing while they carried on a long-winded conversation spiked with lots of laughter. I was pretty happy myself since the idea stuck in my mind they'd escort me out of the jungle. It was dusk now and I was ready to leave. I strapped on my repacked backpack and picked up the re-rolled bed roll. If anyone ever looked ready to get out of Dodge, it was me.

They obviously thought it was time to leave, too, because they were heading into the jungle at a pretty rapid pace—without me. "Wait! Take me with you. I have more stuff you can have."

I was left standing at the edge of the dense brush, dumbfounded. They'd disappeared into the thick wall of green without even a sound. No way could I hope to catch up with them. *Well, shit,* I thought.

It was getting dark. I'd already had enough fun with local critters, so I made my way back to the silo. If I lowered the door and stopped it open with stones just high enough to let me crawl through, it should keep out larger animals that fed at night. I was just thinking to myself *Sure, but it won't keep the bugs out,* when I remembered at no time had I seen bugs of any kind inside the silo.

I put my gear down inside and hurried out to find and position stones under the door before the light disappeared completely. There were plenty of hours between now and having to think about the water again, though I couldn't be certain if the door had to be slightly open or fully open to keep the water out. It didn't matter. As soon as the sun was up, I'd head...somewhere.

The bedroll was still damp, so I unrolled it again and positioned myself against the wall opposite the door; it might be too easy to fall asleep if I used the air mattress. I didn't want to waste a bullet to see if the gun would still fire. If it didn't, I could use the gun to hit something in the head if that was needed. The door being propped open seemed to alter the soundproof effect. I could hear screeches and growls of night animals on the prowl. I felt both somewhat protected and trapped.

I needed sleep, but I fought it. It felt like being at anchor when I was a kid and used to go with one of my uncles on his boat out into the Atlantic. Never did feel comfortable hanging on a rope or swinging on a tide or wind. At night, I was always afraid the anchor would pull loose, or the anchor light would burn out and we'd be hit by a passing ship or some other craft bigger than ours. This was one reason I'd joined the Marines and not the Navy.

Ursula could always sleep straight through the night. Why not? She'd had an anchor watch. Me. I'd have to stand my own watch. No drifting off. Just what I needed, a play on words. Besides, I thought, all that jungle caterwauling would keep me awake.

CHAPTER 20

"Sam."

"What?" Who the hell was waking me up? Damn, I'd fallen asleep.

"Sam."

"Frank?" It was pitch black, which meant I couldn't see a thing. I edged my back up the wall, and used my left hand, the one not holding the pistol, to feel my way along the surface. This had to be what it's like to be blind.

"Sam."

"Frank, is that you?"

"I'm outside."

I felt my way to the door, crawled underneath and stood up. The jungle was silent; the normally stifling air was pleasantly cool.

"Frank, where are you?"

"Here, Sam, on the rock in the middle of the pond."

My eyes adjusted to the bit of light that was coming from somewhere. I couldn't readily see the moon, but assumed that was the source. I recognized his familiar silhouette standing at the center of the flat stone.

"Frank, it's good to see you again. It's good to see anyone again, but especially you. I have a lot of questions, like when are you going to get me the hell out of here, but first, how's Ursula? Do you know where she is?"

"Everything in its time, Sam. Ursula is safe for now; but we have a problem, in fact four of them. The four from one tribe are after you. If they succeed in getting you back to Cuzco, Ursula's plan will fail. If that happens, my people will continue to suffer."

"Sigmund has to leave Peru with her, huh, Frank?"

"Yes."

"They could be anywhere by now."

"They're at the American Embassy in Cuzco, waiting for Sigmund to be well enough to leave."

"What happened? Are you sure Ursula is okay?"

"She's fine. They had to leave the helicopter behind—a mechanical problem—and take a truck to Cuzco instead. On the way, they encountered some very angry men. It seems you both made enemies regarding money that disappeared. They thought Sigmund was you. During the encounter, Sigmund was shot in the leg."

"I can't say I'm really sorry about that; but, Ursula..."

"Dispatched them quite easily."

"Them?"

"The two men who stopped them."

"I don't know from one moment to the next if I really admire her or if I'm terrified of her. You said the four are after me. What makes you think they're looking for me and not Sigmund? I'm a little heavier than he is, but we look enough alike that if they haven't seen him lately, they may not know who's who. If the other two men were confused..."

"They observed Sigmund and Ursula once they landed back at the camp, but realized it was Sigmund with her, not you. It's you they want."

"Why do they want me?"

"They need you so they can present you and Sigmund to authorities at the American Embassy in Cuzco. It's their sure way to ruin the plan to get Sigmund out of Peru. They have their own agenda and will do anything to see that it happens."

"If they succeed, the only problem I see would be that our plan would fall through and Ursula and I would head back to the States. Whether the Cuzco Four or Ursula's organization bring Wasser and son down, and how, doesn't really matter, just that it's done."

"That's not the way it would go in the end. Ursula would be eliminated and so would you. Sigmund or his father would be forced to have it done. Sigmund's still powerful here. You can believe he has some kind of plan ready in case anything goes opposite of the arrangements. He might be temporarily stopped from meeting up with his father, but he'd resume what he was doing before. One way or another, my people would be oppressed by that madman. The four will arrive here tomorrow."

"How can they know to find me here?"

"Marcos will bring them."

"Marcos? Damn it. He's another one I never know whose side he's on. Maybe that explains... He only gave me enough sleeping drug to keep me out for a while. He wanted me to wake up."

"Marcos is confused. Sigmund left him here instead of taking him along as he expected. With the father gone, and now Sigmund, he feels he no longer has a family. It is impossible for him to get back with a tribe. No shaman would allow it, he's become too civilized. But, Marcos needs to tell his stories. The four know this and befriended him. They told him you're the reason Sigmund has left, and without him. Marcos will ask you if it's true. Don't lie to him when he confronts you, and don't look away, if you can help it. You must tell him that Ursula and you have come here to do what Frank has tried to do."

"Marcos knows about you?"

"Don't concern yourself with that now. Whatever you do, make sure he believes you. If he doesn't, you'll be on your way to Cuzco."

"And we know what happens."

"That's why we have to make sure it doesn't. You have to stay out of Cuzco, whatever it takes. Sam, I know a lot of what's happened to you since you got to Peru was unexpected. I also know even when you didn't like what was going on, especially when you were lied to, you still kept going. I don't think you did this just so you could survive or for gold. I think the reason you signed up, all the way back to when you first met Ursula in New York, was because there's a part of you that craves adventure, more adventure than befriending rats in an underground subway tunnel. And, you also want to right a wrong. Am I correct?"

"Frank, you seem to know...You're right. Fuck! I may not be religious, but I'm a Jew, Frank. I owe it to my family and people I never met to do something. And, yeah, I want gold, especially because people decided to put my life at risk, even considered me expendable. Fuck 'em. I'm getting something out of this. And, about adventure... I don't know if it's a left-over adrenaline rush from being in Vietnam or if it's just who I really am, but you're right about that, too. Even when I felt I was up to my eyeballs in deep shit here, every time I got out of it safely, it gave me a rush. Gave me a rush while in it, if I'm honest about it."

"I have a different kind of rush for you, Sam."

"What do you mean by different?"

"Do you trust me?"

"Hell, Frank, yeah, I trust you. So, what's next?"

"The truth…finally the truth."

"The truth, Frank? About fucking time. How about starting by telling me what this place is."

"The end of the tunnel I told you about, Sam. The non-believers from Lake Titicaca dug away the walls, but left two mine shafts, one higher than the other. They did this so they could control the flooding."

"I wondered if that was the stone you described and if this was where the gold was stored. I found gold, all right. You're telling me it's possible to reach Lake Titicaca from here?"

"Even with all you've seen, you're soon going to see things you've never imagined."

"Frank, I saw your…there's no other word for it—grave. I opened the compass you gave me and it fit into the slot on your headstone." I looked down for a moment to pull the compass out from under my shirt. "I have to ask, Frank, are you… Frank?!"

He was gone. I called his name a few more times, not that I expected him to answer. I wished he'd show me how to do his disappearing trick.

I made my way back to the silo and slid under the opening. The only thing left to do was go back to sleep if I could. In the morning, I'd give another look at my inventory. Anything that could stay behind would. I'd leave those items outside for One, Two, and Three to find in case they came back, and wondered if I'd ever see them again.

Marcos and the Four would show up tomorrow. I could leave at first light, but even with the compass, I didn't know which way was best to head. Besides, Frank had just said it was important I speak with Marcos. I'd pretend to go with them and keep my eyes open for the first opportunity to escape. For now, Ursula was safe at the Embassy in Cuzco. All I had to do was get there, connect with her, and hope to convince her to get out of this while we still could. Let others better suited to the task take over.

As long as someone took care of the Wassers, Frank's people would be safe. I'd have to think about the gold silo and what to do about it once things settled down.

Frank had given me a little more information, but there were still a lot of unanswered questions. Again, it was what he hadn't said that gnawed at me. I sat by the wall and propped my back up against it again, tilted my head and looked straight up into the night sky. The full moon was directly overhead. I gave a quick look at my watch in the moonlight. Three hours until dawn.

What if Frank was wrong? Maybe Marcos hadn't been abandoned and was really coming back to finish the job. He was leading the Four to me, or pretending to. What if he meant for the Cuzco Four and me to spend eternity together? There were just way too many strange bedfellows involved, and I was never certain who was *in bed* with whom. If Marcos knew how the water and silo door system worked, he knew a body left inside would be washed out with the water. I couldn't figure it out, but somehow the water level and door were designed to work together.

It felt as though the tapestry seemed to be unraveling without my pulling any particular thread.

It was beyond me; and that was the last thought I had before I fell asleep.

CHAPTER 21

Not one morning I'd awakened in Peru had been a relaxed one. I was always running to the next place with Ursula or away from someone who wanted to kill us, or at least, me.

It doesn't seem to matter where a person is, the body has a particular need to be met as soon as your eyes open. Sometimes that need wakes you. I also felt an unwelcome rumbling in my gut. There are a lot of times a person can get away without toilet paper, but this wasn't going to be one of them. At first, I was surprised when my three native friends didn't reach for the cotton dresses. Now I was glad I hadn't pushed them to take them. One of those dresses was about to serve a purpose it was never designed for.

I was also grateful the shovel had been inside the silo while they were here. They may have wanted it, as well. I took the shovel and one of the dresses and slid under the door. Even though alone, I went around to the other side of the silo for privacy. I wasn't about to go into the jungle and end up with one of those orange caterpillars attached to my nether region. I stayed close to the wall and dug a hole in the dirt. I took a quick look around before I unzipped my pants and squatted down. Nature ran its course. I decided not to worry about any gold nuggets that got away. I knew where I could get more.

There are a lot of ways for a man to feel vulnerable. Being in that position with my pants around my ankles with a wild boar staring me down was one of them. The gun was in my pocket, so I removed it. Images of pork chops came to mind, but had to leave just as quickly. Even if the pistol fired, the other kind of fire was something I didn't have. This Jew eats pork, but not raw.

We watched each other for about a minute. The boar grunted and sniffed the air. It must not have liked what it smelled because it decided to charge me. The distance between us was too close and the boar had the advantage of not having to fumble to get underwear and pants up and zipped. I did the only thing I could; I wait until it was almost on me and toppled over. I was too busy trying to get up to watch this, but heard its head whack straight into the stone wall.

The boar shook its head, gathered its senses and made another charge. I hadn't been fast enough to get out of there, so it caught me between my legs. Both of us got fouled and both of us stunk. Its body covering felt like needles on my bare skin. The two of us wrestled over and over. I lost my grip on the pistol. By this time, my crotch was full of boar's head. It was quite a dance I did trying to protect my privates.

I managed to grab its hind feet. The boar was trembling and we both had blood on us, and I pretty much figured it was mine. As though it might understand me, I said, "If I pull straight back on your feet, that should free your head; and maybe you can go back to where you came from. What do you say?"

I pulled and with a little effort, its tusks got unsnarled from my pants. When I let go, the boar did, indeed, haul butt in the other direction; unfortunately, not for long. The feisty little bastard charged around the silo. I lunged for the gun. *Click!* I tossed the gun aside, got my pants up and zipped in record time and ran for the shovel. In golfer stance, I waited. The boar came at me, head low to strike its blow. I took a back step and cracked it square on the head. The critter was down, but not out. Two more cracks did it, but it was still breathing. No point in killing the creature. I ran back into the silo, grabbed the nylon string, and went back out there to truss its legs. I took the shovel in hand and dragged the boar to the edge of the clearing. My knife cut the string, and a whack with the shovel to its butt finally got rid of it.

I picked up the pistol, ejected the clip, and urged the bullets out—none were missing—and dried them with the cotton dress since I hadn't had a chance to use it as intended. I checked the chamber and found it empty, which was one reason it hadn't fired and also a good thing since during the struggle, the safety had flipped and it might have gone off. It also meant it wasn't the gun

Ursula had used, as had I, on Tinko. I loaded the bullets back into the clip and snapped the clip into place. I considered chambering a round so it would be ready to fire, but changed my mind.

Any concern about messing up the pond water was quickly discarded. I jumped in fully-clothed to clean up as much as I could then climbed out and went back into the silo. Perhaps this was a good time to use some of that deodorant.

CHAPTER 22

While I waited for what was coming, I swallowed some more nuggets just in case I'd lost a few. My boots still had water in them, so I took them off to empty the water out. I noticed a tear in the thin fleece lining and got an idea. I used the knife to make several slits in the lining of both boots, careful to size the nuggets just right. There was enough room for *lots* of nuggets and my calves. When I completed that task, I bundled my gear and used it to cover up the hole I'd dug.

An hour or so went by before I heard sounds of people approaching and French being spoken. My guests had arrived. I'd find out soon enough if they were going to crawl through the opening or open the door all the way. I stayed seated against the wall with my gun in hand, but hidden from view.

"Sam, are you in there?" It was the Frenchman who'd always done most of the talking, Jean-Paul.

One part of me wanted to answer him, another told me to stay quiet. I needed a plan, fast. Acting a little mad might buy me some time. Jean-Paul's face peeked through the opening.

"He's in there; I can see him. Hello, Sam."

I didn't answer, just waited. They weren't going to open the door. I knew this because Jean-Paul was starting to crawl through the opening. As quietly as I could, I got up and stood by the side of the door, gun at the ready.

One-by-one, they entered the silo. And one-by-one, they saw me standing there with my gun aimed in their direction.

"Easy, Sam. We're friends. We're here to help you. Let's talk."

The crazy idea came to me to put the gun to my head. Really let them think I'd lost it. Since the odds were four-to-one, this might work. I hoped the way I was standing wouldn't let them see I'd angled the muzzle so if I did fire it, the most I'd get was a graze to the forehead. Two of them started towards me. I pulled the trigger. *Click! Fuck and double fuck!* I regretted I hadn't chambered a round, so tried then, but got no action.

"Stop him, Francois. We need his head."

"Who the fuck is going to cut it off?" Francois asked.

"Our guide," Jean-Paul answered, a little too calmly, in my opinion.

I'd wondered where Marcos was. He was supposed to have led them here.

"Sam," Francois said, "We're here to take you back to Ursula. She needs you. Tell him, Jean-Paul."

"Sam, let us put our cards on the table. Ursula was fooled into believing the people who asked for her help were the Marada. We know they are not, because we are the Marada. The only way to get to that bastard doctor is to keep Sigmund here in the Amazon. That's the only way we can control his father's every move. There is a strong father-son relationship between them. They don't trust anyone but each other."

They talked a good story. Could it be possible that Ursula had been used and lied to, as well? So many people had lied to me, I decided the only one I could believe was Frank; and for all I knew, he was a damn ghost.

"Do I go with them?" I called out.

"Who are you talking to?" Jean-Paul asked me.

"Do I? Is this what you want me to do? Some kind of sign about now would be pretty helpful!"

"He's mad," Francois said.

I realized how silly it was to still have the gun aimed at my head since it wouldn't fire, so lowered my arm.

One of the women walked over to the wall and touched it with her hand.

"What do you think this is used for?" she asked.

"It looks like some kind of silo," the other woman replied.

I was starting to concern myself about the fact they were going near my gear when I felt a bee sting on the back of my neck.

"Hello, Sam." Marcos had made his appearance.

CHAPTER 23

I was the first to wake up. The other four looked like they hadn't moved from where they fell. I felt my neck, the dart was gone. Marcos was standing in the center of the silo. Behind him were One, Two, and Three, all carrying blowguns. The four of them were covered head-to-toe in some kind of white-wash. Feathers donned their ankles, biceps, and wrists. Everything about them was decked out, except their expressions, which were blank.

"Marcos, this dart business is becoming a pain in the neck." He didn't smile.

"Why did Ursula and Sigmund leave without me?" Marcos asked.

I thought back to what Frank said about eye contact. Before I could answer, though, Marcos shouted, "Why did Sigmund leave without me?"

"Ursula had to get Sigmund away to fulfill Frank's wish to save your people; and if it means Sigmund has to leave Peru without you, then that's what has to happen. I know what you believe about Sigmund, and about Carl, but until he leaves Peru, until both of them sever their ties here, your people will never have control of their own lives."

His angry expression was intensified. "What do you know of Frank?"

"Not a hell of a lot, but we do talk from time to time. Did you recognize his compass when I gave it to you that night?"

"You are the one, Sam, who has to answer questions."

"All right, Marcos, but what about them?" I asked pointing to the four.

"They will wake soon; now tell me what you know about Frank."

"Sure, but I have to start from the beginning."

I explained to Marcos that Frank's story had been told to me by the Cuzco Four lying unconscious at our feet, about Frank finding me and our meeting the next day for our trip on the lake, his wishes and his warnings, including those given during the night. I said that I hadn't known until recently about Ursula's own mission and the reason she'd brought me along.

"So you see, Marcos, Sigmund has to leave Peru, for everybody's sake. I know his father took you in and raised you, but you must understand that he's not a good man, as he had you believe. He comes from a tribe who killed innocent people for their own reasons and rewards, and did so without mercy. His tribe was, and some still are, bent on destroying another tribe with stories that go back thousands of years. His tribe was stopped by a great war. Carl was a doctor who did not live to end suffering, but to create it; and, Sigmund became his willing assistant.

"Marcos, I don't think I can get through this without help. I'm asking for your help. Ursula must be able to continue on with Sigmund. These four from one tribe," I said gesturing downward, "have asked you to help them bring me back to Cuzco. If you do so or allow them to, it will prevent Sigmund from leaving the country with Ursula. That can't happen at any cost, even if it means my life. Only, if I get killed, you have to destroy my head."

"Destroy your head?"

"That's the only part they said they really need to prove to the authorities there's a plan for a swap. In fact, they probably mean to kill me so I can't talk."

Marcos looked down at the four then said something to the three natives.

"Let me show you something outside," I said.

He followed me under the door and stopped where I did, about a yard in front of the silo.

"See the pond?" I said pointing. "That stone is shaped the same as the one Frank was looking for in Lake Titicaca."

"Sigmund calls it a helicopter pad."

"Yes, he used it for that; but it's possible it's something even more important."

"Did Ursula also meet Frank?"

"No. I thought she saw him that day on the rocks, but she said she didn't. In fact, she told me it had to have been a dream I had while unconscious from being ill."

"Didn't you show her Frank's compass?"

"As many times as I thought about doing it to prove Frank was real, something always stopped me."

Marcos got quiet and stared straight at me. Then, almost in a whisper, "Do you think Ursula does believe in Frank…because you do?"

"Ursula has to believe in some of what's happening to me; after all, we both saw the flowing gold and…" Marcos' expression changed and I wasn't sure or not if I'd said the wrong thing.

"You saw the flowing gold, and Ursula did also?"

Frank's words echoed, "Tell Marcos the truth." So I did, including how I'd seen the flowing gold through Ursula's eyes at the sacrificial stone, and in the silo. On impulse, I took Frank's compass from around my neck and gave it to him.

Marcos clutched it to his chest. "Yes, I knew it was Frank's. It was one of the reasons I wanted to hurt you. I told you how I came to live with Carl and Sigmund. Philipe was Carl's shaman and he told me of a white man who'd lived among the tribes. I told you this at the camp. This white man was my father. My father had told them stories of a great war with those of his tribe and another tribe in a land far away from here. Is this the war you spoke of?"

"Yes."

"All the tribes were honored when he would stay with them and tell stories. His stories kept the tribes from fighting. It made me proud and angry to hear the shaman tell my father's story."

"Why did it make you angry?"

"They also spoke of his desire to find the flowing gold, and how sad the day was when he left to look for it. To look for it so you find you're in the gods' favor is honorable. To look for it as treasure is not. Soon after he left, the wars amongst the tribes started again."

"Do they know what happened to your father?"

"The shaman told me my father died when the tribe attacked us. I learned this was not true. He also told me that one day a man would give me a symbol. He said this symbol would answer my unanswered questions."

Marcos handed the compass back to me.

"I think you should keep it, Marcos."

"That would not be right. He gave it to you."

"Look, Marcos, Frank never gave a reason for making me take his compass; but I'll tell you this, I saw his grave. The inscription on his headstone had his name and a phrase, *As I am now, so shall ye be*, the same phrase he said to me on the lake. A slot was cut into the headstone. When the cover is open, the compass fits into it. This compass is important, but he didn't tell me why. I'd like to think this compass is the symbol the shaman spoke of, and if it is… Here," I said thrusting it into his hand. "Frank knew we'd meet. And, he told me to expect you today. I don't understand what's going on, especially with Frank, nor do I know what your unanswered questions are, but maybe this compass answers one of them."

"Frank was my father." Marcos said loudly. He clutched the compass as if it was the most valuable thing in the world, and to him, I imagined it was. "It was only when I heard Carl and Sigmund talk of the gold and of the man named Frank that I knew my father's real name."

"Why didn't the shaman tell you your father's name?"

"A shaman will not hasten destiny. Storytelling to us is more important than many understand. Autheuma had many stories told about him."

"Who?"

"They called my father Autheuma. It means, 'From a place unknown to us.' He was found in the jungle, without a memory. The shaman said that the war finally caught up to him. I wonder what that means." He walked to the door then turned and said, "It is time to go," called something out to the natives still inside, then slid inside under the door.

CHAPTER 24

I followed Marcos into the silo.

"Where are we going, Marcos?"

"You go nowhere; I go to Cuzco."

"Why are you going to Cuzco?"

"To kill the son of the man who killed my father."

"What makes you think Carl killed your father?"

Marcos held out the compass. He opened not just the front cover I had opened, but another one at the back. I hadn't realized it was there. The second cover exposed the same inscription as on Frank's headstone.

"How does this prove Carl killed Frank?"

"Carl gave it to Sigmund before he left Peru. Sigmund always wore it until it disappeared recently. Carl told me once that no one gives their compass away in the jungle. It must be taken, and usually by force. This means Carl killed my father, whether by his own hand or another's. It's also why I hated you. I didn't know how you came to have my father's compass. When you gave it to me, I began to have doubts…to wonder about you. Since I cannot get to Carl to kill him, I must get to Sigmund before he leaves Peru. Move against the wall, Sam."

"You're going to leave me here? To die?"

"You did not die before. I believe you will not die, again. Against the wall, Sam."

Marcos spoke to the three natives and they left through the opening. I moved against the wall. The last thing I wanted was to be drugged by a dart again. Once Marcos was on the other side, I saw hands moving the stones away then heard the familiar thud.

"You're a fool, Sam," I heard Jean-Paul say, "A complete fool. Don't you see? There's another side to this story, one you've been left out of."

"What the fuck are you talking about?" I wondered how long he'd been playing opossum.

Jean-Paul rubbed his eyes and tried to stand. Marcos said they'd wake soon, but this soon surprised me. He must have the sleep potion down to a science. The other three sleeping beauties were stirring, as well.

"What I'm talking about, Sam, is that maybe Ursula was never asked to help get Sigmund out of Peru by Nazi hunters."

"What?"

"Maybe she's a Nazi, herself, and was sent here to get Sigmund safely out of Peru and back with his father. What do you really know about her?"

"Shut the fuck up," I shouted. With everything I'd thought or wondered about Ursula, her being a Nazi was never included in the mix.

"Let me finish. Did she tell you that the Marada recruited her?"

"No, just an organization."

"Since I am Marada, I can tell you this, we would never trust anyone who was not born into our exclusive group. We know only our own, we recruit only our own. I'm very sorry, Sam, but you have been taken in by a very good German agent, a neo-Nazi. Did she not kill? And, how many times that you know of, and times that you don't? So, you see, Sigmund must not leave with Ursula. For that to happen, you must show up in Cuzco. We must prevent him from using your passport which by now has his photo on it."

All four were fully awake. They alternated between speaking to each other in rapid-fire French and trying to convince me to trust them. Jean-Paul was full of himself to think I'd believe he wanted to get me to Cuzco alive. Did he think I'd forgotten he said all they needed was my head?

Francois tried to open the door. Jean-Paul went to help him. It was getting brighter in the silo. I checked my watch—nearly noon—then went over to the air mattress and got on top, and looked like I was ready for a nap. It wouldn't be long before the sun and silo did their thing.

With a little time on my hands, I contemplated matters. Sigmund wasn't considered a war criminal in this country, just the son of one. He could probably come and go as he pleased, if not through Peru, at least Venezuela or Brazil. Sigmund wanted out of Peru to join his father. He looked like me, and with my passport, would have clear passage to the United States, but not to Germany where he might be recognized. It was possible Carl was actually waiting for him in the States.

"Sam, how come you are not worried about being trapped in here?" asked Francois.

"I've been here a while, guys. You might try standing on each others' shoulders like one of those acrobatic acts," I said with a grin. "The sun's going to give us a little show shortly. You guys ever think how nice it would be to go for a swim on a warm day in the jungle?"

"He is crazy," Jean-Paul said. The two men continued to examine and test the door. The two women looked worried. They should.

Shafts of light started to bounce off the walls. The Cuzco Four were fascinated when the silo started to fill with the golden glow. They were so spell-bound by this phenomenon, they weren't looking down.

One of the women took a step. "Water. We're being flooded!"

They were caught by surprise as the silo rapidly filled. The battle for the air mattress I expected didn't happen. They were good swimmers and for the most part, calmly rose with the in-flow.

Reaching the top wasn't as dramatic for me as it had been the first time I'd done it. The Cuzco Four were ecstatic. All four climbed onto the ledge and ran around rattling off in French. All I had to do was trick them into staying up there when the water receded.

Several minutes went by and the glow in the water started to diminish. As I'd hoped, the Cuzco Four were so busy arguing, they didn't notice. Bingo! Down I started to go. They still had their backs turned away from me. Down I went—four feet, five, then six. One of the women noticed and said something to the other three. I needed to keep them from jumping in, so I screamed, "Help me! I'll be trapped again!" That stopped them and bought me more time. The water level was so low now it was too late for them to do anything.

I spun around and around. This time, I was going to ride on the mattress all the way down and out of the silo. I wrapped my arms and legs around it as tightly as I could without losing balance. The four of them were waving their arms and shouting, but I couldn't hear them. I managed a small wave before the air mattress, with me firmly on it, whooshed through the door, with only a few scrapes as I bumped the edge of the opening.

The water carried me straight towards the pond where it was cascading downward. It took a second for me to see that the flat stone at the center was tilted upward and the water was flowing down into the hole, taking me and my raft with it. I squeezed my eyes and every orifice I could, shut. The plunge down was quick and easy, all things considered. Though I leveled off, I kept my grip as tight as I could on the air mattress.

It wasn't a tight enough grip. The air mattress bumped something and I slipped off, but still had a hold of it. I opened my eyes. The current was moving me away from the opening under the stone, which meant also from my only source of light. Around me were small eddies and whirlpools. That made me even more concerned.

Within moments, everything was in total darkness. It felt painfully dark to me. Instant fear hit, and not just because of the absence of light. My legs and most of my torso were dangling in the water as the current continued to move me along. As it had been that night on the lake after Frank disappeared from the boat, anything could be under the water, including rocks that might injure or rip one or both legs off.

The current seemed to carry me for a long time. Fear was being replaced with numbness. My body heat was dropping fast. If I didn't get out of the water soon, I'd fall asleep and drown. A speck of light bounced in front of my eyes. It had to be a trick of my weary mind, like the illusion of an oasis in the desert. *Stay alive*, I told myself.

The light didn't disappear, even after I blinked hard several times. Instead, it seemed to grow larger. I couldn't tell if I was moving towards it, or it and I were moving towards each other. I neared the light and saw a shape. It was a reed boat. Why wasn't it moving with the current? As I neared the boat, it appeared suspended; but, with what? I floated straight to it. Whatever bottom was under the water grabbed my feet. Momentum pushed me forward and my stomach rubbed against a soft, slimy surface. I grabbed onto the boat and tried to stand, but sunk knee-deep into muck. The reed boat was stuck on a mud bank. It seemed nothing was easy to do in the Amazon except get into trouble or find someone who wanted to kill me.

I was able to pull myself free and climb aboard at least half-way. My legs dragged along the mud, but the boat moved; and once again, the current had me. I wrestled my body into the boat and collapsed in a heap. I looked up and saw I was heading into the light shaft. It hurt my eyes when I first looked up, but above me was a perfectly round, wide opening. I could see trees and what looked like four heads peering down at me. With the light in my eyes, it was impossible to see faces.

For a moment, I imagined it was Marcos and the three natives. It was almost comforting. The sudden blackness I was thrust into was stark as I continued to move forward to wherever I was going. I was exhausted, so closed my eyes. I had nodded off because a sound overhead woke me. It was a bellowing. Then a sudden shaft of light burned my eyes and a small deer struggled as it fell through the hole above. Its legs flailed and clumps of dirt fell with it into the water. The splash when it hit the water was loud enough for me to hear it. In my semi-delirium, I yelled out, "Good luck!" to the deer.

Another flash of light hit my eyes, then darkness, then a glint in the boat. I reached my hand out to where the glint was winking at me. First I felt a chill, then something familiar. It was a bottle with a cork in it. One pull on the cork with my teeth and the fragrant bouquet of Pisco filled my senses.

CHAPTER 25

"Don't forget your friend," I heard a voice say.

My heart started to pound so strongly, I could feel the pulse in my throat. "Frank, is that you? I can't see?"

"Couldn't allow you to do this alone, could I? Pass the Pisco, Sam."

Still partially blind, I thrust my hand forward. A strong hand grabbed my wrist and at the same time the bottle was taken from me. Frank's hand was warm. I told him so. He came back with a high-pitched, "Beep-beep." This weird sound was like a memory that itched at the back of my mind. It was familiar, but I couldn't place it.

"What, did you say?"

"Beep-beep," he repeated. "It's the symbol for what you and I have—a bond. How's your fear of the dark now?"

"I was having a hard time with it, but not any longer now that you're here."

"When the war was in its rage and I found myself afraid, two mottos helped me. One was made famous by Franklin Delano Roosevelt which went, 'There is nothing to fear but fear itself.' The other was, 'As I am now, so shall ye be.' I saw that one on a headstone in a French cemetery after we liberated France. I chose it as my epitaph."

"Why that one, Frank?"

"Because it gave me the most strength. I knew that I would always be afraid of my fear; the war didn't give me enough time to learn how to control it. My parents were gone, and I remembered the fears and strengths they had. And, there were my good friends lost in the war. If they could meet their deaths, so could I. At first it seemed naive to think that way, but another friend said to me just before he was killed, 'Frank, the way I handle my fear of death is to realize it's much harder to be born than to die; and, we all made it through our births."

"Is Marcos your son, and as crazy as this will sound, did Carl kill you?"

"To answer the first part, yes, Marcos is my son. As to the second part, all I will say is my grave is empty. I want you to remember something, Sam. It's not how long one lives, but how much living one does that matters."

"I'll take that last part into consideration just as soon as I make it out of here alive. The other two, I'll have to give some thought to, as well. Frank, Marcos is going after Sigmund to kill him."

"My son will not reach Cuzco."

"Marcos wants revenge."

"My son will not get his revenge. Sigmund will leave with Ursula."

"Who or what will stop Marcos." I was worried that Frank was going to say I would.

"His sister is trailing him. Lisa will stop him."

"All this time, I knew you had a daughter and Marcos did mention a sister; but I never stopped to wonder or ask what happened to her."

"Lisa is my daughter and Sigmund's wife."

"Damn, does she know or think that Sigmund and Carl..." I couldn't say the word, but Frank picked up on my thoughts.

"Killed her father, killed me? Lisa knows many stories. Many."

"Frank, this is getting even more complicated as we go along. Also, the Cuzco Four said something about Ursula that disturbs me. They said she's a Nazi."

"Ursula's not what she seems."

"What can you tell me about her?"

"She did use you to get to Sigmund. That was her plan all along, from the moment she learned about you. Her objective is to flush out Carl from where he's hiding."

"And when that happens?"

"Kill them both."

"Frank, I was thinking Carl must be waiting for Sigmund in the United States. So…"

"Ursula must do what she's been trained to do. And whoever gets in her way, which by the way, means you..."

"Ursula would never..." I didn't finish. I really didn't want to think of it.

"Sam, Ursula will avenge me. That's a part of the story you haven't been told. You will help Marcos and Lisa take whatever is left at Sigmund's camp and move deeper into the jungle. A new disease is sweeping Peru. Without Sigmund or Carl here to support it, there's a chance the Peruvian government and its people may survive."

"What disease?" I blinked hard because my eyesight was starting to clear.

"The Shining Path that was started and supported by Carl and Sigmund. When Sigmund goes, so does the money. Pockets of small drug dealers will emerge to take over the empire that the Wassers created; but, they will spend most of the time fighting each other. During this time of unrest, it will be easier to disband them. But all of this depends on Ursula getting Sigmund out of Peru."

"Difficult to believe that Sigmund and Carl would leave behind all this power and money."

"For forty-plus years, the burning desire of world domination and the ethnic cleansing of the races controlled Carl's thoughts. Just the fact of their control over the tribes and the surrounding mountain people should show you what is deep inside them both."

"But the people will remember they created schools, health facilities, and gave jobs of a kind to the natives."

"Ask what the natives gave up to receive such wonderful things. These people were rich. Not in the way you think. Life, as a force, streamed through them. Fathers taught sons the way of the jungle. Mothers taught their ways to their daughters. They sometimes died of the simplest reasons easily cured in our civilization; but to them, death was expected and therefore accepted as a natural part of life.

"The young grew as a unit. War games played daily, picked out the strong and also the weak, because each were equally important. The guarantee of the next generation depended on everyone knowing what to expect from each other. Sure, the good doctor taught them to read, but he also made certain the books were hand-picked by him. He wanted to control every step in their learning process. What you see around the camp is a very strong cult following not unlike the one that Hitler created.

"Carl, however, did not include Marcos and Lisa in this exact training. Carl, and Sigmund, gave them the choice of independence, but more as a test of loyalty than fact. He convinced them they were more like family than they ever would be. He taught them to see into other societies, according to his views, of course, but he was careful to make certain they didn't learn to read and write. He got away with this by telling them they were above it, chosen for a special purpose. No mention of the Nazis, though, to anyone he brought into his circle from the jungle.

"Carl had one problem that haunted him, that of being the killer of the father of Marcos and Lisa. This was a difficult thing to keep from them in a culture that survives by telling stories. Carl and Sigmund felt it necessary to kill all who knew what had really happened to me. And, he needed a shaman who could be bought and controlled. This in place, and after enough years passing, he believed everything would be made right.

"But, there was great wrong and my soul was not at rest…until you and Ursula saw the flowing gold."

CHAPTER 26

Coldness crept through my soul as I thought of all the lives that had been affected by Carl and Sigmund across the decades. I squeezed my eyes shut. When I opened them, I turned my head to look at Frank. He was gone. Was I mad after all? Maybe not, since the bottle of Pisco was in my hand.

The sound of the rushing current caught my attention. It was odd, but I could feel the noise it made. It was loud and kept getting louder. Something was about to happen, I could sense it. I lay flat on the bottom of the boat and pushed against the sides with my arms. The boat was spinning and I was getting really dizzy. I felt too weak to fight throwing up. My body lurched upright as I began to heave all over myself. More sounds in front of me.

I couldn't make out what the sounds were, but the boat started to slow down. The spinning ceased. It grew quiet. The water was just barely moving, and the boat seemed to have stopped. A new sound, like grunting or mumbling, was in front of me. Dripping water hit me; it was hot. I heard sounds behind me, then from another direction. Sounds were all around me now. Mumbling—no, more like odd grunts...throat grunts.

A putrid smell assaulted me, like really bad body odor mixed with decaying leaves and food. I heard a splash to my left. Another splash, and another. The water sounded alive. I couldn't see. What the fuck was it? Something got into the boat with me. Whatever it was had company, lots of it. Water splashed over me as these things continued to fill the boat. Whatever they were, they were landing on me. As I knocked them away, I felt my body coated in slime. There were so many of them, I was covered with them and more kept coming. It began to feel like I was being crushed.

I tried to protect my face. The boat passed under another opening and once the light stopped blinding me, I got a look at what was in the boat with me. I was covered with the largest frogs I'd ever seen. They wouldn't move unless I nudged them, and not always then. The boat moved past the light and I was, once again, in total darkness. I began to wonder if it was an abyss and I was trapped in it. The grunts were so loud; so was the sound of rushing water. I felt the strong current, but at least I wasn't spinning. As the water seemed to become less turbulent, I passed out.

CHAPTER 27

I woke with a start. How long had I slept? My eyes were still closed, but I ran my hands across the top of my body and around me. The frogs were gone. I could smell dank leaves. The feeling created in the stomach when some elevators start their descent, hit me. I felt myself dropping and again pressed my arms and feet against the sides of the boat. Water engulfed me, but I surfaced and took in a large gulp of air. The boat was gone.

Suddenly, I was submerged again. There was pressure. I was moving up this time instead of down. The pressure got worse. My lungs felt ready to burst. I needed air, soon. When I thought it was all over, meaning I was about to drown, I broke through the watery surroundings. My lungs sucked in air. Large bubbles burst the water's surface all around me.

It was nighttime, but at least my vision had returned. I looked up and felt like screaming with joy when I saw the sky filled with stars above me. I gulped the fresh air and looked around. I couldn't see land, and the water was frigid. I became furious and shouted, "I'm going to drown? After all this, I'm going to drown?!" I hit the water with both fists. *Calm down. Take it easy. Tread water and wait for dawn. Land may be right there and you just can't see it.* I decided to listen to my own voice of reason.

I alternated treading water and floating on my back. This was the best course of action so I wouldn't wear myself out or risk falling asleep. Out on the water, it was quiet. More quiet than any night on land would be. That's why I was surprised when I heard a creaking sound behind me. I maneuvered my way around in the water and watched as a reed boat emerged from the darkness. It was difficult, but I climb into it, exhausted. When I went to lie back, something stuck in my side and I pulled it out. It couldn't get any better than this at the moment. I pulled the cork and took a heavy drink of Pisco. The chill started to leave my body immediately.

Calmer now, I took a look around. This boat was like the one Frank and I used that night on Lake Titicaca. "Frank!" I called out. No answer. Was this Lake Titicaca? Had I traveled the underground tunnel? Was this Frank's mythical door-to-door water taxi service? Figuring I was delirious, I took a few more hits of Pisco. Might as well be drunk, too.

I finished the bottle and it was lights out, Sam.

CHAPTER 28

It was the easiest wake-up I'd had my entire time in Peru. I was sore, but felt rested.

It wasn't too much after dawn. I stretched; then sat up. In front of me was the island, and it was close. There was a paddle at the bottom of the boat. I started to row.

An overwhelming urgency to get to Cuzco and find Ursula consumed me. I began to row harder. The harder I rowed, the sicker my stomach felt.

"Stop, Ursula!" I shouted.

"Sam! Sam! Oh, thank God, you're awake."

"Ursula? Where are we? What's happened? I was just in the lake. You're supposed to be in Cuzco. Are we in Cuzco?"

"No, Sam, not Cuzco. Don't you remember anything?"

"What should I remember?"

"Of course, how could you? You're in Miami General Hospital, Sam. You've been here for a month."

"Who found me on the lake? How did they know to get you and where you were? And what about Sigmund, is he dead?"

"Sigmund?"

"Yeah, Sigmund. Ursula, for God's sake! Don't try this on me again!"

"Calm down, Sam. I have no idea what you're talking about. You really don't know how you got here?" I didn't answer her, just glared, so she continued. "You ordered an exotic eel-like fish caught on some lake in the Andes."

"Lake Titicaca?"

"I think that's where it came from. It almost killed you. You've been in a coma for the last month. I know this is probably too much for you to learn just when you wake up. Go back to sleep, Sam. It'll really help."

I didn't remember finding Ursula after I rowed to shore, much less rowing to shore. Had I forgotten all of it or was she right—nothing but a bad fish dinner had ever happened? Any ability to know what was true and what was false seemed to leave me at that moment. Did I believe what I heard or what I felt? No ready or certain answer came to me, so I closed my eyes.

CHAPTER 29

"Hello, Mr. Paris. Ready to rise and shine?" It was an unfamiliar voice.

I opened my eyes. "Who are you?" Ursula wasn't there. "Where's Ursula?"

"Easy, Mr. Paris. Ursula is taking care of a few details so you can get discharged from the hospital today. I know you're still experiencing some confusion; that's understandable considering what you've been through. But physically, you're well enough to leave."

"Who are you?"

"I'm your attending physician. I've been taking care of you since you arrived a month ago. My name is Dr. Carl Wasser."

"You're... Why am I in Miami?"

"This hospital was best suited for your case. It was a little involved, but Ms. Jung did what was necessary to fly you here from New York. However, this is not the time to concern yourself with such details."

"New York? You mean Peru."

"Ah, of course, the delusions. No, Mr. Paris. You and Miss Jung planned to go to Peru, but you never made it. You both thought it was a good idea to dine at a Peruvian restaurant in New York the night before you were to leave. You ended up here, instead."

"But, I know things..."

"When your delusions began, Miss Jung explained that you'd read many books to become familiar with your destination. The mind is a remarkable thing; but I assure you that you never made it there. Perhaps one day you will visit the place in your dreams.

Best if you don't trouble yourself about this any more. I don't want you to cause a relapse of the brain fever."

Was this the truth? Was everything I thought had happened, actually a delusion caused by bad fish and the coma it put me in? Every experience I believed I'd had in Peru was always tinged with craziness. This would explain it. It would certainly make sense of things that never seemed to fully piece together. Like a video on fast-forward, a film flashed through my mind of the flowing gold, Frank, Marcos—everyone and everything about Peru was a dream, just a dream.

"Dr. Wasser, do you have a son named Sigmund?"

"Well, maybe you do remember a few things. Yes. He was in your room almost every day while you were in the coma and was very helpful in your recovery."

"Can I see him before I leave?"

"I'm sorry, Sam, but he's not available today. I promise to tell him you…"

"Hi, Sam!" Ursula rushed in and leaned over and kissed me on the lips. "How is he, Carl?"

"Ready to go; but he must stay off of exotic fish for a while." He was more amused by his comment than I was. I didn't join the two of them as they laughed

Ursula had called him Carl, not Dr. Wasser or even just Doctor. Was that because after seeing each other daily for a month they'd gotten on a first-name basis or did she know him prior to my stay here? If it was all a delusion, did it matter?

Ursula had come in with a couple of large shopping bags. She'd bought a gym bag, which she stuffed my clothes and boots into.

"What am I supposed to wear out of here?" I asked her.

"Pick something from this bag." She pulled out a couple of pairs of shorts, some T-shirts, and two pairs of flip-flops. "These are for hanging around at the hotel we're going to. If you need to wear anything dressier, I got you these." She held up a couple of pairs of slacks in navy and dark brown and a few regular button-up shirts, and a pair of brown deck shoes.

After my discharge from the hospital, we went to a nearby hotel and spent the next several days hanging out by the pool or walking on the beach. Dr. Wasser's orders were for me to relax, which included not discussing what I thought had happened or to ask questions. He said to do so would probably keep me confused, but that I should write my thoughts in a journal, which would help.

Following those orders, Ursula and I engaged in small talk; and she read lots of paperback novels while I scribbled in a notebook or stared at whatever. The doctor had wanted me nearby for several more days in case any complications arose and I needed treatment. The worse part was he also advised I wasn't to have any alcohol during that time.

Almost a full week later, Dr. Wasser signed off on my release and Ursula and I were at the Miami airport, ready to board a flight to New York. I was feeling much better. I'd even started to accept that I'd imagined everything, just as Ursula and Dr. Wasser had explained. It was a relief, actually.

"Sam, I need to go to the restroom before we board."

"Me, too."

I went into the Men's room and took my position in front of a urinal. The door opened. Following the code of all Men's rooms and a natural instinct to watch your back, I only took a quick glance as a man wearing a flight captain's uniform came in.

He walked up next to me as I was washing my hands. I still didn't look at him.

"Where are you flying to?" he asked.

"New York," I answered, still not looking at him. "Time for me to get back to…" I paused because what I was going back to hadn't entered my mind. That struck me as odd. "I'm not actually sure what I'm going back to yet."

"Well, have a nice flight," he said.

His voice was familiar. I glanced at his at his reflection in the mirror, not at him actually, at his name tag and saw asnahtfuL, oreuB knarF niatpaC—Captain Frank Buero, Lufthansa.

He finished drying his hands and started to walk out. I shook my head hard and rushed to follow him. When he got to my flight's departing gate, he turned to look at me, smiled and gave me a salute before continuing on.

An announcement came over the speakers, "American Airlines, Flight 803 to New York, is now boarding at Gate 17." She continued on with the usual details, but I blocked her out. Our flight was starting to board and I didn't see Ursula. I scanned the sea of faces lining up to get on the plane; she wasn't there. I walked into the wide passageway and looked in the direction of the Ladies' room thinking, hoping, I'd see her hurrying to join me.

Another flight message came over the speaker system. "Lufthansa corporate private jet party, please meet at Gate 3 to be led out to the plane."

Nausea hit me suddenly. I rushed through the crowd of people and headed to Gate 3. At the window near the boarding gate, the private jet was close enough for me to see Ursula make her way up the steps into the small jet. On the tarmac, just about to start the climb up, was Dr. Wasser. Another man was right behind him. The second man turned, and for a moment, I thought I was truly insane. This man had my face. I knew I was looking at Sigmund.

The jet's stairs swung up and I saw the captain peer through his little window. Again, Frank Buero saluted me and I saw him mouth, "Beep-beep," and wink. The Roadrunner cartoon character flashed into mind. I recalled that he told me, or I'd imagined he'd told me, that the sound the Roadrunner cartoon character made represented our bond. What bond had he meant? In Peru, it hadn't made much sense when he said it. Here and now, I didn't know what it made, other than me feel crazy.

The jet started to taxi. Ursula looked out one of the windows and said something. Sigmund's face appeared at another window, followed by Carl at another. They were laughing, laughing at me.

My eyes followed the jet until it left my field of view. I felt numb and in shock, and sick to my stomach. I stumbled to a chair and fell into it. I sat there bent over, my head cupped in my hands.

My name was being paged. My flight at Gate 17 had boarded and I wasn't on it yet. The airline was allowing all the time it could for me to make the flight. I realized the announcement didn't include Ursula's name. Not knowing what else I should or could do, I made my way to Gate 17.

I never boarded, though, just watched the plane pull away. I hung out in Miami long enough to know I didn't like it there. Hitched a ride with a trucker and got off at Port Salerno.

I found a shit job and a room to stay in. Once I had a little cash saved up, I bought some jeans, new shirts, a new cowboy hat, and slipped my boots back on in case I could recover a piece of my former self by wearing something familiar, and got rid of the clothes Ursula had bought for me. I'd been wearing them like a life preserver, as though they verified that she was real and not just an illusion—that all of it was real.

CHAPTER 30

"And, that was that, Harry. The end."

"What the hell kind of an ending is that?"

"That's it, Harry. There's no more."

"That's no kind of fucking ending, Sam. You want me to believe there wasn't more?"

"It's just a story, Harry. You said you wanted me to tell you my story, entertain you; and, that's what I did."

"This is total bullshit! Come on Sam, work with me, here. I know there's more."

"Harry, stories never really end. They have only a beginning; that's a given. The end can be whatever you want it to be. I gave my story to you. Now, you fill it in, you write it, you do what you want with it. Write your own ending, Harry. And, keep your money. I'm headed to bed. Thanks for the beer."

I leave Harry sitting at the table. He looks as frustrated and unhappy as I've felt many times. The bar's patrons are stirring about now that the depression they'd hoped to ease with alcohol is either gone or worse. Some will stay until Jake kicks them out. Others will soon drag their sorry asses home for some sleep before the sun comes up and they have to start all over again.

Outside the Peckerwood, I step onto the street that's part of A1A. The heat and humidity make my shirt stick to my skin almost immediately. I look back through the bar's window and see Harry staring at me. His woman is now next to him, also watching me. I told him, and meant it, that it was up to him to put the ending on this story.

Harry wanted my story, and its conclusion, but he didn't ask me any specific questions. A journalist or writer would've had questions, and would've taken notes or used a tape recorder. He'd done none of these.

I make my way down the street and turn left at the corner onto the crushed clamshell and sand Salerno Road. There are no streetlights, just the shadow of whatever lights are on nearby. The winding road leads to the water, past the processing plant that turns fish waste into cat food. On the left, just past the plant, is a small boatyard and where I'm headed.

Footsteps start to rush up behind me. I start to run towards the processing plant to take refuge and push on the first door I come to. It opens. I push the steel door shut, feel for the deadbolt and lock it. The door has one small window at my eye-level, like a ship's porthole. It's opaque and all I can see are dark shapes moving around outside. There are also two small windows with clear, but heavily grimed glass on both sides of the door.

No lights are on, but all along the top edge of the tall warehouse are windows—the sole source of light, dim but better than nothing. Some of the windows are open, some are broken. This is probably why I hear when Harry's voice calls out, "Sigmund! Sigmund, come out. We only want your father, not you. Don't be a fool. Let's end this now. Let's make it a good ending to a long story. Let's bring the truth out for the good of mankind. You'll be a hero instead of a criminal."

Trusting they won't see me, I lean as close to the edge of one of the small windows as I can to peer out. Four indistinct shapes. They know I'm in here. Might as well take a risk.

I move a few feet away and aim my voice up, hoping they won't be able to tell where I'm standing. "Harry, you have it all wrong. I'm Sam Paris, not Sigmund," I yell out.

"No more lies, Sigmund."

"What makes you think I'm Sigmund?"

"Because Sam would never have killed. After his time in Vietnam, he became a passivist. His psychological profile indicated this to be a fact. You said you shot Tinko. You left the four French people to die at the silo. Only Sigmund would have done that. We won't harm you. Let us help you stop the running and hiding. You must be very tired of it, Sigmund. Quite weary, in fact."

I glance back outside. Only one shape is there now. The other three must be looking for a way in. I bend at the waist and quickly walk to the other window to get a different view. I see a man's face trying to look in from the opposite side.

My right hand reaches for the .32 caliber Beretta nestled in the shoulder holster under my jacket. It's too small to do any real damage unless I get right up on someone and don't miss when I fire.

As I try to figure how to safely get out of the warehouse, a loud *bam-bam* and glass shattering behind me splinters my thoughts. My thumb flips the safety off, and I chamber a round.

The silky voice of the woman calls out, "Sigmund, please come out. Sigmund... Sigmund... Come with us. Come out and play a different game, Sigmund, with those who only want to help you."

I move to the center of the steel door, put my back against it, and bend my knees so my head is below the round window. "I'm not Sigmund and I can prove it."

The crash made me look to my left. I see a hammer breaking the window into shards. Someone starts to batter the door with something heavy. Shit.

An arm comes in through the window, a gun is aimed in my general direction, and its holder starts to fire. I run up, grab the wrist, and shoot my gun. Adrenaline is pumping so hard and fast through my system, I barely hear the screaming when my bullet shatters the man's elbow. His gun falls to the ground. I let go of the arm and the man disappears. I pick up his gun, a 9MM Glock. I stick the Beretta back in its holster and check the clip on the Glock. It's more than half full. They didn't come here to work a deal with Sigmund, they came here to execute him. That would certainly send a message to the right people. Killing me would only send certain people into fits of laughter.

Well, one down or at least out of commission. I carefully maneuver my way around the window. I don't see anyone out there, which is good and not good.

A noise from an adjoining room at the back of the warehouse gets my attention. Someone is coming. Time to move. I make my way towards the back. I know better than to try to exit through the steel door. Just because I can't see anyone out there, doesn't mean they aren't hiding and waiting for me. The back way is the only way. I've walked all through the inside and all around the outside of the plant, so know the nooks and crannies.

I listen at the back door. Nothing. Gun at the ready, I ease the door open, praying the salt water and humidity hasn't rusted the hinges. No bullets fly at me, so I move low, but fast through the door and head to the right. Only ambient light from outside offers any illumination, but I know the room is full of equipment and shelves. Any path I choose could be dangerous, but I decide to go as far right as possible and walk between rows of stocked metal shelves and the far wall.

My foot catches on something and I fall over. It's a man, unconscious. Even without much light, I can see the dark puddle on the floor. It's blood from his head. He must have run into something hard. His gun is just inches from his hand; so I figure he's one of Harry's bunch, not a worker. The plant shuts down at night and all workers go home. This guy's in slacks and a jacket, so he's definitely not a security guard. The nighttime guard here always wears a uniform. Thinking about the guard, Joe, I wonder where he is. I wonder if they killed him. Then I notice the right elbow of the man on the floor. It's shattered and spreading its own red pool. He must have been carrying two weapons. *What kind of fucking mutants does Harry have working with him?* I jump when the guy on the floor moans and shifts his body.

"I told Ursula that her people's evaluation of me from my profile was wrong. Now, you're about to find out the same thing."

I place the Glock right behind his ear and pull the trigger. I feel my face and clothes get splattered.

I don't want anyone to find him soon or ever, so I stick his extra gun into my waistband and drag his body into the next room where the processing machines are. I move at warp speed and remove his watch and all of his clothes so nothing can block the gears, and heave him into the open chopper. When the machine runs again, he'll be turned into mush. No cats will be harmed though; at this point, he's no different than fish waste.

Time to get my butt in gear and out of this place. I keep low, run to the back, and find the door the guy left ajar. I know this door opens to an alley that leads to the parking lot in back. I use my body to push it open and hit the ground in a roll just as I was taught in the Marines. Of course, back then I had no beer rolls at my middle and was usually sober.

My breath is just returning when a gun fires in my direction and misses, but just barely. I hear the *zing* as the bullet flies next to my right ear. I glance up and see it's Harry's woman. Damn, if she were any closer she'd be on top of me. Did she deliberately miss me or is she that bad a shot?

I see her taking aim again. I throw my body forward and fire two rounds into her just under her ribcage. Only she doesn't fall, just stares at me with a bewildered expression. Her arm with the gun still in it comes up, but doesn't aim at me. She fires repeatedly at the door I just came through until nothing comes out but the *click*, then she falls to the ground. I look towards the door, but don't see anyone. Maybe she just fired all the rounds out of her gun as a reflex before death.

No time to dawdle here. I run, still crouching low, until I hit the parking lot. I have to run across the clamshell road to get where I'm going. Harry appears from behind a shrub, takes aim and fires. I feel the sting as the bullet grazes my head above my right temple. I fire point-blank into his chest then start running and don't stop until I reach the back door of the Peckerwood. I thank God or Buddha or whoever might be listening that Jake left it unlocked. Again. I was the one who always nagged him not to do that.

I race into the bar, gun in one hand, blood running down my face, covered in bits and pieces of gore. Everyone turns to look in my direction. Jake nods at someone near the front door, who quickly locks it. Then he hands me a dirty bar rag that I press against my head wound. We stand there looking at each other. Everybody's looking at me, and you could've heard the proverbial pin drop.

"The usual, Sam?" Typical Jake. But why not? He's seen it all.

I stand there for a moment, then walk to my bar stool and sit.

"What I'm really thirsty for, Jake, is a cold bottle of Pisco."

"I don't serve piss anything here."

"Tequila. Three fingers."

I gulp it down and he refills my glass which I empty again. "Might as well leave it out, Jake."

Across from me is no-neck, big ears. He's looking at me, but trying not to stare. All of them are trying not to stare. Behind no-neck is a mirror. I see my reflection. For a moment, I think it's

Sigmund I'm looking at. The difference is I only kill people who try to kill me. As far as I'm concerned, that's a big difference.

My hand moves to my pocket and I pull out all the cash I have on me. I throw it on the bar.

"Ladies and gentlemen, I have to leave you now. Here's enough cash for one hell of a big send-off and finish to what's been an interesting association and one hell of a night. I'm going to need your help. I imagine that quite soon, some not-too-happy people with guns are going to come to visit you here at the Peckerwood, and they'll be looking for me."

What happens is exactly why I love this crowd and am really going to miss them. As soon as I say people with guns are coming, handguns and knives of all sizes and shapes appear out of pants, pockets, and purses. Jake pulls his sawed-off shotgun from under the bar, along with a box of shells, and rests them on top the oak surface next to the bottle of tequila.

"So, you're leaving us," he says.

"Got to, my friend."

"I'm gonna miss seeing your ugly old drunkin' face sitting at my bar."

"And I'm gonna miss your butt-ugly face just as much."

"Any chance you want to tell me what you're up to?"

"I think it's time for a little adventure. It's too damn quiet around here."

Jake snorts a laugh out and shakes his head. "Fuuuck, Sam. You're a real shit piece of work. You know that?"

He pours both of us a shot of tequila, raises his glass and shouts out, "Listen up, all you Peckerwood peckers and peckerettes, raise your glass in a toast to Sam Paris."

Glasses go up, cheers ring out, and liquid is tossed back.

"Shouldn't you already be gone?" Jake asks.

"I'm outta here," I answer.

"Wait up." He looks at the Glock I placed on the bar and pulls out a box of 9MM bullets, three bottles of the red Peckerwood sauce—all with the Roadrunner label, and an unopened bottle of tequila. He shoves them into a canvas bag he had stashed under the bar and hands it to me.

"Can't let you leave without something for the road. How are you for cash?"

"I'm covered. And... Jake," I say, holding the bag up.

"Do *not* go wuss on me, man. Get the fuck outta here before I shoot you myself."

I leave the Peckerwood knowing whoever tries to get in there to look for me is going to find a different kind of surprise party than they've ever been to. It takes an extra ten minutes using the back way, to get to where my trawler is docked. I can't see anyone lurking around at the dock. I'm not even sure if they know about my boat or not. A little extra caution won't hurt though.

I slip the Glock and the Beretta into the canvas bag, and sneak my way into the water. Holding the bag above the surface, I dogpaddle to the boat. No one is on it or near it. I use the makeshift ladder on the dock and move as fast as I can to get onto the boat and set it free from its moorings.

I make my way quietly out of the harbor and head towards the Atlantic Ocean. I glance down at my boots and smile as I press my hands to the leather and feel the rest of the gold nuggets that I haven't cashed in yet, which are quite a lot.

Who knows what kind of adventure I'll find or will find me, but I know it probably won't take long. I'm older, but life still has a lot to offer; and I've still got a lot of life left in me. As Frank said, "It's not how long one lives, but how much living one does." I'd certainly done a good deal of it and intended to do even more. Maybe I'll even stop drinking. Nah. Fuck that.

I open the bottle of tequila Jake packed for me and take a swig, and another…and another. And, I wonder what the other four—Carl, Sigmund, Ursula, and Frank are up to.

Maybe it's time to find out.

ABOUT THE AUTHOR

Captain Nathan Lichtwar began his over 45-year life on the sea as a young sailor for the U.S. Coast Guard then moved to tug boats, including a stint as a New York Harbor ferryboat operator. Lichtwar is the owner-operator of Cielo e Mar Charter Service and New York Boat Charter, and is publisher-owner of *CROSS UP, Long Island's Motorcycle Scene*. Called the Old Man of the Sea, he has traveled extensively throughout the world, on and off the beaten tract. He's been a guest on *Oprah* twice. His travels and adventures inspired the writing of *Peckerwood Twist*, and is, as Nat likes to say, "...either 90% true and 10% false, or just the opposite." Contact the author at pwt@peckerwoodtwist.com and visit his website at http://www.peckerwoodtwist.com.

www.ingramcontent.com/pod-product-compliance
Lightning Source LLC
Chambersburg PA
CBHW020950180626
46814CB00003B/1024